SNOW

MIKE BOND

CRITICS' PRAISE FOR MIKE BOND

Assassins

"An exhilarating spy novel that offers equal amounts of ingenuity and intrigue." – *Kirkus*

"Packs one thrilling punch after the other...A first-rate thriller. – *Book Chase*

"Powerful, true to life, and explosive...The energy is palpable and the danger is real...A story that could be ripped right out of the headlines." – *Just Reviews*

"Mike Bond is one of America's best thriller writers...You need to get this book...It's an eye-opener, a page-turner...very strongly based in reality." – *Culture Buzz*

"Riveting, thrilling...so realistic and fast-paced that the reader felt as if they were actually there." – *NetGalley*

"The action is outstanding and realistic. The suspense flows from page to page...The background is provided by recent events we have all lived through. The flow of the writing is almost musical as romance and horrors share equal billing." – *Goodreads*

Killing Maine

FIRST PRIZE FOR FICTION, 2016, *New England Book Festival*: "A gripping tale of murders, manhunts and other crimes set amidst today's dirty politics and corporate graft, an unforgettable hero facing enormous dangers as he tries to save a friend, protect the women he loves, and defend a beautiful, endangered place."

"Another stellar ride from Bond; checking out Pono's first adventure isn't a prerequisite, but this will make readers want to." – *Kirkus*

"Another terrifically entertaining read from a master of the storytelling craft... A work of compelling fiction... Very highly recommended." – *Midwest Book Review*

"Quite a ride for those who love good crime thrillers... I can't recommend this one strongly enough." – *Book Chase*

"Sucks in the reader and makes it difficult to put the book down until the very last page... A winner of a thriller." – *Mystery Maven*

Tibetan Cross

"Grips the reader from the very first chapter until the climactic ending." – *UPI*

"A taut, tense tale of pursuit through exotic and unsavory locales." – *Publishers Weekly*

"An astonishing thriller." – *San Francisco Examiner*

"It *is* a thriller... Incredible, but also believable." – *Associated Press*

"Bond never loses the reader's attention... working that fatalistic margin where life and death are one and the existential reality leaves one caring only to survive." – *Sunday Oregonian*

"Murderous intensity... A tense and graphically written story." – *Richmond Times*

"The most jaundiced adventure fan will be held by **Tibetan Cross**." – *Sacramento Bee*

"Grips the reader from the opening chapter and never lets go." – *Miami Herald*

Holy War

"The suspense-laden novel has a never-ending sense of impending doom... An unyielding tension leaves a lasting impression." – *Kirkus*

"A profound tale of war... Literally impossible to stop reading." – *British Armed Forces Broadcasting*

"A terrific book... The smells, taste, noise, dust, and fear are communicated so clearly." – *Great Book Escapes*

"A supercharged thriller...A story to chill and haunt you." – *Peterborough Evening Telegraph (UK)*

"If you are looking to get a driver's seat look at the landscape of modern conflict, holy wars, and the Middle East then this is the perfect book to do so." – *Masterful Book Reviews*

"A stunning novel of love and loss, good and evil, of real people who live in our hearts after the last page is done...Unusual and profound." – *Greater London Radio*

The Last Savanna

FIRST PRIZE FOR FICTION, 2016, *Los Angeles Book Festival*: "One of the best books yet on Africa, a stunning tale of love and loss amid a magnificent wilderness and its myriad animals, and a deadly man-hunt through savage jungles, steep mountains and fierce deserts as an SAS commando tries to save the elephants, the woman he loves and the soul of Africa itself."

"Dynamic, heart-breaking and timely to current events...a must-read." – *Yahoo Reviews*

"Sheer intensity, depicting the immense, arid land and never-ending scenes...but it's the volatile nature of nature itself that gives the story its greatest distinction." – *Kirkus*

"A powerful love story set in the savage jungles and deserts of East Africa." – *Daily Examiner (UK)*

"The central figure is not human; it is the barren, terrifying landscape of Northern Kenya and the deadly creatures who inhabit it." – *Daily Telegraph (UK)*

"An entrancing, terrifying vision of Africa." – *BBC*

"From the opening page maintains an exhilarating pace until the closing line...A highly entertaining and gripping read." – *East African Wild Life Society*

House of Jaguar

"A high-octane story rife with action, from U.S. streets to Guatemalan jungles." – *Kirkus*

"A terrifying depiction of one man's battle against the CIA and Latin American death squads." – *BBC*

"With detailed descriptions of actual jungle battles and man-hunts, vanishing rain forests and the ferocity of guerrilla war, **House of Jaguar** also reveals the CIA's role in both death squads and drug running, twin scourges of Central America." – *Newton Chronicle (UK)*

"Bond grips the reader from the very first page. An ideal thriller for the beach, but be prepared to be there when the sun goes down." – *Herald Express (UK)*

Saving Paradise

"Bond is one of the 21st Century's most exciting authors... An action-packed, must read novel... taking readers behind the alluring façade of Hawaii's pristine beaches and tourist traps into a festering underworld of murder, intrigue and corruption." – *Washington Times*

"A complex, entertaining... lusciously convoluted story." – *Kirkus*

"Highly recommended." – *Midwest Book Review*

"A highly atmospheric thriller focusing on a side of Hawaiian life that tourists seldom see." – *Book Chase*

"He's a tough guy, a cynic who describes the problems of the world as a bottomless pit, but can't stop trying to solve them. He's Pono Hawkins, the hero of Mike Bond's new Hawaii-based thriller, **Saving Paradise**... an intersection of fiction and real life." – *Hawaii Public Radio*

"A complex murder mystery about political and corporate greed and corruption... Bond's vivid descriptions of Hawaii bring **Saving Paradise** vibrantly to life." – *Book Reviews and More*

SNOW

MIKE BOND

MANDEVILLA
PRESS

Weston, CT 06883

MANDEVILLA PRESS

Weston, CT 06883

Published in the United States by Mandevilla Press

LIBRARY OF CONGRESS CATALOGING-IN-PUBLICATION DATA
Bond, Mike — author
Snow: a novel/Mike Bond

p. cm.

ISBN 978-1-62704-037-2

1. Thriller – Fiction. 2. Drugs – Fiction. 3. Las Vegas – Fiction. 4. Wall Street – Fiction. 5. NFL – Fiction. 6. TV Sports – Fiction. 7. Gambling – Fiction. I. Title

10 9 8 7 6 5 4 3 2 1

Author photo by Peggy Lucas Bond
Cover design: Asha Hossain Design, Inc.

Printed in the United States of America

www.MikeBondBooks.com

I want it all,
and I want it now.
– *Queen*

What I love is to go too far.
– *Charlotte Gainsbourg*

She don't lie,
cocaine.
– *JJ Cale*

What is not sought in the right way
is not found.
– *I Ching*

to
Peggy

GOOD KILLERS

THE RAVEN TUCKED its wings tighter to its body and shivered. It tugged one foot from the frozen bough, then the other, scanned across the snowy treetops to the distant icy peaks. Nothing moved but the sweep of bitter wind in the pine boughs.

Far too cold for life. Rabbits, mice and chipmunks all gone to earth, chickadees taking a last refuge in the firs. Coyotes denned, none leaving prey – no guts, no skins, no bones. Deer yarding up in the young spruce but none starving yet.

The early hunger season, before the men come. When they come they kill everything – elk, moose, deer, bear, wolves, coyotes, grouse, raccoons and many others, leaving guts, lungs, heads, skins and legs all over the blood-blackened snow. Many more animals get away injured and die later. So the men make food for all winter. Marrow bones and frozen innards to dig out when cold cracks the trees.

Now that the cold had returned the men would come. And this season of early hunger would be done.

Men bringing death. Good men. Good killers.

THE MAN followed the blood trail up the mountain through deep snow toward a steep ridge of young aspen. Frothy lung blood spattered the white crust: the elk wouldn't last much longer.

The man halted gasping, bent over hands on knees, sucking in the thin air, and wiped frozen sweat from his face. He stood wearily, rifle in his right hand, and climbed toward the ridge.

Below the top he turned to look out over thousands of miles of conifered crests, glaciated cliffs and valleys of firs and lodgepoles all covered in white, and beyond them the faraway mountains shimmering in their blankets of snow and ice. It felt sacred and deep, this ice and cliffs and forests of wild creatures, this frozen wind, the sighing pines and scurrying drifts. It wakened something deep inside him. How the whole earth once was, when people were in a better place.

He took a deep breath, loving its icy sting in his lungs. Almost like a drug, this air. How it changes you. Renews you. He climbed the last few hundred feet to the ridgetop where in a little saddle fringed by oak brush the elk stood huffing out his blood.

The man faced him, forty yards apart. "I'm sorry." He raised the Winchester and aimed for the elk's brain.

Their eyes locked, and in that instant he was sure the elk understood, and his last glance was eternal hatred.

THE REGRET was always like this. You hunted because you loved it, to be back in our primeval life, how we've lived for millions of years… And the elk so overpopulated that they eroded the stream channels and ate down the willows and cottonwoods to the bone. But it was always painful to kill, he hated it. Life lives on death – but he still regretted it.

He leaned the Winchester against an aspen trunk and knelt beside the dead elk. "Thank you, for giving your life." That was how Curt, their half-Cheyenne guide, would say it. To reach out to the elk's spirit on its way to the death world.

He cut the elk's throat and dragged him headfirst downhill to let him bleed out, sliced down the chest and belly and down each leg. The guts steamed in the subzero sun when he pulled them out. But already the elk was cooling and lines of ticks were running down his legs and halting at the snow.

When the man heard the sound behind him he paid it no mind, busy cutting the elk's thick-furred skin away from the ribs. Then he heard it again, turned and leaped to his feet, the skinning knife useless in his hand.

A big grizzly. The kind so huge he towers over everything, his thick fur copper-bright, his shoulders so wide they crush down trees, his jaws like steel, enormous teeth.

2

The grizzly trotted down the slope toward the man, a dreamy cold look in his black eyes.

The man stumbled backwards from the elk, realized the Winchester was too far to reach, turned and ran knowing you're not supposed to run because a griz can outrun a race horse, and running makes it mad.

He had to reach the trees.

The bear smashed him down. He curled in the fetal position with his arms covering his head as the grizzly's great snout burrowed into his neck, the hot black lips and grating teeth rasped his skin, hot saliva down his neck.

The griz moved away. The man didn't breathe. The griz ambled to the elk. The man ran for a tree, jumped into the low branches and scrambled up the trunk. Looking back he saw the griz squat leisurely beside the elk and start to eat.

Clouds sifted across the sun; the snow turned gray, lifeless, the long-limbed conifers shorn of light. The grizzly finished eating the elk guts and with a shake of his jaws ripped a rear leg from the body and chewed it down, bones crunching like tinder.

The light thinned, seeming to rise up the mountain and fade into the sky. The grizzly dragged the elk's body into a spruce thicket, swished his huge muzzle back and forth in a drift to clean it, sat to scratch behind an ear with a rear paw, stood, shook himself and slowly wandered uphill till he was a far golden tinge between the aspen trunks.

The man slid down the tree, grabbed the Winchester and ran downhill toward a northwest-draining valley with deep drifts between the scattered lodgepole pines.

Panting, he halted to look back but the griz wasn't coming. He realized he didn't know this valley, but if he climbed the left side and headed southwest he should find camp.

He rubbed at his neck but there was no blood, just soreness where the grizzly's lips had abraded it. He felt less fear, deeply moved and alive. The drifts underfoot felt weightless. *Thank you*, he told the grizzly. *Thank you for letting me live.*

Ahead of him trees had been snapped off, shattered; he worried maybe the grizzly had done it. No, this was a wide gouge in the forest as if a huge boulder had smashed through it.

It scared him though he didn't know why. And because it scared him he went closer.

A crashed plane lay on one crushed wing, nose buried in the snow, the other wing raised toward the sky as if in supplication, the propeller twisted and the tail torn half off.

The man edged forward and peered in the shattered windshield expecting to see death, but both pilot seats were empty. In the rear behind them were two long dark wooden shapes he realized were coffins. One coffin had cracked open and snow had drifted over it.

As he backed away he saw tracks: human, heading downhill. Strides wide apart, no blood, a person moving fast, practically running from the plane.

He followed the tracks to the bottom of this valley where they dove over another ridge into the lower forests of lodgepole, aspen and spruce toward distant Highway 191, the road from Bozeman to West Yellowstone.

Whoever had made these tracks needed no help. He hiked back up the valley and climbed through the dark timber toward the next valleys and camp. He was tired now, the late afternoon sun bouncing off the white drifts and icy trees glared into his eyes; his legs were leaden, his feet wet and numb. He thought of what he'd tell Steve and Curt in camp: this plane, the grizzly, the dead elk.

Motion ahead made him flinch – the griz? No, a lynx staring at him with yellow slit eyes. It hissed and trotted away on wide fluffy feet. *It scorned me*, he realized. *But how could it not? We're destroying their world, and they know it.*

It began to snow, tiny glittering flakes against the blue sky.

Didn't matter. Soon he'd be sitting round the fire with Steve and Curt, warmed not only by the flames but by this special companionship, guys you rarely saw but with whom it was a joy to be. To like and respect them as they do you. A brotherhood, almost.

In a way it was these ten days of hunting he looked forward to most, every year.

He crossed wearily over the crest into the next valley, and across that up through another steep slope of firs and aspens, the snow-flakes tumbling faster, darkening the trees.

A bullet smashed into the aspen beside him as a rifle roared uphill. "*Stop!*" he screamed. "*Don't shoot!*"

His voice echoed away through the forest of ridges and cliffs; chunks of ice fell from branches down his neck.

"Zack!" a voice yelled uphill. "That you?"

"Steve? You nearly *shot* me!"

"You aren't supposed to *be* here!" Steve came running downhill rolling clods of snow before him.

"You *shot* at me."

Steve threw down his rifle and dropped to his knees, head in his hands. "Holy shit! I thought you were the elk I was tracking." He stood, wild-eyed. "*Christ,* you weren't supposed to *be* in this valley. That's how we divided things up this morning."

"You can't tell an elk from me?"

"You were coming through dark timber where there'd been an elk a minute ago. I thought you were him –"

Zack lowered his gun. "Damn!" he spat, fierce in some way he didn't understand; more than being shot at, it was fury at the type of person who made these mistakes. Not like Steve.

"I'm truly sorry, man," Steve was saying. "I'm gonna regret this all my life."

Zack nodded, not mollified. There was no way to explain or forget.

"Really sorry, man." Steve repeated. "Really sorry." He jacked the empty cartridge out of his gun and put his thumb over the breech to keep another from entering from the magazine. He took a bullet from his pocket and shoved it down into the breech.

"Forget it." Zack said. For some reason he didn't want to mention the bear and the plane but did anyway.

"A crashed plane?" Steve stared uphill. "Why didn't you say?"

"With two coffins in the back." Zack glanced at the aspen trunk smashed by Steve's bullet. "Let's get to camp and tell Curt. That's where I was headed."

A hesitant smile crossed Steve's rangy, lean face. "You call 911?"

"Uphill's like here, no coverage."

"Weird there's no bodies. Coffins? Spooky." Steve slung his rifle. "Can you show me?"

Zack leaned against the aspen. "What for?"

"Hell of a pilot, to survive a crash landing up here."

"We need to tell Curt."

"It's what, half mile away?"

"A mile. At least."

Steve brushed new snow from his shoulders. "Let's do it. Or I have to follow your footprints all the way down the valley where you tracked that pilot, then up again to wherever the plane is. And by then it'll be all covered with snow."

As they climbed the ridge in last light toward the plane, Zack could not stop thinking how close it had been, that bullet hitting the aspen.

I could be dead now.

NEW SNOW half-covered the plane, giving it a sepulchral air in the deepening darkness.

"Holy shit!" Steve circled it, wiped aside snow to peer in the windows, leaned his rifle against the smashed tail and climbed the fuselage.

He tugged open the starboard door till it pointed straight up like a broken cross. "How the pilot got out." He dropped feet-first into the cabin, checked the instruments and squirmed over the seats toward the coffins.

"Don't worry," Zack called. "They're already dead."

Steve reached the broken coffin with the snow atop it. But where had that come from, Zack wondered: there was no break in the fuselage where it could have drifted in.

Steve licked a finger, touched the snow and tasted it. "*Snow!*" he called. "The real stuff."

"Snow?" Zack still could not figure how it had landed on the coffin.

"*Whooeee!* We just found ourselves a plane full of cocaine!"

LADY COKE

"*THIRTY GRAND* A kilo!" Steve tugged a plastic bag of powder from the broken coffin and jumped down from the plane. "What *this*," he held it up. "is *worth* on the street! And there's a ton of kilos in these coffins!"

"So w*hat?*"

"It's a *fortune!*" Steve stared out at the fading landscape, the white snow almost dark now, the black trees and dark night. "Imagine, if *we* could sell this…"

Zack laughed. "You *nuts?* It's not even ours."

"So do we *care?*" Steve nodded at the plane. "These guys are drug dealers. Crooks."

"What would *we* be, if we took it?"

Steve grinned. "Could make us rich."

"We're already rich." A black scorpion logo, Zack saw, was printed on the bag: *A warning.* The bag was torn on one end and the powder trickling out made him want to cup it in his hands. He glanced up at the glacial peaks, the lofty darkening trees, the hills of deep silent snow, the horizon empty of humans. "What would *we* do with it?"

"*Sell* it!" Steve tipped powder onto the blade of his Buck knife. "Oh *Jesus* this is good." He sniffed again, head back, inhaled. "Absolutely *pure.*"

"If we take it, then *these* guys," Zack nodded at the plane, "they come after us."

"You're telling me *you* are afraid of some scumbag coke dealers?"

"It's an added hassle, that's all."

Steve smiled at him with affection. "You know, in all my life, all the shit I've done, all that's happened, Lady Coke's done me more good than bad."

"I don't care. Let's get back to camp."

Steve tipped more powder on his knife and held it blade-first to Zack. "*Try* it."

"Giving it a break for a while. You know that."

"Because Monica told you to?"

"You know she wouldn't."

Steve withdrew the blade. "*Never* have you had coke like *this*. We're on vacation...don't tell me you don't do it when you're going live."

"Not anymore."

"You, the great white linebacker, and now the handsome TV guy with all the answers – and you're *afraid* of a little snow?" Steve took another hit. "Is *that* why you're losing your edge? Why they're not offering you another season?"

"I didn't say they weren't. I said it was possible. I've got a meeting next week, after we get back..."

"*Are* you're losing your edge? You're in a wicked business, every instant have to have the right words, the fast talk...Be looking *good*..."

Zack laughed. "I can retire now. I told you."

"You don't want to. Not when the market's this hot." Steve snorted some coke, tipped more on the blade. "Just *try* it. We do this right, we can make so much money you won't need to sell our portfolio."

"It's not *our* portfolio. It's *mine*. Money *I* made breaking bones and pissing blood."

Steve gave him a curious look. "So what's the difference between doing that and selling coke?"

"Maybe nothing." Zack unsheathed his own knife, with a fingernail scraped dried elk blood from the blade, shook on some powder. "This ain't so unusual."

Then it seared into his bones, electrified his muscles, drove pure oxygen deep into his lungs, exploded his vision to infinity.

Everything grew clear. He sat on the snow. It felt warm and cradling, fit his body like a glove. He looked out over the vast horizon, the great sweeping white plateaus, the raw black peaks and tree-thick ridges under the near-black sky, and sensed the magnificence of it all.

Jesus life is magical. What a great gift. He smiled at the white plateaus, sharp cliffs and endless forests. *Thank God for this.*

With this God inside him, he could do anything. So what was he afraid for? "Holy shit!"

"Yeah," Steve chuckled. "*Holy* shit."

"How much you say?"

"Thirty grand a kilo, Wall Street or Vegas."

It always amazed Zack how coke instantly hones your judgment and will power. You can do whatever you decide to.

But does it hurt you? He couldn't tell. *Is it evil, to steal what's evil? Or is coke even evil? It's always been good to me.* Or maybe coke hurt one person inside him but helped another. Helped the athlete facing endless pain from so many battered places in his body, helped the TV anchor deal with the endless fraud and hustle. But hurt the other side, the one Monica loved, the one she called *the real you.*

What seemed impossible an hour ago now looked easy. As if you can move the earth with one hand.

True, a century ago lots of folks did coke. It was in every bottle of Coca Cola – how Coke got its name. It's been the basis of so many medicines that have done so much good – why forbid it?

Funny how so many government prohibitions were not to protect the citizen but rather the powerful interests that could be financially harmed by the item proscribed. Like it's okay to smoke cigarettes that kill half a million Americans a year – the industry even gets government subsidies. But smoking marijuana, which kills no one, is against federal law. How funny. How tragic.

"Is it better to be poor and honest?" Steve grinned, "or rich and crooked?" He hunched into his black parka against the thickening snowfall. "Is coke even crooked? Anyway," he chuckled, "if it comes down to a choice, I'll take rich and crooked any time."

Zack laughed. And felt a blade drop between his past and now.

"All I'm saying," Steve added, "is what if there's a way to do this? Think what we're doing with our lives. You want to spend thirty more years like this? Or do you want to *live?*"

"It's insane. How would we get it out of here?"

Snow began to fall harder, twirling down through the green-black treetops and blotting out the early stars.

FIRELIGHT flickering through the trees ahead made Steve think of ancient hunters returning home out of the cold darkness, generations after generations over thousands, millions of years.

"You boys been gone a while," Curt said. He stood from the fire and helped them shake snow off their coats. "I was even thinking of looking for you."

"Beautiful night out there," Zack said, excited from the coke and trying not to show it.

They unloaded their rifles and slid them into their tents, knelt by the fire. Curt handed them each a cup of coffee and Jack Daniels. "This'll warm you up."

"You're not going to believe what I found," Zack said.

"Zack killed an elk," Steve broke in, "but a griz got it."

Curt glanced at him. "What griz?"

"That's not all I found," Zack said.

Steve slapped Zack's shoulder. "A big griz. Chased Zack, knocked him down ... Then he chewed on the elk and Zack got up a tree."

Curt turned to Zack. "You okay?"

"Fine. Just scared for a while." Zack looked down at his snow-soaked, still-bloody boots. "But the griz got my elk. Six-pointer."

"That's a damn shame." Curt chewed on a grass stalk. "But at least he's fed for the winter and won't bother us now." He stood and stretched. "I'll get you boys some more coffee and Jack. Then we'll have dinner."

Zack stared at Steve. "That's not all I found."

Curt halted. "What else?"

Feeling as if he'd transgressed somehow, Zack told him about the plane.

"Why didn't you say before?"

"The pilot got away fine," Steve put in. "Zack followed his tracks part way down toward 191. No emergency."

"So what was in this plane?"

"Nothing," Steve said. "Just a couple coffins in the back."

"Coffins?" Curt half-smiled, as if this might be a joke.

"If there's bodies in them," Steve chuckled, "they won't rot at twenty below... And that pilot was obviously okay, probably on his way to where he came from by now."

Curt took the grass stalk from his teeth, tossed it. "We'll have to ride down to the road, call it in."

"Tonight?" Steve raised his hands, palms up, collecting the fast-falling flakes. "In this?"

"Tomorrow morning." Curt took off his hat to dump snow from the brim. "If this weather keeps up, we should go down anyway. Getting too deep for the horses."

"It's not that bad," Steve said.

"We agree every year, if there's too much snow we cut it short."

"We paid for a full hunt," Steve said.

Zack glanced at their tracks entering camp. "It's only knee-deep."

Curt nodded. "So far."

"I don't see any reason to ride out because of that plane," Steve added. "The pilot's surely reported it by now. And like I said, those corpses..."

Curt smiled. "Maybe those coffins're empty."

"Yeah," Zack said. "Maybe."

"If it stops snowing," Curt said, "I'll ride down in the morning, call it in. You boys can keep hunting."

"Too bad there's no service up here," Zack said. "Or we could call it in now."

"Yeah, too bad," Curt said, "that a little bit of this world's still natural."

"When I climbed that ridge," Zack said, "chasing my elk, I looked out at these mountains and forest…" he halted, not knowing what to say. "It was the most beautiful sight I'd ever seen."

"Be nice to keep it that way." Curt shook more snow off his jacket, clapped his hat against his knee. "Time I get you boys some dinner."

"What we got, chef?"

"Elk liver'n onions."

"*Elk* liver? Where from?"

"I shot him as he was coming right through camp. Must've been running from you guys." Curt pointed a thumb toward the kitchen tent. "There's liver and heart in that pail, and four quarters hanging from the crossbar behind the tent."

"We hire you to find us elk," Steve half-laughed, "and *you* shoot them instead?"

"What was I going to do? Tie him down till you got here?"

"What you shoot him with?" Zack broke in.

Curt patted his thigh. "Ruger."

"Anyway there's plenty more elk out there," Zack said.

"That's not the point," Steve tailed off, as if not sure what the point was. "Anyway, I'm not leaving tomorrow just because of a little snow."

"If we have to we have to." Curt grinned. "Unless you want to stay up here without a tent or food or sleeping bags or horses."

"Hell, Curt, how many seasons you've guided us up here? You know we're not afraid of a little bad weather."

Curt walked back to the cook tent whacking snow off the low branches, not answering.

Is it true, Zack wondered, that every snowflake is unique? A multi-infinite paradigm, an endlessly varying geometry? How could there be so infinitely many?

Steve turned on him. "What you tell him about the plane for?"

Zack drained his Jack Daniels. "It could be an emergency, maybe that pilot didn't get to the highway."

"You said he was fine."

"I said his tracks looked like he was fine."

"And now we've got Curt wanting to go down? We paid him for the whole trip."

Zack glanced at the fast-falling snow, blinking as it hit his eyes. "Not his fault if this keeps up. Four years now we've hunted with him, he's always been fair."

As a football announcer Zack had a bye week every year, when the team didn't have a game and he could get away for ten days. He and Steve had always hired Curt, who picked them up at Bozeman airport, drove them up here and had camp ready. Any meat they shot was packed on horses down to Curt's truck and driven to a game butcher in Bozeman. Two weeks later it was shipped, frozen, to Steve in New York and Zack in LA. Elk they had killed high in the wilds of Montana now fed to rich friends in a huge city, on a table set with silver, crystal and fine Bordeaux.

But this year felt different. It wasn't just the foolishness about the cocaine. Steve seemed tense, less reachable, worried about something Zack couldn't decode. Steve had made him a fortune when he broke into the NFL, and since then they'd always been close; now Zack found himself almost nervous around him, but didn't know why.

"TO THE CHEYENNE," Curt said, "Bear is mother or father, sister or brother. We – what's your word – we *revere* Bear. And Bear takes care of us. Even Griz. We tell each other stories." He jostled the fire with a scrub oak branch and laid it on the flames. "*True* stories."

They'd finished the elk liver, onions and pan-fried potatoes and two bags of chocolate chip cookies and had opened another bottle of Jack. Curt brushed new snow off his shoulders and leaned toward Steve and Zack. "Guess how come Bear has no tail."

"Hell, yes," Zack said, remembering where he was. "How come?"

"One winter day Bear was fishing in a hole in the ice when Fox came by. Fox asked him if he was having any luck, and Bear said no. So Fox said, 'Stick your long tail down through that hole in the ice and you'll surely catch a fish.' So Bear stuck his tail down through the hole, and Fox went off, saying 'Don't pull your tail out till I tell you.'

"Bear sat there a long time, till finally Fox called him to pull his tail out. But now the ice had completely frozen around his tail, and it broke off when he pulled it out…"

"Ouch," Steve said.

"So *that's* how it happened," Zack laughed.

"That's how the ancestors tell it," Curt said. "But speaking of bears, I've had a bear lick my ear, a bear eat out of my hand, I've had a bear cub sitting in my kitchen sink…"

"What'd you do?"

"Opened the door and let him out. The one who licked my ear was when I was sleeping, out in the woods somewhere, but that woke me up. I yelled at him and he ran off. The one who ate out of my hand – it was a buffalo rib – I called him Boston. For the Boston Bruins, you know… And I think he took that rib from my hand out of kindness, not wanting to hurt my feelings by refusing."

"In LA," Zack said, "we don't have bears."

"That's because you killed them all… You even got a grizzly on the California state flag." For a moment Curt said nothing more, then, "Friend of mine once was chased by a griz, it got him down, clawing his backpack, the pain getting worse and worse, then the bear suddenly took off. My friend rolled over, realized his backpack was on fire, the bear had lit a box of safety matches when he clawed it…"

"Holy shit," Steve laughed, still high on the coke.

Zack thought of the grizzly today ripping the elk leg apart, how when he walked the mountain seemed to tremble. "He meant me no harm, that griz. He just sniffed me and went away. He wanted the elk."

"He recognized your spirit. That you're a good man. That's why he didn't kill you." Curt huddled over the fire with his cup of Jack, his shoulders touching Zack's and Steve's, the fast-falling snow blanketing them, "Just think, how many thousands of years, we humans, in dark caves, in the cold, the fear of the bear coming in…"

Zack smiled, seeing Curt as he was, entirely without subterfuge or bullshit. Slim, tall and muscular in his white-tanned elk vest, long black ponytail, high hard cheeks and wide black eyes, an elkhorn knife at his belt and an eagle-feathered white Stetson on his head, impervious to the biting cold, unafraid of grizzlies...Yet human too, with a wife, a ranch, a truck that didn't run right.

They'd always been close, Curt more friend than guide. Someone you care about beyond normal human connections. Who had your back, and out of respect and gratitude you had his.

Maybe it was the woods, the wilderness. Hunting. Made you closer in the old way. He glanced at Steve, grinned. Steve telling another of his funny stories. Closer to him too.

TREADMILL

WHILE CURT FED his horses Steve and Zack scrubbed the iron skillet in which Curt had cooked the elk liver and onions and the tin pail in which he'd boiled the potatoes. They washed the plates and silverware and dumped them in boiling water so nobody came down with the shits, and rinsed their coffee cups and turned them upside down so snow wouldn't freeze inside them.

They sat close to the fire, which always leaves you too hot in front, Steve said, and too cold behind. But better than the deadly night. That kills you if you stray from warmth.

The thought of dying out there in the cold made Zack shiver. His body was worn and aching – from the miles hiked through deep snow in subzero winds, from slinking silently through dark timber seeking the distant flicker of an elk's tail between the trees, from kneeling to peer beneath the low boughs for the glimpse of a deer leg between the trunks...Intense and exhausting. But how lovely to come home to the fire's brave heat and light, to booze and hot food, good friends, a warm sleeping bag. To be rescued another night from cold death.

He thought of the feeling he'd had seeing the firelight through the trees on their way back to camp. Out of the cold darkness. Back to our roots.

But this year his body was paying the price.

It was harder to do what he used to do easily.

On TV he'd always encouraged kids to play football, but was that right? Wasn't he enticing them into an impossible lottery, a hundred thousand to one? But making them pay the dues anyway, the broken bones and dislocations and battered muscles, the torn cartilage and tendons, the smashed knees, the jaw that won't shut right, the ringing in your ears and the confusion in your head, with the knowledge that every year the pain and soreness just get worse?

He was here now, whatever it took. He hadn't tagged the elk the griz had eaten, so he could hunt another. Tomorrow he'd climb above 9,600 feet, where the big bulls hid in dark timber on the north-facing slopes.

He tugged off his boots and socks and stretched bare feet toward the fire. How funny and pale his toes looked, like white worms. "How blissful this is." Then, as if to explain: "Leaving LA, getting out of that weird scene for a week."

Steve smiled. "That's why we do this, every year."

"And to stay in touch."

Standing with his back to the fire Steve hunched his shoulders into the heat. "How you doing, your other investments?"

"Not so good, why?"

"Just wondering... The world out there is changing. Money's getting hard to find."

IN THE LOG-POLE CORRAL Curt opened a bag of oat cookies and gave each horse three. You had to be careful to give them all the same number or there'd be trouble. He rubbed down each horse, along the neck across the withers and back, murmuring, "You good buddy, Tom, my beautiful gray baby," or "You too Kiwa, don't you act jealous, I'm giving you a good rub too, and you got three cookies just like he did..."

Then he gave each a muzzle bag of oats, marveling as always how warm they stayed, how the snow melted off their muscular backs, their short hair. He gave each a hug and a kiss on the ear, sniffing their lovely odors, and from each got a warm nuzzle in response.

He checked each hoof for impacted ice or a wedged stone in the frog, rubbed their legs to make sure each horse was warm and comfortable, broke free a chunk of new alfalfa for each from one of the two bales Tom had carried on his packsaddle up the mountain.

Not wanting to return to camp, he sat on a corral pole enjoying the evening and the bitter stars cutting through the branches. It was so free, this, so open, so wild. What the ancestors had.

What was bothering him, he realized, was Zack and Steve. Something different about them this year. A tension, distance. Out of touch.

Though you couldn't live in a place like Lost Angeles or New York and have any connection to the earth. When you move away from nature, like the ancestors said, your heart becomes hard. No matter how real you think you are. How much money you have.

Our first teacher is our own heart, the ancestors also said. But how can it teach us if it becomes hard?

Zack seemed to love the wild country. But if you did, how could you go back to what he did? Curt had seen him on TV, the famous linebacker talking football between commercials. Tall, rugged with a hard jaw, square-faced under a blond crew cut.

Not a guy you want to mess with. Not ever.

But who *was* he? Sometimes a real person who then faded into his TV talk, looking at you with those deep blue eyes.

Never ever trust a guy who looks you sincerely in the eye.

And Steve this millionaire banker, an ultra-marathoner, whatever that is, still complaining there's no cell service up here and he can't call his wife and kids every night. Give them a break, buddy, away from you.

Though in his own way just as tough as Zack, runs ten miles on a treadmill every morning, he says. Dark-haired and narrow-faced, the opposite of Zack.

Where did he get time to run on a treadmill, with all this investing he did?

Isn't their entire life a treadmill?

"The markets are a scam," Steve had once said. "The world would be better off without them."

How, Curt had wondered, *can you keep doing something the world would be better off without?*

And Zack had said the same thing about TV football. How you got into high school football because you loved it, loved it despite the pain. Then college, and if you work like a demon, are very good and very lucky, the NFL. But then, maybe after a few years and many injuries, you start to see it's fake, unreal. Has no real value. Just hurts lots of people … In more ways than one.

So how can you keep doing it?

Back in camp he checked that everything was covered and safe from the deepening snow. For morning he put the coffee and filters, the big pot, and the bread all under a tarp, and tucked the dozen eggs by the foot of his sleeping bag so they wouldn't freeze.

FOR FOUR DAYS Steve hadn't talked to Marcie and the kids. It had become a gnawing desire, as if he couldn't breathe without the reassurance of their voices. He turned on his phone, fingers numb. *No service.* 8:12 pm, so just after ten in New York. Marcie'd be checking the kids' homework, keeping them off the internet. Telling them good night stories about real life.

Did he really need to call, or was he just lonely?

He *could* call. To say what? That we've been up here in the snow and I'm freezing. I miss you. Why am I here? Yes, I know why: to better hone myself as a man.

"You don't need to hone yourself," Marcie said inside his head. "You already *are.*"

I knew that, he realized. *Then why call?*

I love you, that's why.

To call he'd have to go down the mountain. But couldn't tell Curt he was going. Or Curt would say call 911 about the crashed plane.

"In the old days," Curt had once joked, "guys left for months on hunting trips. No cell phones back then. No talkin with the wife every day, back then."

No, Steve had thought, just the pure white light of every moment in elegant untouchable nature. Skies thick with birds, prairies dark with antelope and bison, nights bright with many thousand stars, cold clear water in every creek… "Yeah. I wish we could be back there."

Curt had glanced at him, surprised. "*You* would be back there?"

"Thinking it over, what we've gained and what we've lost, I think we lived better back then. Trouble is, we didn't understand the universe. Inside the body. Inside life."

Curt had looked away, back at him. "And we do now?"

IT SEEMED A BAD OMEN to Zack that Curt had shot the first elk. When he was supposed to be finding the elk for *them*. Not that Zack wanted to be guided. Or be with Steve. What he really wanted was to be alone. Why, after all these years? These ten days they'd looked forward to, every year.

"Keeps us in touch," he'd said. But did it?

He hadn't told Steve about last Friday in Malibu, the two Vegas toughs who showed up at his front door the morning before he flew to Bozeman. "You got a week," they said. Plus their boss Haney the Rat calling Zack every day. "Pay us or we drop the bomb on you."

The Vegas guys don't invite you to the high money tables because they like you. You were stupid to think they did. It was because they needed you there to pull the suckers in, to *legitimize* the place. And because maybe you'd be stupid enough to lose your own money there too. Like you were inciting everybody else to do.

Other gamblers, the rich spenders and wannabees, so idiotically impressed that Zack was there. The future Hall of Famer, the famous linebacker, the TV sports guy with the solid shoulders, strong jaw and winner's smile. The guy everybody trusted because they thought football makes you noble. Giving gambling a veneer of cool respectability.

How they fought for a chance to kiss his ass. What was wrong with people?

Now despite all this he owed the Vegas guys two million. No big deal in real terms. But no more gorgeous hookers. No more frothing hot tubs with two magnificent women fighting over his prick.

No matter what Steve recommended, Zack *had* to cash out his portfolio, pay Haney the Rat and the other Vegas guys their two million before they got mean. And the transactions should please Steve, with all the commissions he'd get.

Like so much in life, you do what you have to.

But how do we find happiness? Despite all the lies of modern life, the ads, the TV, the corporations and politicians, the distractions and "entertainments" that turn us into serfs?

What is good, and what evil? When cocaine is money, does that change how we see it? When money's an option, don't we embrace and defend what we used to call sin?

And come to love it.

Why was he worried?

What am I here for, he'd used to wonder. But could never find an answer so gave up asking.

Is it true, that you have to do what you have to?

The bullet snapped past his head.

STEVE WAITED ten minutes after Curt and Zack had gone to their tents before he shouldered his rifle and headed down the mountain. The snow was deep and the air very cold, burning his cheeks and the inside of his mouth when he opened it.

But it felt lovely, prehistoric, primal. Just him and the night and the cold and the mountain. The ancient battle. Which in the end life always lost.

For now it was joyous. The black trunks and white snow, the delicate mist of crystals sifting down from the boughs, the air a razor in his nostrils, So good. A challenge: live or die.

"Way too much snow," he said when he finally reached Marcie. "We may have to leave camp, go down."

"You poor thing...Are you staying warm?"

"It's warm in the tent. And once you're out hunting you don't mind the cold."

"If you have to go down, you'll be home sooner?"

"Yeah, why? Everything okay?"

"No worse than before. No, yes. It is. It *is* worse."

His chest went hollow. "What?"

"Those securities you were going to sell? Merrill Lynch says we can't cash them." She said nothing for a moment, gathering herself. "They're worthless."

"They *can't be!* They're cash equivalent. Oh shit." He turned from the phone, staring at the black firs against the white night, his chest crushed by this news as by a bullet, something he could not survive. "Oh Jesus Marcie."

"So all your clients…"

"Zack – I put all his money there."

"You put lots of people's money there."

"How will I ever…"

"It gets worse."

He shook his head, as if she could see him. "It can't."

"The Lefkowitz deal just fell through."

"Fuck!" Her 1.2 percent broker's take on a $9.3 million apartment, next month's rent and expenses down the drain. "*Why?*"

"Parnell found them a place. Gramercy Park for God's sake!"

The air burned his throat, pierced his lungs. For an instant he thought of the climb he had to make back up the mountain to camp. When what he wanted was to sit down and die.

"Steve, what are we going to *do?*"

"Don't give up, baby. Don't give up. I'll be home soon." He shut off, wondering how he could tell her not to give up when he already had.

STEAL FROM A THIEF

AFTER FOUR CUPS of whisky when Zack had crawled into his tent he hadn't even bothered to turn on his ebook, not caring about what went on in some imaginary world. Over-weary, weirdly unsettled, he wanted to talk to Monica but there was no damn service up here.

The griz, the wrecked plane, the cocaine.

The meeting next week that would decide his future.

Steve's bullet smashing into the aspen.

What had Steve been shooting at? There'd been no elk, no nearby tracks.

He thought of the two Vegas debt collectors who'd shown up at his door last week. One tall and muscular with a tiny mustache. The other short and swarthy, light on his feet.

He could've taken them both out, but what then? And then it's in the news...

He'd tell Steve to sell his auction rate securities. Get those assholes off his back.

He tried to find a more comfortable position in his sleeping bag but kept sliding off the foam mat. A root underneath bit into his ribs, he pushed it down but it kept popping back up.

How many years had Steve been like a brother? Believed in Zack when nobody else would. Told him, "You're the best out there. And I'm going to make you more money than you ever even *imagined.*" And so he had.

When Zack hit the NFL, chances were that like most guys he'd be finished in a year. From horrendous injuries during training camp inflicted by older guys on your own team protecting their buddies whose position you were trying to take. Didn't matter if you were better. There were always better players coming up – by that they meant *less injured.*

Like everyone he'd compared football to the Coliseum. You survive by killing others. But back then there was no way out. You were a slave and this was your fate. Was he somehow still a slave?

After his first year Zack was locked into the NFL. Till the injuries took him out. A dance of fate: if somebody's helmet had been two inches lower it wouldn't have blown out your knee ... that kind of thing ... millions of injuries every year – for what? What did the TV viewer *not get?*

And now nearly 2,000 NFL veterans suing all 32 teams for violating Federal drug prescription laws, for handing out opioids, narcotics, like candy. Here, pop these Vicodins, these Percocets and OxyContins before you go out on the field. And more at half time. Take home another handful to deal with the pain tonight. We'll have more for you tomorrow.

And here's a shot of Toradol before every game, and another at half time. All season long, every time you were hurt. When you were hurting all the time. When the drug company says don't use Toradol more than five times in a row or it can give you a heart attack or stroke.

Guys who played a whole season with a broken leg and the team docs didn't tell them it was broken. "A bone bruise," the docs said. "Play through it."

How many times had he played through it? How many concussions had he had? Back in the days when you shook them off, maybe a couple a game. Whacked the holy Hell out of your head. You hopped up, headed back to where you thought the huddle might be, realizing that the guys in the white were your team, not the guys in brown. Trying to remember what the fuck you were doing, could you possibly run the next play.

You're in the huddle, body screaming with pain, your eyesight fuzzy, a cascade of wavering images before you. Over the razor howl in your ears you can't hear what the defensive captain's saying. You clap like the others, but a little slower, turn to O'Donnely, the nose tackle. "What the fuck is the play?"

You're strong on the tight end but it's a weak side pass play so you make a quick run at the QB till he throws and now your head is clearing a bit and you realize how lucky you are that the offense didn't come at you…

It had always seemed to him hilarious that the Federal government had its knickers in a knot about cocaine but never says a word about the thousands of NFL players with deadly concussions, narcotics damage, and who can barely walk and talk.

That the government doesn't even tax the NFL.

After seven years, too injured to play anymore, Zack *had* found his way out: TV Sports Analysis – *hilarious, that idea.* That well-trained violence was worthy of analysis, like some important historical event, a new triumph in medicine.

And the wannabees can even play "fantasy" football. Pretend they're their favorite player. Go out there and hit, while you sit in your armchair with a sixpack of Bud Lite. When one single real hit would take you down for life.

Football's a mix of ballet and chess, he'd always said. But watching it is just sports porn, as Monica had once told him: seeing others do what you'd like to do yourself. And it panders to the viewers' love of violence. And pain.

As long as the violence and pain doesn't happen to them.

CURT WATCHED the dancing voluptuous flicker of the dying fire on the tent over his head.

How lovely to lie in this lingering smoke of lodgepole and scrub oak, the frigid wind sifting between bare oak boughs and tall swinging firs, the cold metallic snow, the bitter air and the whisper of distant stars, the warmer upwind scent of horses standing asleep in the corral. The memory of fire on mossy rock in rooted soil, of the lives lived here for many thousand years, Blackfoot, Arapahoe, Sioux, Nez Perce, Cheyenne – all the way back to the first adventurers into this huge land between the towering glaciers, hunting the reindeer, mammoth and buffalo south.

When the spirits were with them.

Till the white man came the buffalo herds so huge it took three days to walk through one herd, antelope in hundreds of thousands, the earth white and tan with their backs to the horizons, a sky thick with eagles and hawks, and darkened for days by flights of geese, cranes, ducks, swans, passenger pigeons, and a hundred other bird tribes that had vanished since the white man. Or so few in numbers that everyone celebrates when one is seen.

And wolves far as the eye could see. And their raven twin spirits watching over them.

So many wolves that a two-mile road in Montana is built up entirely on their bones...

Unending forests.

Infinite prairies soaring into clean blue sky.

Rivers like diamonds, wide and pure, tasting of every good thing they'd come from.

All gone now.

Was that world better? What if he'd lived back then, he and Diana, instead of running a ten-section cattle ranch in Judith Basin County, up in the Little Belt Mountains an hour north on bad roads from White Sulfur Springs, itself a forgotten dot on the vast map of Montana? With only two alfalfa cuttings this year because of the drought? The cattle market in the tank and the industrial wind bastards hunting down every rancher in Judith Basin.

Now the industrial wind bastards had a lien on his ranch.

And it would take two hundred thousand dollars to buy them out. When he and Diana had, what, maybe seven hundred dollars in their Bank of the Rockies account in White Sulphur Springs?

This land had belonged to the people till Wihio the white man came. Came with his lies, guns and diseases. Just as Sweet Medicine, the ancient prophet of the people had predicted. *A white man, a trickster, will come to destroy the world.*

At first the people had welcomed the white man, the ancient Cheyenne courtesy toward visitors. Then the land stealing, the slaughter of the buffalo, the liquor madness, the endless battles, the last murderous conflicts at the Washita and hundreds of other places, and Sand Creek massacre, the death march to Oklahoma and the deadly escape back to Montana…

Where are you, Maheo the Creator? Why did you let this happen?

He had to forget all this. Pretend it had never been.

This was how the world is.

Stop thinking.

He settled into the sleeping bag's warmth. Both his dudes jumpy tonight, mostly Steve. Who knew what disasters went on in his life? Maybe not even he.

Even though Curt had spent ten days with them in each of the last three years, he realized he didn't really know them. In fact they seemed suddenly like strangers.

BACK in his tent, Steve tried to digest what Marcie had told him. But it was too horrible, too awesomely encompassing. To be damaged in so many places, all at once.

The auction rate securities had been sold to everyone as liquid cash equivalent. Citigroup, UBS, Merrill Lynch, JPMorgan Chase, Morgan Stanley, RBC Group – all too big to fail… "The single greatest fraud ever perpetrated on investors," Marcie'd said some financial analyst had just called them. And he'd dropped his clients into them. Like giving them AIDS.

How was he going to tell Zack? Why was Zack pushing to sell out, anyway?

If he could convince Zack to postpone selling them, maybe they'd come back? In the meantime, how were he and Marcie going to live? The apartment, the cars, the private schools… all that going up in flames?

The SEC, why hadn't they overseen this, like they were supposed to? When the government agency you pay taxes for doesn't protect you, why have it?

And up the hill, in the deepening snow, a plane of cocaine worth ten million.

Maybe more.

Under maritime law, when a ship is abandoned the cargo belongs to whoever finds it first. Was that true too for air cargo?

Is it wrong to steal from a thief?

He rolled up on one elbow, tipped some coke on his knife and sniffed it. *Oh God good.* How lucky he'd pocketed some when he'd left the plane, because he needed to stay high for what he now had to do. The coke felt lovely and warm sinking through his chest, his stomach, his arms and legs. This golden glow.

Lady Coke I love you. How many times have I buried myself in your luscious flesh, felt your lissome skin against my chest? How many times I've kissed every inch of your tantalizing body? Tasted every cell of your sacred heat?

How many times have I inhaled you with the dedication of a lover? Made you mine?

How many times have I followed your counsel, to grave success?

I'm not giving you up again. Never again. I promise.

He turned over restlessly in his sleeping bag. Must have hiked twenty-five miles today, most of it through deep snow. How come he wasn't tired?

How come he was trying to sleep when he knew he couldn't?

Zack would go apeshit about his portfolio. Like it was a big thing, twelve million bucks. That wasn't *real* money. And he, Steve, had done his best to make it grow.

Zack had said no risks. But no risks didn't grow it, and Steve's job was to grow it. Not his fault the markets went sideways. Not his fault at all.

But it *was* his fault. He couldn't deny it, didn't want to.

Zack had wanted the money protected and now it was gone.

He had savaged his friend's well-being.

You can't blame yourself for everything, Marcie had said.

But that's how you get ahead, he'd told her. Taking responsibility for everything.

Trying to fix everything.

He had to tell Zack about his lost money.

The tent above his head sank toward him with the weight of new snow.

ZACK WOKE, wondered why. A sound, an absence? Had to piss.

He banged on the tent sides to shake off the new snow, squirmed out of his sleeping bag, tugged on his unlaced boots, unzipped the tent fly and crawled out.

The snow had stopped. A carious moon glared through the branches. Cold stung his nostrils like fire. He shivered, had a moment's sorrow for all the animals out in this frozen night, without a sleeping bag or tent or fire or even a gun to protect them.

And death comes fast, at the tiniest mistake.

Or even no mistake.

He shuffled to the side of the tent and pissed with a long deep sigh, burning a hole in the snow.

From Steve's tent a faint line of tracks led down toward the distant highway and came back up again. And new tracks led up the mountain toward the plane. He must have gone uphill to piss, Zack decided. But why so far?

Was he crazy, out in this deadly night?

Zack checked Steve's tent. Empty.

Steve's rifle and the pack frame he normally stowed down one side of the tent were gone.

Zack ducked back into his tent for his coat, hat, gloves, gun and headlamp, laced his boots, zipped his tent shut and followed Steve's tracks uphill over the ridge toward the plane.

THE CAVE

THE MOON was crystal, the wind like dry ice in his lungs. Steve's tracks were following the same trail he and Zack had made coming back from the plane, now just a trace under the new-fallen snow. Steve was moving fast, sure of being alone.

When Zack followed him to the ridge above the plane he could see the dark thread of Steve's tracks but no sign of the plane, realized it was now nearly buried in snow. From it another set of tracks climbed the far side of the valley, a tiny figure toiling up it, bent under something on his back.

Zack reached the plane as Steve came running downhill, an empty pack frame slung over one shoulder. The plane's door was open, in the light of his headlamp Zack could see that one coffin was empty, the other half-gone.

Steve came up panting, bent over to catch his breath. "Too high up here. Can't breathe."

"*What* are you doing?"

Steve huffed a laugh. "Moving our coke. You can help with what's left."

"*Our* coke?" Zack sat down in the snow. "*You* are *nuts!*"

"I hid it in that cave up there we found last year." Steve sucked in a breath. "Now it's ours. *All* ours."

Zack remembered the cave, undiscovered, a few arrowheads on a stone ledge, blackened earth from ancient fires. It had seemed sacred, and they had touched nothing. "We have to put it back!"

"Are you totally crazy?" Steve shook him. "We're going to be rich!"

"I already am rich, soon as I cash out. I don't need your stolen drugs."

"Yes you do." Steve clapped him on the shoulder. "Look, man, it's hard to tell you, but I've just learned your money isn't available right now."

Zack felt his muscles tighten. "Isn't *available?*"

"We put it in auction rate securities, remember? Citigroup? Now they're saying they won't release it."

"You said it was cash *equivalent!* You promised me! Buy however many millions you want, they give us one-fifty over Libor and a seven-day redeem." Zack held himself back from hitting Steve, smashing him down. "That's what you *said!*"

"That's what *they* said. It's in the prospectus. The SEC backed it. S&P and Moody's rated it Triple A, no risk. But now with other values going south there's been a run on them. Merrill Lynch, UBS, Citigroup, they're all getting hit. Trouble is, the cover's only eight percent, and they've already blown past it. So it's sucking money, money they don't have."

Zack nearly fell to his knees. All his years, all the work, all the pain and the freedom it had bought, gone. "You're saying they're *worth*less?"

"For the moment." Steve waved a hand at the plane, uphill toward the cave. "So this coke, it can make us whole again."

"*You,*" Zack tried to hold down the wrath rising inside him, "you're saying you've *lost* my money?"

"Mine too. I'm in as deep as you. I'm suing them, but…" he waved a hand uselessly, "you know…"

Zack looked away, head spinning, the night black and ominous. At the future with no money. The job he was losing.

At Haney the Rat and the Vegas guys who wanted their two million bucks.

He glanced at Steve, this guy he'd trusted absolutely. Wanted to smash him down. Wanted to understand *what is it I'm not understanding? Maybe it isn't Steve's fault?*

"Give me time," Steve said. "I'll figure a way."

Zack realized he wasn't breathing, inhaled. Already the shock was wearing down: *This is the new reality. Deal with it.* "Who's this lawyer?"

"He's a securities specialist. Used to work for the SEC. Says we have a chance of getting some of it back."

"*Some* of it?"

"Thirty cents on the dollar. Maybe. And I'm pushing the New York and Massachusetts DA's to look into it. They don't like it either, it drives up their muni rates." Steve crawled into the plane. "Here," he called, voice muffled, "take these bricks as I hand them out and stack them on that tarp. When we get thirty we'll tie them on the pack frame and carry it up the mountain."

"Curt's going down to the cops, remember?"

"Yeah, but we didn't tell him about the coke." Steve's head popped out of the plane. "Though you were going to, you idiot."

"They're gonna know, soon as they look in those coffins. You can't get all that powder out."

"No they won't." Steve glanced around, spoke low as if it were a secret. "Gasoline on hot metal, eventually, guess what?"

"Fuck you, you *are* crazy –"

"It's the *only* solution, man. That way the cops don't know about the coke, and even the owners, if they come back, they might think it *all* burned … with six feet of snow on it, it'll be hard to tell …"

"Your tracks," Zack nodded uphill, toward the cave, "they're visible to anyone."

Steve pointed up. "You been watching this snow? More's coming. Lots more. There won't be a trace of our tracks by morning."

"And you think you can *sell* it? What are you going to do, run ads in the papers?"

"Wall Street folks are always buying … And you, with all your friends in Vegas, what are you worried about? Coke is Vegas and Vegas is coke. All you have to do is ask around."

All I have to do, Zack thought, is hike down to the highway and call the cops. But then Steve and I get arrested for trying to steal the coke, or I get accessory because I didn't tell Curt about the coke, I lose my job, and never get back my portfolio Steve invested for me.

And the coke's owners will know who we are and come after us. And Haney the Rat and his Vegas guys want theirs now.

THE INSTANT he heard it Curt knew. Grizzly in the horses. He tore from his sleeping bag, grabbed his flashlight and Ruger and sprinted barefoot through the snow for the corral, the horses stamping, neighing and kicking, a deep growl.

He fired a shot in the air as he ran, hoping to scare the griz but it kept snarling like it had a horse down, killing it.

Curt leaped the corral into the mix of swirling kicking horses, the griz twenty yards away, red-eyed, jaws wide as it swung its massive head from side to side, ready to charge. Curt fired a shot past its head, worrying as he fired again that the shots would just madden it, and even if he hit it between the eyes a .357 slug would just piss it off. He fired again, just past its ear, yelling as he ran toward it, and with a strange hiss the griz turned and shambled into the night.

"YOU HEAR THAT?" Zack cupped his ear with a frozen glove. They were taking turns with the pack frame, each carrying it a few hundred yards uphill, then the other. "Maybe Curt sees we're missing, wants us back?"

"Why?"

"Worries we're out here, that's all."

"Snowing harder." Steve held out a palmful. "Maybe he's worried about that."

Zack halted, pack frame on one shoulder. "Our doing this could screw Curt up, somehow."

"No way he'll ever know."

"In the morning he's going to want us all to go down."

"All the more reason to move this stuff now."

Zack followed him uphill. He thought of going down the mountain also, to call Monica. But it was too late now, unless she was on late shift... He imagined pretending he'd just wanted to call her to say hi and how much he missed her. Not mentioning this weird and deadly scene he had somehow stumbled into.

BY THE TIME Curt had calmed the horses and got back to his tent his bare feet were blue and numb. He pulled on socks and boots and stumbled to the fire but it was out.

He waded into the forest snatching low dead branches then remembered he'd already stacked the morning's kindling under a tarp, went to it and shoved some into the fire pit, ran feet aching to the slit trench and grabbed toilet paper and pushed it under the kindling, tugged a box of matches from his pocket and struck one on the box.

It dragged a damp furrow in the tinder strip, snapped.

Damnation, the kicking horses had dumped snow on him, soaked his pocket. He ran back to the cook tent and snatched a lighter, lit the toilet paper but a gust knocked snow from a bough on it. He dashed back to the slit trench, grabbed more toilet paper and lit it under the sticks again but now they were wet from the fallen snow.

Damn again. He stood, took a breath, stumbling on numb feet. He was going to have bad frostbite. "Zack! Steve! Come give me a hand!"

Silence of new snow sifting down through the boughs and piling on the ground. "Where *are* you?"

He waded through the snow to Steve's tent. Empty. Zack's too.

"Steve! Zack!" His voice echoed through the hills and in its echo he recognized fear. *You're being stupid*, he told himself. *You could die.* He ran back to the cook tent, lit the propane cooktop and put his bare numb feet on its edge.

Where were Steve and Zack, the damn fools?

Then he smelled it. Upwind. Rank, rotten meat, thick hot damp fur.

The griz was back.

He yanked on his boots, snatched the flashlight and scrambled out the cook tent grabbing at his hip holster but the Ruger was gone.

He checked his pockets, the cook tent floor.

The Ruger was truly gone.

Maybe he'd lost it in the corral, trying to quiet the horses.

Head down, ears back, with a deep grunting growl the grizzly shuffled toward him out of the forest.

THE PLANE BLEW in a tall orange ball turning the night incandescent and driving them back with its heat. Snow swirled down on it in great hissing clouds that the flames steamed and drove upwards. They watched till the coffins were cinders at the bottom of the bare black fuselage. The snow fell harder, dampening the blaze, obscuring it as they trudged away, till the plane was a glimmer on the horizon, then gone.

The blizzard wailed across the valley, erased the line between earth and sky and hid the tracks they'd made coming from camp. They could see nothing but stinging snow in their eyes, snow and ice packed to their bodies and swirling past their feet. Zack went first, probing with his boots for their old tracks under the new drifts, a gloved hand like a visor over his eyes to keep them from freezing.

Soon he could no longer find their tracks under the snow. He wandered side to side, feeling with his toes, finding nothing. The blizzard hailing down had hidden Steve; Zack yelled for him but the answer seemed to come from everywhere.

"I am not going to lose you," Zack said aloud, crawling through the snow looking for his back tracks till there was a fudge of gray in the whiteness ahead, a blur that became Steve bent over, hiding his face from the wind. "Where the fuck were you?" he yelled.

They wandered on, in circles, lost before the beginning of time, in howling snow and deadly cold. Zack imagined them dying here, to be found in the spring, half-gnawed by animals. He thought of all the people down through time who'd died in frozen wildernesses.

He thought of his sleeping bag, the Jack Daniels in his morning coffee. Live for that.

Behind him Steve followed with the dumb obedience of the dying. One foot in front of the other, in the same holes. Easy, humans had been doing it for millions of years.

WHEN THE GRIZ kept coming Curt had grabbed a plastic tarp, twisted it round a pole, lit it on the propane cooktop and run yelling at him. Surprised, the great bear had risen up on rear legs, taller than the low trees, monstrous in the dark. Expecting to be slapped dead Curt shoved the blazing tarp against the grizzly's chest and the bear gave a high grunt and scrambled into the woods.

Curt still couldn't find the Ruger. He kicked at the snow leading to the corral, then in the corral among the nervous agitated horses, but it had vanished.

He heard a distant thud, straightened up to listen but it didn't come again. From up where the dudes had said the plane was. Maybe he'd imagined it.

Didn't matter. Whatever those two idiots were doing out there in this frigid night he would find them. Because if they died he'd never get another guide job. Blacklisted.

Nobody hired guys who let their clients die.

Unless the griz got them. Even then.

But when he tried to follow Steve's and Zack's tracks uphill they vanished under the blinding new snow, and finally he turned back.

"Steve!" he yelled till he couldn't yell any longer, "Zack! Where are you?"

When he got back to camp his watch said 02:41. Five hours till dawn.

THE SNOW CAME AT THEM horizontally, then down, then sideways. It ate into their iced-up faces, froze their eyes shut and their ears numb. Each breath was a knife down the throat.

"Maybe here," Steve called, his words snatched by the wind.

"This ridge, has to be the one above camp."

"If he'd only shoot again –"

So much seemed familiar, the sloping snow, the firs nestled close, a tall pine, the tinkle of a stream under its ice. "Here," Zack called. "We've found it."

But it led to a waterfall off a cliff that would have killed them had they gone five more steps.

Snowing so hard Zack couldn't tell up or down, wished he'd brought a compass, realized he could use his phone, stepped back to reach in his pocket and slipped off the cliff down into the crown of a tree and grabbed a bough that snapped but slowed him enough to grab another and clamp his legs around the tree's trunk as it teetered over the void.

Not to Worry

H E WAS SHAKING so hard he could barely hold, realized he was biting a branch but didn't dare let go, hugged the tree to his chest till the teetering slowed. He could hear Steve's yells but couldn't tell from where, could see only this cage of boughs encasing him in howling snow, realized he was in the top of a fir tree that stood on a tiny ledge with a cliff beneath it.

"Steve!" he screamed, "*Help!*"

"Zack!" Steve's voice wavered. "Zack! *Zack!*"

He tried to climb higher but the tree grew thin and tipped him out over the cliff. The snowstorm cleared for an instant and he could see gut-wrenching black rock and vertical ice below the tree. Somehow he had to climb down the tree then up the cliff. And not slip and fall into the dark emptiness below.

The terror was like a deer's in a tiger's jaws. When there's no hope. *You will do this.* One step at a time.

And if a step seems dangerous you pull back, find another way.

Till you get to the top.

It wasn't so bad going down the fir tree, stepping from limb to limb, sometimes slipping on icy bark but always able to hold on to the limbs above.

"Zack!" Steve's voice, tiny on the wind.

"I'm coming!" Zack yelled, but Steve kept calling.

The rock face he had to climb was vertical and icy. Black granite ribs stuck from it, too slick to grip.

He'd always hated heights. Since he was a kid stuck on a ladder and his Dad called, "You big sissy get down from there."

It was Death, this aching vertical rock. This fir tree like a monastic companion, saving your soul. But you can't leave it: there's no way up or down this cliff.

Maybe there was. One point at a time.

One point was ice that he hammered from the rock with his fist, another a slim frozen ledge his foot kept skidding off, then a vertical slit he could jam his fingers into. Once he looked down, the trunk of the fir tree descending below him into darkness, into death, and the looking down nearly made him slip off the cliff.

Twenty feet from the top there was no way to climb further. A pure sheet of black rock, tilted past vertical.

A headlamp flashed down. "Zack!" Steve shouted over the wind, "Hold tight."

He held on, fingers quivering, breathing fast, shuddering with cold and fear.

The headlamp came back. "I'm sending down a pole. I'll hold it. You grab it and climb."

Steve slid a slender spruce trunk down over the cliff. It was just long enough, sticky with resin where Steve had cut off the branches. It was impossibly hard to climb. With each lunge he feared pulling Steve off the cliff.

When he slithered over the top to safety he lay breathing hard into the snow, unable to speak. Steve sat beside him saying nothing, his hand on Zack's shoulder.

STUMBLING BLINDLY downhill through the new drifts and dark timber Zack tripped over a low branch and fell face-first into something soft and snow-covered. He couldn't believe it, didn't dare. His tent. In the flailing snow he'd walked into camp and tripped over a guy line.

They were home.

He brushed ice from his face and clothes and crawled into his sleeping bag and slept.

He woke. For a few seconds he wasn't sure where he was, what he was. Coffee odor on the biting cold air, the tang of bacon and scrub oak smoke. There'd be pancakes with maple syrup, and fried eggs, and Jack Daniels for the coffee.

What life had been like just a few hours ago, before he'd learned his money was gone and they'd stolen the coke. Then he remembered the cliff, the wandering in the snowstorm, the wicked cold, the burning plane, the cocaine hidden where it could be easily found.

His stomach clenched. How did this happen so fast?

He crawled out of his bag and unzipped his tent and a wall of snow fell in on him.

"You should whack the tent wall first." Curt called from the fire pit, laying bacon on a cast iron griddle on the coals.

Zack felt an instant of anger, dismissed it. He stretched to full height, arcing his back. Felt all the muscles pull, tired but lithe.

"Where were you two?" Curt said.

Zack stretched more, tightened his coat round his shoulders. "I couldn't sleep. When the moon came out I decided to hike up the ridge, see the view. Then Steve got up to piss, saw my tracks and followed them, make sure I was okay. We've always been like that, watching each other's backs."

"Is that so?"

"It was beautiful, till it started snowing. Then we heard a shot so we came back. Was that you?"

"Your damn grizzly got in the horses. I shot to scare him, lost my gun in the snow."

"He's gone?"

"He'll be back. So one of us has to stay here. With the horses."

"After yesterday and last night," Zack said, "I don't need to go anywhere."

"Yep," Curt said, "you had quite a time."

"You can't imagine."

Curt smiled. "Maybe I can."

Zack woke Steve, told him what he'd said to Curt about last night.

"Good, that was smart." Steve rubbed his face, his words muffled.

"And when we heard his shot we started back, but got lost in the snowstorm."

"Why'd he shoot?"

"Grizzly."

"He's back?"

"He's back. Curt wants us to stay with the horses. He's leaving after breakfast to go down and call about the plane. He'll wait for the cops to come, then show them the way to the plane. They'll be on snowmobiles…"

Steve slid into his trousers. "Fuck."

"If they trace it to the cave –"

"YOU COULD'VE DIED up there," Curt snapped as they wolfed down bacon, eggs, coffee and Jack Daniels. "What the Hell got into you guys?"

"Nah," Zack smiled. "It was beautiful."

Curt stared at him. "This isn't New York City." He turned to Zack. "This isn't Lost Angeles. You guys can't wander off at two a.m. and thirty below and expect to live."

"It's probably safer here," Steve chuckled, "than New York."

"You ever been to LA at two a.m.?" Zack said, backing him up.

"No and I don't want to. But if you boys want to hunt with me you got to be reasonable. If you die it's bad for my reputation."

Zack laughed, stood and slapped Curt's shoulder, tossed his coffee dregs on the snow. "We'll keep that in mind."

"Not to worry," Steve added. "We won't die on you."

"WE HAVE TO MOVE FAST!" Steve said to Zack when Curt had saddled Kiwa and started down the mountain.

"Let's find that Ruger." Zack started tromping the snow on the way to the corral.

"Fuck the Ruger! Once Curt calls this in, it's on the cop radio, and the folks who owned that plane will come after us. The cops'll come too, they'll be all over the place." Steve made a helpless gesture with his hands. "They're not going to be fooled by a burned plane."

"You said they would."

"I said it was the best option. At the time. Now we got to move it."

"Move *what?*"

"The coke, you idiot."

Zack felt a hard shape in the snow underfoot. Reached down. *The Ruger.*

He wiped snow from the barrel and grip. It felt cold and solid in his palm. He looked up at Steve. "Did you *really* call me an idiot?"

"Sometimes you are." Steve smiled grandly. "Me too. But you're still my friend." He shrugged, raised his hands: maybe.

Zack slipped the Ruger into his coat pocket. "You said the burnt plane would stop them."

"So should we sit on our ass hoping for the best?" Steve gave him a questioning look. "Or shall we be proactive?"

"Your being proactive is how I lost my money."

"The Securities Exchange Commission and the Federal Reserve lost your money. Them and S&P and Moody's – the rating agencies. They're all bankers. They do what's best for the banks and big bondholders. Notice how every time the Fed raises rates the bank stocks go up? With higher rates the banks make more money for doing the same thing. Their job, all these guys, is protecting the rich, not the average American."

"I don't care about that." Zack took a breath, tried to think. "So you want to move the coke down the mountain then rent a truck? How we going to get to Bozeman to do that?"

"One of us will have to hitch."

"Curt and the cops will follow our tracks –"

"Let's worry about that when the time comes." Steve was already walking toward the corral. "You saddle the gray, I'll get the pinto."

"And you think Curt's not going to see we've used his horses?"

"Maybe not."

"Steve, we've hunted with this guy four years now…I don't want to screw him over."

Steve looked at Zack, shook his head. "We won't hurt them."

To put a packsaddle on a horse looked easy; like a regular saddle you cinched it under the horse's belly while the horse inhaled and bulged its belly to keep the cinch loose – but if the cinch stayed loose the load could shift and slide down under its belly.

So he let the gray exhale then cinched him tight while the horse groaned in response, then tightened the straps around his chest and rump. Towing him at a half run he followed Steve and the pinto horse up the ridge and along it eastward, above the crashed plane and up to the Paleolithic cave that now held their worldly goods.

FROM HIGHWAY 191 Curt called his wife's cousin, Kenny Stauffenberg, the Gallatin County Sheriff. Even here the reception was bad and Kenny had a hard time understanding.

"I been hunting with two dudes up by the Buffalo Horns, that valley that peters out in the cliffs, about fifteen miles in, going east?"

"Where you got that seven-pointer."

"Exactly. Well, a plane's gone down, just north of there. In that next valley."

"What kind of plane?"

"Single engine, apparently. You had any news?"

"About it? Not a damn thing." Kenny cleared his throat. "You see bodies?"

"I didn't see the plane. One of my dudes did. You know, that football guy, played for the Broncos?"

"Zack Wilson? The one who's now a sports announcer?"

"He found the plane, the valley going north toward Goose Creek. North of Lone Indian Peak, about fourteen miles in. Says there were no bodies, just the track of one guy walking out, who seemed okay."

"We'll get on it. When'd he find it?"

"Late yesterday. He told me last night. I got out soon's I could."

"I know that, Curt."

"I'll wait down here for your guys. Who you sending?"

Kenny busied himself for a moment, a clicking keyboard and rustle of paper. "We're gonna put four Arctic Cats on a trailer.

Three guys plus me. Be there fast as we can, hopefully an hour. I'll have Myrtle check the Hospital, see if the pilot's come in."

"Zack said the guy was walking fine."

"You've talked to Diana?"

"That's my next call. Why?"

"No reason. What's the latest on that windmill company?"

"The industrial wind bastards? It'll take two hundred grand to get rid of them."

"They got you sewed up, huh?"

"They bought my loan, found a way to foreclose."

"They're all over the country, putting up these hideous turbines that do no good, just make them rich on taxpayer money."

"They kill birds, millions of them. Bats too. Destroy property values, drive people crazy..."

"You know the family's going to pitch in."

"That's real kind, Kenny, but it wouldn't be right. And nowhere near enough."

"We'll find a way. We always do."

PAIN KILLERS

CURT CALLED DIANA from the highway but she didn't answer. Out with the chickens, maybe. Bringing in the heifers, it's so cold, giving them extra hay.

"It's me," he said when the message signal beeped. "I'm down the mountain to meet cousin Kenny, we had a crashed plane up here, nobody hurt apparently. Got a couple more days with these dudes then I'm coming home. Miss you. Miss you all the time ..."

He short-roped Kiwa to a lodgepole and sat beside 191 watching the few trucks and cars go by. Thought of how it was once, a beautiful canyon made by the River over millions of years, how it was when his people travelled up and down its well-worn paths, paths that went everywhere through the back country. When everything was back country.

Now it was a highway of hardened oil that carried the cars and trucks between Bozeman, Big Sky and Yellowstone. There'd been a time, thirty years ago, he'd thought Big Sky would die a natural death. How many city folks, after all, would come up here to the snow and ice just to titillate themselves? Then that Democratic Senator, Melcher, passed a back-room law allowing logging in wilderness areas, and soon the single most beautiful place on this planet, Jack Creek, fifty thousand acres of primeval wilderness, fell to the Plum Creek chainsaws. For no reason whatsoever. Death to the wilderness.

He'd wearied over this so many times he was determined to do it no more.

THE CAVE was covered in new snow. They tied the horses to the trees and took turns handing out the kilos and stacking them in the paniers. When all four paniers were full they loaded them on horses' packsaddles while the horses snorted and stamped, their eyes white with anger.

They bundled the leftover kilos in two tarps and tied the tarps across the packsaddles. The horses, overburdened now, shook their bodies to undo the loads, swinging their backsides ominously.

Steve pulled at the pinto, trying to turn her. In a frozen instant Zack saw the pinto's hoof pulled back to strike, come fast at his face as he dove aside raising his right arm that the pinto's hoof smashed knocking him down.

His arm raged with pain. He rolled over and over yelling then caught himself.

"Zack! Zack!" Steve was shaking him, grabbed his arm. Zack screamed and passed out.

Steve rubbed snow on his face. "Are you okay? Are you okay?"

"Oh Jesus Christ!" Zack sat up, cradling his arm. "Both bones. Just like football." He glared at Steve. "You did it. You spooked that damn horse."

"Oh shit. Oh damn." Steve sat beside him. "I'm sorry, man ..."

The horses had quieted, huffing under their loads. "Maybe we should just get out," Steve said, "leave the coke, take the horses back, forget all this."

Zack stood, holding his arm. "Cut some of that extra tarp, make me a sling."

"Like I said –"

"Move the coke back down? What about the burned plane?"

"I know, but –"

"We can't quit now. It's already way too late."

KENNY STAUFFENBERG parked his cruiser on the shoulder of 191, got out tugging his pistol belt up around his hips and sauntered over to Curt. "The snowmobiles are right behind me." He glanced at Kiwa. "She okay while we're gone?"

"She don't like to be in the trailer by herself."

"So your dude found this plane? And told you where?"

"Up the long valley above Goose Creek, like I said."

"You can ride with me, on the first snowmobile. Show the way."

"Fine. What you think happened?"

"That's what we'll find out."

"Planes don't normal fly over here."

"Not normal." Kenny spat tobacco, glanced down 191. "Here come the Cats."

The big black Ford towing the trailer with the four snowmobiles pulled to the shoulder. When they were unloaded Curt climbed on behind Kenny and they rode up into the mountains toward the crashed plane, more snow starting to fall.

BEFORE ZACK AND STEVE reached camp their horses began to whinny and the ones in camp answered. They snatched their gear from their tents, piled them into their pack frames, tied them atop the heavy tarps on the horses' saddles and followed the same trail Curt had taken down the mountain toward 191, the horses shaking their heads angrily and rattling their halters.

Steve went first leading the pinto then Zack with the gray. Every time the gray tugged its halter the pain in his broken arm was unbearable. There was no position he could hold the arm where it didn't hurt beyond belief. So he just kept going, one foot in front of the other. Like a bad hit in football and you hop to your feet and jog back to the huddle, twisting your head from side to side to see through the pain.

By now Curt would have reached the Highway. Called it in. But wouldn't be coming back up this trail. He'd take the cops straight for the crashed plane, then maybe follow the tracks Steve and he had made with the two horses.

Behind Steve the pinto skidded sideways, banged a panier into a tree and fell to its knees. It staggered up, the paniers spilling kilos that the horse stepped on as it tried to stand. It jerked its head back pulling Steve off his feet and knocked him down. "Zack, you got to hold him," Steve called. "So I can reload him. Hold them both."

Zack led the gray around the pinto and took its halter. "What's that?"

"*What?*"

"The noise."

"A plane maybe? Already they're doing flyovers?"

"They'll see your goddamn burnt plane."

"Maybe they won't."

The noise wasn't a plane, Zack realized. "Snowmobile. Coming up the trail."

"Shit. See those junipers? We'll hide the horses!"

"He'll see our tracks."

"Give me the gun."

"No, I'll keep it."

"Gimme, now!"

They ran the horses into the junipers, dashed back, laid down a tarp and piled it with fallen kilos. Some had broken, the powder melted into the snow. They dragged it back to the junipers, Zack reeling in pain, telling himself the way he always did, *the pain's happening to someone else. Keep going.*

THE SNOWMOBILE clattered to a stop fifty yards downhill. As if the driver sensed something.

The engine died.

This meant the guy was walking up the trail toward them. Steve turned to Zack, gestured for the gun.

Zack shook his head. With his good hand took out the Ruger.

No sound but the smallest of breezes flicking through the massive trees, its whisper over needles and bark, the heartbeat of all the lives crouching in the cold.

Zack checked that the Ruger's safety was off, and waited. Steve watched him, looking for a moment to grab the gun.

The snowmobile coughed, revved. Zack raised the Ruger. His heart thundered, he couldn't hear. He went forward till he could see down through the trees. A blue machine, one rider. It revved again, turned and wandered across the hillside toward the crashed plane as if the guy knew where it was.

FROM AFAR the burnt spar of the plane's wing seemed to stand up like a cross. "They didn't tell me it burned," Curt said. Everything but the up-jutting blackened wing was snow-covered. "C'mon you guys," Kenny said to the three deputies. "Let's dig it down."

They had good shovels on the machines so it didn't take long to reach the flame-twisted fuselage. "Enough," Kenny said. "We have to get forensics in on this."

"Wait a minute," a deputy named Lopez said. "What's that sound?"

Lopez turned and stared up the mountain, shading his eyes. "A machine," he pointed. "Up in those aspen. See it?"

Curt heard the sound, faint but steady. Saw a flash of blue snowmobile among the trees.

"Some recreational guy," Lopez said, "out for a ride."

"Or a hunter," Curt said.

"This's a Roadless Area," Kenny said. "No machines allowed except for search and rescue."

"You want we apprehend him?" Lopez said.

Kenny shook his head. "We got plenty here. Let's take four ninety-degree sectors and search them. Work our way to the ridge. First I'm going to radio for Weismann to get his crew up here. Then I'll ride up that ridge and check where that guy on that blue snowmobile was, see if he's still around."

ZACK AND STEVE TIED the horses in thick trees by Highway 191. "We stash the kilos here." Steve panted, "get a truck and disappear."

Zack nodded, thinking that till now he'd never had a reason to disappear. His life had been constantly having *to* appear: TV football, charity shows, Vegas high tables, college games. Now all that seemed bizarre, artificial.

They piled the kilos on the two tarps and set the horses free to find their way back to camp. "If that snowmobile returns," Steve said, "he'll track us here, find the coke."

Bent over with pain, Zack stared at him. "So we don't have the time to get a ride into Bozeman, rent a truck and come back."

Steve nodded at the trailhead where Curt's big Ford 250 was parked, still hitched to the six-horse trailer. "We have to borrow *that*."

"Curt's truck? You nuts?"

"Otherwise we can throw this coke away. Plus still be prosecuted for having tried to take it. A lose-lose situation."

Zack sat on the trampled snow. The pain made him dizzy, he couldn't think. "This just gets crazier and crazier."

"I remember where Curt keeps the spare key. We'll leave him a note that you broke your arm and I took his truck to drive you to the hospital. We leave the truck in Bozeman and rent a U-Haul, like we planned. Curt'll understand."

Steve ran down the road toward Curt's truck. In the distance Zack could hear a snowmobile, wondered if it was the guy on the blue machine who'd come up the trail. Out for a ride, maybe. Probably no danger.

If the snowmobiler kept going straight, he'd hit their tracks coming back from the cave. *Hurry up*, he told Steve, who was having trouble unhitching the horse trailer.

Maybe the snowmobile was one of the cops, Zack thought. And maybe Curt was with him, would arrive just as they were taking his truck.

What if they tried to give the coke back? Take it back up the mountain? No, the horses were gone. Where to put it, anyway? The cops would catch them. And if they left it here they'd be caught for that too.

Something vibrated against his chest, snakelike. His phone. Monica. "Hey you," he said.

"How are you?"

"Good. I'm good. You?"

"I had this dream last night you were in trouble. Just checking it out."

"You believe too much in dreams, Monica."

"I'm missing you...When you coming home?"

"Wait!" he put her on hold, listening to the snowmobile come nearer. "Hurry up!" he yelled at Steve, who was bent under the truck's front wheel well looking for Curt's spare key.

When Zack switched back to Monica she was gone, and didn't answer when he called.

"SOMEBODY burned this plane," Kenny said, peering down the hole where the plane lay.

"No shit," Deputy Lopez said, caught himself.

"Don't touch anything," Kenny said.

"I'm not even going in that hole," Lopez said.

"We leave it for Weismann." Kenny scanned the horizon. "Let's spread out. I got a feeling we'll find something. Maybe up on that ridge."

Curt climbed on the back of the Arctic Cat and Kenny accelerated toward the ridge. When they got there they found the track of the blue snowmobile and followed it westward and down, joining the tracks of two men leading two horses.

"These are my horses!" Curt yelled. "Suzie and Tom. These are my dudes – what the Hell?"

"What are they doing up here?"

"I have no idea. This is crazy," Curt leaned out from the snowmobile to check the tracks. "They've loaded down my horses."

They followed the snowmobile down the mountain along the trail that Zack, Steve and the two horses had made with the paniers full of kilos.

"You give your horses white man names?" Kenny called back. "What's with that?"

STEVE AND ZACK had piled half the kilos into the back of Curt's truck when Zack raised his good hand: *silence.*

The snowmobile. Coming down the mountain. Toward them.

One-handed, Zack dumped more kilos into Curt's truck. "It's the blue machine, the guy we heard this morning. Who stopped below us."

"Leave the rest!" Steve shouted as the snowmobile crested the ridge above them.

Zack glanced at the pile of kilos they hadn't yet moved and ran to the truck, jumped in the passenger seat as Steve accelerated south toward Bozeman, a blue snowmobile racing down the road behind them, losing ground, then giving up.

"That's him," Zack said. "Who came up the trail. Then turned away below us."

"You think I haven't figured that out?" Steve said, crouched over the wheel, scanning the road.

"Yeah, yeah I forgot. You're a fuckin genius."

Steve checked the mirror. "So who is he?"

"The plane." Zack doubled up as a spasm hit his broken arm. "Somebody from the plane."

"There wasn't any snowmobile trailer, just the cop truck."

"So where'd he come from?"

Contra Todos

CURT AND KENNY FOLLOWED the prints of the two dudes and two pack horses and the blue snowmobile back down the mountain toward camp.

Racing along on the back of Kenny's Arctic Cat, Curt couldn't figure why his dudes would have brought the pack horses up here. Unless one of them had shot an elk and was bringing the meat back to camp.

But why would they be hunting when he'd asked them to stay in camp in case the grizzly came back? And who was the blue snowmobile and why was he following them?

When they reached camp he saw with sudden fury that the corral had been broken down and his four other horses had vanished down the trail toward the highway. Grizzly tracks wandered the trampled snow. In the corner of the broken corral his two pack horses, Tom and Suzie, stood huffing, packsaddles askew.

They'd obviously just arrived, after the griz had left. And whatever they'd had in their packsaddles was gone.

Tom was holding up his left rear leg, hurt.

Fury rose like bile up Curt's throat, the urge to kill. Zack and Steve hadn't guarded the horses and the grizzly stampeded them. Then Zack and Steve had taken Tom and Suzie up the mountain, loaded them down, then brought them back empty? It didn't make sense.

Then he saw that Tom and Suzie's tracks went down the mountain loaded, but had come back up empty.

Why? This was crazy.

And where were Zack and Steve now?

Tom was truly hurt, holding his left rear leg up against his belly, the hoof hanging down. He danced away when Curt touched his fetlock.

Broken leg.

Curt walked in circles on the trampled snow, rubbing the back of his neck, trying to see through his anger to what had happened.

He gave up and turned to Tom. "Now don't you worry," he said, holding in his rage. "It's not like they used to say, a horse with a broken leg can't be cured, just shoot him. Remember Belle, when she broke her leg? Remember how I massaged it with alcohol every morning and night for three months and she turned out good as before? I'll massage your leg just like Belle, every morning and night. And you can have that back pasture and those young mares to yourself."

The horse sniffed and rubbed his cheek up and down Curt's shoulder. Curt hugged him, thinking of Steve and Zack and what he would do to them.

"WE CAN'T GO TO THE HOSPITAL in Bozeman," Steve said. "The cops'll catch us."

"We have to. This arm's killing me."

"We'll switch to a U-Haul, put Curt's truck somewhere, then head for Denver."

"Denver?"

"Hide the coke there, no one'll know."

"I need to have this arm fixed."

"Sheridan, maybe. Buffalo, somewhere in Wyoming. Even Billings is too close."

"Then I need meds in Bozeman. Morphine."

"It's not over the counter."

"So *climb* over the counter. *Rob* the place. Just get me some." Zack eased himself up in the seat. "I can wait on the doctors. I can wait till Wyoming. Just get me meds."

Steve tugged something from his shirt pocket, handed it to Zack. "Stick this in your nose."

A clump of wet coke. It burned his nostril, ate into his heart. He saw flaming dragons and naked women. Whatever he had to do, he realized, he could make it through. "I had this same injury at Notre Dame," he said. "The other arm."

"From a game?"

"Car wreck."

A few cars passed the other way, a cop with lights flashing.

"Get whatever pain meds you can," Zack added. "Vodka too. Lots of vodka."

THE MAN ON THE BLUE SNOWMOBILE drove it south alongside 191 then up a newly-plowed dirt road and parked it beside a red KIA. He drove the KIA back down the dirt road and parked where Steve and Zack had abandoned the fifty kilos. He loaded them into the KIA's trunk and called a Big Sky number. "I left it up a road half mile south of the trailhead."

"That's Durkitt Road," the man on the other end said. "I'll come get it."

"*Gracias, hermano. Gracias por todo.*"

"*Nosotros,*" the other man answered. "*Contra todos.*"

As he drove the KIA north toward Bozeman he keyed another number into his iPhone. "It's Diego," he said.

"I know," she said. "What new?"

"Two guys took our mail."

"*Took* it? From the machine?"

"Yes."

"Achh." There was silence while she thought about this. "There is no honor in this country any more. No justice."

"So we make our own justice."

"Like always."

"I got back forty-seven pieces. These two guys, they're in a red Ford 250 pickup truck Montana plate number 6Z9851F. They're in Bozeman by now, or beyond."

"We are listening to the Sheriff's office, in that town, Bozeman. They don't know yet about what was in our machine."

"Our machine is burned –"

"Ahhh." She was quiet a moment. "It wasn't burned, though, when Tranquilo left it –"

"It is now very burned. How is he, Tranquilo?"

"Just bumps and bruises. But he is very angry about the machine."

"He's the one who broke it."

"So we lose our machine and maybe the rest of our mail that was inside it. Plus the cost of you finding these guys. The cost of getting it back. If we can."

"We won't lose it." He wanted to console her, remind her of his total devotion. "Do not worry, María Christina," he said softly. "I will find them."

STEVE BOUGHT TWO FIFTHS of Stolichnaya at the Hideaway Lounge on Main Street in Bozeman and two bottles of Advil at Price Rite Drugs on North 7th. One-handed Zack broke open the Advil bottle and shoved some into his mouth, unscrewed a vodka bottle and drank it half down. He eased back in his seat and sighed, cradled his broken arm tighter against his chest. "Already better."

At U-Haul on North 7th Steve rented a van, reserving it for three days for a local move. "Now what do we do," Zack said, "with Curt's truck?"

"We have to hide it. If they find it here at U-Haul they'll trace us right away."

Driving the U-Haul one-handed Zack followed Steve in Curt's truck across I-90 and up Bridger Canyon where Steve pulled into a logging road and they transferred the kilos from Curt's truck to the van.

Steve drove Curt's truck further up the logging road till it curved round a steep bend and the truck's rear wheels skidded sideways. The truck tipped off the shoulder, slid downhill and crunched into a tree.

"No way they'll find it till spring," Steve said, climbing back up to the logging road.

"You wrecked his truck?" Zack shook his head, nauseated by it all, the pain, the misery. "You did that on purpose?"

"We needed to hide it."

"Curt's been our friend..."

Steve grimaced. "Drink more vodka."

ZACK HAD A GOOD BUZZ going from the vodka and Advil and the intoxicating pain. His broken bones had subsided to a fiery ache which didn't bother him. What did bother him was he couldn't move his fingers.

"What do you mean you can't move your fingers?" Steve turned from the steering wheel. "Show me."

"It won't." Zack peered down at the fingers of his broken arm as if they had betrayed him.

"Oh Jesus," Steve said. "Maybe we better stop in Billings."

"Maybe the kick broke the nerve?"

They were going down Bozeman Pass, the route John Bozeman had broken through the mountains in 1864 and then led thousands of wagons westward across it, dooming the northern tribes. Zack stared out the window at the snowy afternoon light across the roadside ponderosas. "What a place this must have been, when they had it."

"They?"

"The Blackfeet, Cheyenne, whoever lived here. Curt's people. Imagine when all of this was free, open, there were no fences, the land went on forever, the earth and sky –"

"You are *stoned*."

"I don't believe we can sell all this coke." Zack turned to him. "What then?"

Steve snickered. "What then?"

"Yeah, what *then*?"

"We *will* sell it." Steve patted Zack's knee. "Trust me."

Zack tugged away. "Trusting you is how I lost my money."

"Wasn't me that lost it. Try Wall Street, the politicians and the fucking Federal Reserve."

"I don't give a fuck who. I want it back."

"That's why we're doing this. To get it back."

KENNY RODE the Arctic Cat following the blue snowmobile and the tracks of the two dudes and loaded packhorses down toward 191. At 191 he parked the Cat where the two dudes had unloaded the horses and stacked things on two ten-by-ten tarps. One of the dudes had stayed there – his tracks wandered in close circles – then the two of them had walked back and forth many times to the road-side where a truck with heavy-lugged steel snows had been parked. Then the snowmobile followed them out on the Highway, then a car stopped here and someone took the tarp and the rest of the stacked things. All of it made sense, so it was time to call Curt's two dudes in for questioning.

He took out his notebook and called the cell numbers Curt had given him. Both went to voicemail.

He called Undersheriff Nick Holsein to set up a team. "Let's background these guys, send out a five-state, see if anybody locates them."

"Shall do. And FAA's on the way. DEA too, they want to have a look, see if that plane was carrying drugs."

"The plane burned. No numbers, nothing left."

"Heck."

"Let's check vehicle rentals and hotels. Try to get credit card numbers and track them that way … And the pilot, let's go back two weeks on airport departures, hospitals, doctors, taxis, rentals, all that stuff."

"The guy on the snowmobile, him too … Let's check snowmobile rentals, see what's gone out."

"Good idea. Maybe he's the missing pilot?"

"Whatever this is," Nick said, "it doesn't look local anymore."

Kenny tried Steve's and Zack's numbers again, got voicemail.

He glanced down Highway 191 and saw Curt's truck was gone. For a second he wondered if somehow Curt had got here before him, driven off.

Impossible.

He ran to where Curt's truck had been parked and saw the same pattern of heavy-lugged steel snows.

"Bastards!" Kenny stood astonished at the side of the road, wiping cold dirty palms on his thighs. "I will get you."

WHEN HIS PHONE RANG Zack thought it was Monica then saw it was his agent Rob O'Brien. "Hey, Rob!"

"Where the hell are you?"

"Montana. Hunting trip. I told you."

"You coming back in plenty time to prep for Sunday?"

"Of course, of course." Zack tried to keep the pain and vodka out of his voice. "Look, can I call you back?"

"Call me back? You want to hear about their new offer or don't you?"

"Sorry, real tired. Just got out of the woods."

"They're willing to take you on, Zack. For another year."

"Willing? What's that mean? I've been good."

"Ratings don't show it. You're down fifteen."

"That's seasonal – you know that! Wait till three weeks before playoffs –"

"We're almost there."

Zack crunched his body in a new spasm of pain. "So *what's* the deal?"

"They're offering four-fifty..."

"Four hundred fifty thousand? A cut of a hundred thousand? Why?" Zack tried to move his broken arm into a better position. "You want me to *take* that?"

"Calm down. Be glad they're keeping you."

"I can get another deal. They're not the only game in town."

"Your contract has a two-year non-compete – you know that – so you *can't* get another deal."

"Fuck them. I can."

"This isn't like you, Zack. And it spills over into how you treat them, the network, gives them the wrong feeling. That you're in it just for *you*. A prima donna. I tell them no, you're just a tough guy who won't take excuses. And they know the viewers love you. It pisses them off, but they know it."

"You said I was down fifteen…"

"What they'd like from you is a little respect, a dedication to helping the network prosper. Commitment, not just *financial* commitment but an emotional and moral priority to work for their benefit. You as a part of *them*."

"Don't lecture me, man. Not now."

"Not now? When am I supposed to lecture you? When it's too late?"

There was no way to ease the arm pain like a knife sawing through the bones. "Tell them I want the same as last year. That I am totally committed to them and determined to help them succeed. That I love the network and though I can go elsewhere I'd rather be with them. Tell them all that."

"Only elsewhere you're likely to go, you don't take this deal, is nowhere."

LITTLE BIG HORN

CURT FOUND THE HORSES the griz had chased, packed up camp and loaded it plus the four quarters of the elk he'd shot on all the horses except Tom, and led them down the trail to 191. He looked up and down the road, trying to figure where his truck had gone.

At first he thought maybe Kenny had needed it, but there was no way. He checked his phone, and yes there was a voice mail from Kenny: *Call me when you reach the Highway... Bastards took your damn truck. I will trailer your horses to my place, but I am going to bring the vengeance of the Lord down on those guys.*

"Well I'll be damned." Curt looked back at his weary, laden horses, the limping Tom. From the lodgepoles where he'd tied her earlier Kiwa nickered.

In a daze he went to her. She shivered snow off her back and snuffled at his coat, looking for oat cookies. He caressed her soft nose and warm ears, inhaling her lovely horse scent, patted her hair back from her forehead as she rubbed her jaw against his and put her head on his shoulder. He untied her and led her back toward the others, her hooves plodding softly behind him, her breath warm on his neck.

"Can you believe it?" he said to her. "Those idiots stole our truck."

Nobody steals pickups in Montana, she reminded him. Because if you do, sooner or later the owner will find you and kill you. She rubbed his shoulder with her jaw and nickered softly as if to say *that's how life is.*

"And they broke Tom's leg. And they didn't wait in camp like I told them, so the other four horses got chased by that damn grizzly."

Yes, she told him, clear as a bell. *You go after those bastards. And get them.*

"WE'LL SELL IT in New York. Promise," Steve peered over the steering wheel into the dusk of oncoming headlights. "What about Vegas, like I said? You're the one with all these casino buddies, the guys with the high-priced chips and free women?"

"Nothing in Vegas is ever free."

"You are so *negative*! Why not talk to them, see what they say?"

Zack eased back in the seat, Stolichnaya bottle between his thighs. "They'll take our coke and kill us."

"All the coke in this van wouldn't last one night in Vegas. It'll sell, they'll love you for it."

"Vegas doesn't love you for anything."

"Wow, the Little Big Horn, that sign. Where the Sioux and Cheyenne beat the US Cavalry. And killed Custer."

"Unbelievable."

"And we're going to do the same thing. We're going to win."

"Yeah, but think about what happened to them, afterwards."

"Who?"

"The Sioux and Cheyenne. Curt's people."

"Yeah. That's true." Steve glanced at the dash display. "Fifty-nine miles to Sheridan. What are we going to say happened to you?"

"A horse kicked me, you idiot."

"No, no, don't say anything near the truth. You slipped on your front steps, put out your arm, hit a stair edge ..."

"And where would these front steps be?"

"Yeah, didn't think of that."

"Maybe we can sell it back to them, the coke."

"The owners? How?"

"I don't know. But maybe we can figure it out."

"You fell on the ice in a parking lot in Cheyenne and your arm hit a bumper."

"I can't use my ID."

"You're going to have to. In and out before anybody knows."

"Curt's going to know. The cops're gonna know." Zack winced at a bump in the road. "They're going to know it was coke ... or they'll track down the plane, find out when they go after the owners."

"Maybe."

"And they're going to ask us why we took those horses up there and what was in the plane and where did we take it."

"We took the horses because we decided to hunt up there and wanted the horses in case we got something."

"But Curt asked us to stay in camp, in case the griz came back."

"We don't always have to do what he says." Steve bit his lip, staring at the road, the oncoming headlights flitting over his face. "That griz wasn't coming back. And with all the snow that *was* coming, we were afraid it was the last day we could hunt. So we went out there with the horses, hoping to find an elk."

"Why'd we stop at the cave?"

"We were freezing, remember? We stumbled on the cave, stamped down the snow to make a fire, then decided not to. Saw some elk on the next ridge, whatever."

WHEN STEVE'S PHONE rang again it showed area code 406, Montana.

"Is it Curt?" Zack said. "Don't answer."

"It's a different number." Steve punched on the speaker. "Yeah?"

"Mr. Montclair this is Ken Stauffenberg, Gallatin County Sheriff. I need to know why you haven't answered my calls."

"Calls? Why Mr. *Stoffen*berg –"

"Sheriff."

"*Sheriff* Stauffenblad, I just found my phone. We've been on a hunting trip. Just now found it when it rang. All day I've been looking for it."

"And your buddy Zack Wilson, he lost his phone too?"

"I don't know ... he took off for LA, had some meeting. I do too, heading back to New York as we speak."

"In Curt Weathers' truck?"

"Curt's truck? Why no Sir."

"What are you driving?"

"Rental car, Sir."

"What were you doing up on that ridge?"

"What ridge?"

"Where you went with Curt's horses."

"You didn't ask Zack?"

"We would if we could find him."

"It was in case we got an elk, you know. So we could carry two quarters on each horse. But it started to snow so we went back down and packed out our gear, it was time to go home, and with the weather getting bad…"

"What about the plane?"

"What about it?"

"You're the one who saw it?"

"No, Zack did."

"What did it look like?"

"Like a crashed plane I guess. I don't know."

"Did he say it was burned?"

"Yeah, I think so."

"You *think* so?"

"Like I said. Yeah."

"Trouble is we can't reach him right now. So we need to talk with you."

"I'll try him," Steve said, "tell him to call you."

"Forget about New York, Mr. Montclair. I want you back in Bozeman for questioning."

"Questioning? I just answered all your questions."

"Where are you now? This minute?"

Steve tried to remember the map of western Wyoming. "Rock Springs."

"Your cell phone is between Billings and Sheridan. I'm sure you're with it."

"Yes, Sir. I am. I don't want trouble."

"Then you turn around and drive back to Bozeman. Or I put out an Arrest Order on you. For grand auto theft."

"That's crazy. Curt said we could take the truck –"

"Where'd you leave it?"

"Leave it? I'm not sure. Zack dropped it off, somewhere. He must've called Curt, told him."

"He didn't tell Curt anything."

"If you're tracking my phone you know I can't drive all the way back to Bozeman tonight. If you insist, I'll head back there tomorrow. But you'll have to pay for my time – why should I lose money, and valuable time, just because you can't ask questions over the phone?"

"Be here by noon tomorrow. Or the Arrest Order goes out. And I'm sure you don't want that, Mr. Montclair."

If we get arrested, Zack thought bitterly as he listened to Kenny's unfriendly voice on the cellphone speaker, at least the Vegas guys can't do anything to me.

Oh yes they can, he remembered. *Even if you're in jail, Mr. Bigtime,* Haney the Rat had once said, *we got plenty friends there, will do what we want.*

"No sweat," Steve told Kenny. "I'll be there." He shut off his phone, turned to Zack. "Since I'm driving, you have to figure out how to turn off the GPS on our phones. So these bastards can't track us."

THE EMERGENCY ROOM at Sheridan Hospital was bright and cold. "Thank goodness when it's this chilly most folks stay home," the heavy dark-faced woman at the desk said. "So we don't have so much car wrecks."

Because of the broken arm they took him ahead of the others with the flu and colds and bad backs and broken fingers and knife cuts and all the other daily bread of the Sheridan Emergency Room.

The doc came back with Zack's X-rays. "We're going to have to operate."

"Operate?" Zack realized his voice was a whisper. "No way."

The doc laughed, a quick huff, as if there were no end to insanity among the hordes who invaded the Emergency Room.

"The radius is shattered," he said, "with pieces stuck in the ulnar artery." He was a tall skinny guy, bent over in his white coat, with a dark narrow moustache which made Zack distrust him. "That's what brings blood to your forearm, wrist and hands. You could bleed to death if it's severed. In addition, there are bone chips stuck in your ulnar nerve, that extends all the way to your fingertips. You could lose it all. Do you hear me, Mr. Wilson?"

"I have to get back to LA," Zack felt drunk, couldn't modulate his words, speak normally. "For a work conference. It's essential, it's my future ... I'm a TV sports announcer."

"You think that makes you immune to the dangers everyone else faces?"

"No, not at all ... I'm just telling you why I have to leave, that's all. Splint it and I'll get it done in LA, no problem."

"I can't splint you like this," the doc said. "You can't get on a plane ..."

"Fuck it." Zack hopped jauntily off the examining table and headed for the door.

"Wait!" the doctor called. "I'll put it in a protective sling. With bubble wrap. That'll keep you till LA."

"Good." Zack turned back. "And get me some pain meds. Before I go crazy."

LIKE HANGING OFF A CLIFF, you're fine till you start worrying about it. But the more Zack worried about it, the more he wanted to get away from these kilos of coke with their evil scorpion logos. Wanted to give the coke back and resurrect their lives.

No, he realized, scanning but not seeing the flitting Highway signs – Chugwater 162 miles, Cheyenne 210, the empty road ahead with its dashed lines flashing under the van, the jackrabbits splattered on the asphalt, the sagebrush crouching along the shoulders, their dancing shadows in the headlights, the huge wind turbines motionless on the hills, their red strobes blotting out the stars – he and Steve had already passed the point of no return.

Whoever owned the coke would kill them if they turned it in to the cops. And the cops would sell it anyway. Then jail him and Steve for withholding evidence. And no matter what they did, the coke was going back into the system. No reason to be a hero.

"Maybe we *can* give it back to them," Zack said.

"How can I give it to them when we don't know who they are?" Steve protested, hands off the steering wheel.

"Figure it out," Zack said. "Otherwise they'll kill us."

"GOT THEM!" María Christina said. "They just talked with this Montana sheriff, they're heading south on I-90, probably headed for I-25 and Denver."

"Denver?" Diego said. "I'll have to drive all night."

"Too late for that. We have to figure another way."

"Are they still in that Ford truck?"

"I don't think so, from what they said. We will check if DEA is on them yet. So you hire a plane, get to Denver. Let me know when you're there."

"I have some of our mail. Forty-seven pieces."

"Get a couple suitcases, take it with you."

Diego glanced out the ice-clad motel window at the frozen streets of Bozeman. *Who could live in such a place?* He sat on the edge of the king-size bed, found the number for Signet Air and punched it in.

"I need to get to Denver," he told the cheerful young lady. "Tonight."

"I can't find a pilot tonight," she said. "But I can probably set it up tomorrow."

"Tonight. Call whoever you want. Tell them I need to be in Denver," Diego checked his Rolex, "by midnight. And I'll pay five grand extra to whoever gets me there."

A Gun for Life

Zack and Steve got to Denver at 2:12 a.m. and paid cash for a room at the Rawhide Arms Motel on South Santa Fe. In the morning they hid the coke in a storage unit at Maxi Self-Rent on Wadsworth, $79 a month, first month free.

"We should keep some kilos out," Steve said.

"What for? So we can get arrested?"

"Maybe we can unload some – I know a guy in New York who has contacts here in Denver. And we need to take some with us when we head to Vegas. Or New York."

In the shadowy back of the storage unit the pile of scorpion-topped kilos looked insignificant. "Most people put their old clothes and sofas in this place," Steve said. "And we're putting in ten million."

"Like I said, we should split it in half, I take half to Vegas, you take half to New York. We each keep what we get for our half. And then," Zack smiled, "you pay me back my portfolio you lost."

Before they turned in the U-Haul they rented Steve a blue Denali with tinted windows from Nationwide, and Zack a white Pathfinder from Avis, using Zack's credit card billed to Pigskin Events, a company you could hire to bring football players to your marriage reception, divorce party, birthday, Bar Mitzvah, or anniversary. For tax reasons he'd put the company in an LLC, and, he told Steve, there was no way to trace it to them.

A block after they left Avis Steve pulled into a Burger King lot and came back to Zack's Pathfinder. "Get out a minute."

"What for?"

"Just do it."

Zack got out of the Pathfinder and Steve leaned into the driver seat and tugged a small gray plastic box from under the steering wheel and handed it to him.

"What the hell is this?"

"GPS tracking device. Most rental cars and fleet vehicles have them. They plug into the car's onboard diagnostic port – the one the dealer uses when you bring the car in for maintenance. With it the company can track the car in real time, even get a street or satellite view."

Zack stared at it. "I never knew."

Steve shrugged. "Now you do." He went to a trash can and tossed them in. "I don't think they work when they're not plugged in, but no need to take chances."

Zack felt a strange surge of optimism. No reason they couldn't pull off this deal. Sure, ten million bucks wasn't a lot, but it was a starting point.

Though you had to split it two ways.

From the lone pay phone outside the motel lobby Steve called Princeton Securities at 33 Liberty Street, three blocks from Wall Street. "Roger," he said. "I'm in Colorado, and may have a market story for you. Is there anyone here you'd like me to call?"

Roger thought about it. "Is it Colorado-based, or nationwide?"

"Could be nationwide."

"A big story or a little story?"

"It could go 250 words. You got anybody here might like to see it?"

Roger thought a bit more. "If they are they'll call you. What's this number?"

"Hotel pay phone."

"Go buy a throwaway phone. Then call me back."

Steve bought two phones at a Broadway electronics shop and tossed one on the bed beside Zack. "Go call your people."

Numb with morphine and oxycodone, Zack couldn't figure what Steve meant, or really who he was, and couldn't figure why he disliked him.

"DO I HAVE A STORY for you!" Kenny said over his cell phone to Duane McCord, the DEA Field Division Office director in Denver.

"You Montana rednecks're always full of stories," Duane said. "What is it now?"

"I may have a couple of amateur coke hustlers coming your way." Kenny smiled, thinking of the two dudes and what would happen to them when Duane got them. "They took maybe two hundred kilos from a crashed plane and stole my wife's cousin's red Ford 250, plate 6Z9851F –"

"Damn!"

"– and wrecked a packhorse and caused all kinds of other commotion. So we want them."

"How they get your cousin's truck?"

"My *wife's* cousin's. He was guiding them up in the Buffalo Horns north of Yellowstone."

"I know where the Buffalo Horns is." Duane swung his cowboy boots off his desk and started taking notes. "You're not making this up?"

"Hell no I'm not making this up."

"If it didn't sound so unreal I wouldn't believe it."

"Our forensics guy's found cocaine traces in what's left of the plane. Kilos in what seemed to be two coffins, best we can tell –"

"A metaphor," Duane chuckled, "to remind us that coke kills."

"And a couple of plastic kilo wrappers that blew out of the plane when it burned. They've got a black scorpion logo on the top. Anyway, we think the whole damn plane was full of cocaine."

"So maybe it all burned."

"No, these guys seem to have moved it down to Highway 191, the road from Bozeman to West Yellowstone –"

"I do know about 191, Kenny. Have you traced the plane?"

"Bonanza G36, no markings, no numbers. A coke truck."

"Who are these guys?"

"One's from New York, some kind of Wall Street investor, the other's from LA, used to play linebacker for the Broncos, now a TV guy."

"Zack Wilson?"

"You said it."

"And he's shipping *cocaine*?"

"Seems like it."

"Well I'll be..." Duane chuckled. "We got a special place for guys like that."

After Kenny had rung off, Duane looked over his notes then made an internal call. "Whitney, you want to come up here a minute?"

"I'm working on something," she said. "Do I have to?"

"Well of course not. I'll just have to arrest these two dudes all by myself."

"Arrest *what* two dudes? I'm coming!"

WITH HIS NEW THROWAWAY phone Zack called an old girl-friend, Emily Rausch, now living with Wally Greene, who'd been a defensive coach when Zack had broken into the League. "Is he still in the market?"

"Wally?"

"Who else?"

"A little, sure."

"I have a deal he might like."

"Sweetie I don't want you caught up in that."

He shook his head, as if she could see him. "Just *tell* him."

"You really want me to?" Her voice turned studied, less accented. "You don't know what you're getting into –"

"You already said that."

"Okay but I think you're crazy. So where are you?"

"Far away."

"Why don't you come up to Aspen?"

"Love to. Sometime."

"I get cold up here, sweetie. Wally's gone all the time. There's way too much snow..."

Zack realized he wanted to, thought with shame of Monica. "Tell him call me."

"If he calls you, it'll be another phone, no caller ID."

"Whatever turns him on."

"Remember, sweetie, how you used to turn *me* on –"

"I know. It was wonderful. But I'm hooked up now, might even get married –"

"With that doctor in LA? Yeah, it was in *People*."

"I hate how our lives are so public. I want all that to go away."

"You sound real tired, honey. Are you in pain?"

"Nah, just a little older."

"We can fix that, you know –"

Pain surged up his arm. "Just have him call me."

A REMINGTON 700P. Long and lean and weighed only nine pounds plus a pound for the scope. Diego couldn't believe he'd found it, right here in a trailer park in South Denver, sold by a young guy with a red beard, Rockies hat and bulging stomach. One of the world's best long-range rifles yet easy to use in short-range combat. Better yet, chambered for the .338 Lapua Magnum, and anybody hit with that wasn't going anywhere. And an Army Leupold Mark IV 10x40 mm telescopic sight, so what you see is what you get.

"Two thousand three hundred," the young guy said. "That's what I paid for it."

"So how come you selling?"

A heavy-armed shrug, hands slapping thighs. "Need the money, man. Hardly ever shot it, you know…"

They settled on two thousand one hundred including two boxes of bullets. Diego didn't care, had bargained just to put the guy's mind at ease, that he was just another shooter looking for a new toy.

Back in his motel he took the gun apart and cleaned it but it was already super-clean. He checked and polished each cartridge, reassembled it all and replaced it in its tan EuroOptic case.

The only thing that bothered him was when he'd used it how to get it home to Miami.

A gun like this you kept for life.

STEVE CALLED ROGER in New York and gave him the number of the phone he'd just bought.

Half an hour later it rang. "This is Radar," a man said, a heavy Hispanic accent, "I'm interested in your story, we should talk."

"Where?"

"Come down to Fountain, seven tonight. When you get to the exit give me a call, I'll tell you the address."

"'ll only be able to tell you a little bit about the story, without some kind of agreement –"

"Not to worry. We like your story, we give you a good agreement."

"YOU'LL GET KILLED," Zack said. "You don't *know* this guy –"

"Friend of a friend."

"You have great friends. Like Citigroup."

"Fuck you, I *like* my friends." Steve bent his head from side to side, loosening his stiff neck. "So I take twenty kilos to Fountain but it's hid under the seat, and I'll only show them a little …"

"It's your twenty kilos." Zack grimaced. "I get all the rest if you die."

Steve tucked his rifle under the bed – it wasn't something you could bring to a meeting like this. He drove to Maxi Self-Rent on Santa Fe, took twenty kilos from the pile and hid them under the back seat of the Denali. He drove south from Littleton on 85, the old wagon train trail that once went the 400 miles to Santa Fe, thinking how ironic that this festering of factories, malls, coal trains, box stores and cheap condos was called *Holy Spirit.*

"Holy Spirit!" he yelled, a little drunk with fear. He could imagine it, the slow melting of his body into spirit. *But I love my body. If it works don't fix it. So no reason to kill me, Lord. No reason at all…*

Highway 85 switched from two lanes to four and back to two again, lots of oncoming traffic whose lights seemed to shatter the frosted windshield and whose steel vehicles whisked past at a combined speed of 140 miles an hour. Then came Castle Rock, more subdivisions and 6-lane highways in a place he remembered ten years ago as open prairie.

Then the vast gleaming arena of Colorado Springs – probably could be seen by a naked eye in some faraway constellation: the Air Force Academy, the endless stores and subdivisions, the vast parking lots and traffic lights, and hovering over it all an exalted haze of pollution like mist in the eyes, a veil over the world.

He took the exit for Wagner's Warfare Heaven and paid cash for a nice 9 mm Beretta – "the self-defense resource for those who know" – and two boxes of hollow points, loaded the gun and tucked it and the spare ammo under the driver's seat.

WHEN ZACK SAW it was Emily he answered his phone. "He says okay," she said.

"Okay what?"

"You come to Aspen, he checks out what you have, takes it from there."

"When?"

"He's leaving for Miami tomorrow. So he says ten tonight. If you're interested."

"Of course I'm interested."

"He says call when you get to Tamarack Way."

"Shall do."

"Be on time."

IT TOOK STEVE twenty minutes to get from Wagner's Warfare Heaven to the Fountain exit, where he called the number Radar had given him. A woman answered. "You have GPS on your car?"

"I have a map."

"Go to 6995 Hermito."

"Okay, but what's there?" he asked but she was gone.

He followed the main street east across a dark river through the town which looked like an old movie set, past new subdivisions, more roads, then rolling snow-dusted prairies.

Hermito was easy to find, an old road wandering east between rusty barbed wire and lichen-gray fence posts, here and there a ranch house, big barns and huge round white-wrapped hay bales stacked in muddy piles.

6995 Hermito sat close to the road, a pale green aluminum-sided shop building with four vehicle bays and a steel-barred office door and picture window. The lights were on and a black Mercedes and a blue Toyota TRD pickup sat out front, new snow atop them. Steve wished Zack were here, wished *he* weren't here, and pulled into the parking lot.

But Roger in New York had said it was okay. So it couldn't be bad. Couldn't be dangerous. How many years had he known him?

He realized he didn't really know Roger at all but let that pass, wondered should he pocket the Beretta and decided no, got out of the Denali and flicked the lock, shuffled his shoulders into his black North Face jacket and reached between the steel bars to knock on the office's icy glass door.

He waited, knocked again. A face at the door, a tall skinny blonde with a sharp mouth, very pretty in a cold way, dressed in a thin pink silk blouse and short black skirt. "Come on in," she smiled, holding the door wide in false welcome, as if she were a high-priced hooker and he her new john. "Tony wants to see you."

"Tony?"

She smiled sweetly. "The man you talked to."

"His name was Radar."

"Hey, get over it." She danced down the hallway ahead of him, skirt swirling, opened the double doors and called, "He's here."

A swarthy man, a little hunched as if from an old wound, in his fifties maybe, gray-haired but ominous, a cold black light in his eyes. "Come, sit down," he waved at a low table of dark wood and leather. "So, you have something to show me."

"I spoke with my friend in New York –"

"No, no, no," the man waved an admonitory finger. "No such talk."

"Right." Steve sat back. "So?"

Tony chuckled, sat back. "Please, show us your stuff."

Steve tugged a vial from his North Face jacket. "Check it out."

Tony laid a line on the polished mahogany table and sucked it up with a silver tube from his pocket. He sniffed, looked out the window, faraway. He tucked the silver tube back in his pocket. "Okay. You have how much of this?"

"How much can you take?"

"We can go ten keys, maybe fifteen."

"They're not cheap."

"They never are. We can do twenty-five."

"Twenty-five grand a kilo? Are you nuts?"

Tony tut-tutted. "That's very rude, you know, Mr....?" He cocked an ear. "What was the name again?"

"How many you want, now?" This was brazen and stupid but Steve did it anyway. Had to get out of here. *Do the deal and run.* Roger'd said this guy was safe.

"You are deaf? You did not hear? I said maybe fifteen keys, at twenty-five thousand dollars each. That is three hundred seventy-five thousand dollars, no? Not bad for an evening's work."

Steve tucked the vial back in his pocket. "I'm sorry, I was told to get thirty a kilo ... It's not up to me to decide ..."

Tony glanced at Emerald. "You like her, this girl? We make a deal, you can have her tonight. Extra bonus."

Steve imagined this, thought of Marcie. "I'm not here to get laid. I'm here to make a deal."

"You will never get laid better than Emerald. Not in your whole life."

The girl was there, at his elbow. Tall and statuesque and totally without kindness. It would be like screwing the cold depths of Hell – how could you not want to?

She handed him a brandy glass and gave Tony another. "Azteca de Oro, 1999. Back when everything was always going to get better."

He could see her breast through the cleavage of her pink silk blouse. Small and perfectly curved, soft-nippled. How lovely to feel that against his chest.

He waited till Tony drank his glass then drank his down, the ceiling bulb a rainbowed aura in the upturned bottom of the glass, imagined the silky place between her thighs and everything went dark. He couldn't breathe, knew he should care but couldn't.

TAMARACK WAY

THE MORPHINE made Zack oversleep and he woke late for the meeting with Wally in Aspen. Swearing at himself he shoved ten kilos into a Safeway shopping bag, hid it under the donut tire in the Pathfinder's trunk, and was doing 85 past the Buffalo Lookout when a Colorado State Trooper hit the flashers and pulled him over.

Half-drunk with pain, he tugged his license from his wallet and the rental contract from the glove box. The trooper walked up to the car, hand on his pistol in the open holster.

He was tall and stern in a blue uniform. A small blond mustache, thin lips in a grim face. "I was going too fast," Zack said. If he was nice maybe it wouldn't take too long for the trooper to give him a ticket so he wouldn't be even later for Wally. But if the trooper had seen an arrest alert from that Bozeman Sheriff? And then he'd find the ten kilos in the back?

"I think I recognize you," the trooper said, "but let's check that license and registration anyway. This a rental car?"

Zack handed him his license and the rental contract. "Yes it is."

The trooper glanced at the license. "Thought it was you." He handed it and the contract back through the window. "I played football all the way through college, seen thousands of games, and some of the best linebacker plays I've ever seen were yours."

"Thank you," Zack glanced down. "That's very kind."

"What happened to your arm?"

"Slipped in a parking lot." Zack smiled at the irony of it. "Stuck out my arm to catch myself and broke it on somebody's bumper."

"Well you take care, Broncos may need you again someday."

"I'd love that, officer."

"So, keep it under 75 and you won't get ticketed. And you'll live longer." He turned back to his cruiser, "And tell Avis the rear right tail light has a short... That's why I pulled you over."

Zack watched the cruiser's lights fade into the distance and then accelerated toward Aspen. 8:21 – now he'd be half an hour late. *Damn.*

But the trooper obviously hadn't seen any arrest warrant. Zack imagined what the trooper would feel when he found out that this famous athlete he'd respected was actually a crook.

That was wrong. On every level.

There must be a way out of this.

WHEN CURT'S PHONE buzzed with a 303 area code he thought it was maybe his brother's stepson at Denver University, but it was a soft sedulous black woman's voice. "This is Whitney Castro, with the DEA in Denver. I work for Duane McCord –"

"Well hi!" he said, more innocently than he'd wanted, she had that effect already. "Kenny Stauffenberg said you might call."

"Sorry it's so late – do you have a few minutes?"

"Of course, of course."

"We've been trying to track your truck but can't... Did it have a GPS beacon?"

"No."

"These two guys, how'd they get *into* this? I'm recording, so talk all you want..."

"It astonishes me, the whole thing. They've always been good guys. They've been close for years, since Steve started by investing Zack's bonus when he broke into the NFL."

"The Broncos," she said. "I remember."

"Zack's a bit of a wild man but he's slowing down. First year I guided them was when he'd just left the NFL. He was tough, in a lot of pain. Last couple years he's been better... The TV job, he doesn't like it. This new girlfriend, well, since last year... she's changed him a lot... Yet he seemed stressed, this time, wrought up." Curt thought a minute. "They both did."

"What about Steve?"

"He's a big Wall Street guy, invests other people's money. Seems like a fair guy, for the business he's in. Loves his kids, crazy about his wife – they met when they were six years old, been together ever since … Tries to call them every night …"

"We have their backgrounds – Steve at Harvard and a Wharton MBA, the rich kid who's smart enough to get even richer. Zack the Notre Dame hero, then the NFL, now the sports announcer, funny and slightly off-color, the viewers call him the Jon Stewart of TV football. A bit of an icon, our Zack …"

"You wouldn't know it to be with him. He never speaks about it. Always ready to help, to pitch in." He paused. "If I had to think about it, I'd say he cares about other people."

"And Steve?"

"Him too. But he's in a nasty business. Investment management, he calls it. What I've learned in my life is the only way to make lots of money is take it from someone else."

"They ever talk about drugs?"

"Zack once said that to play football in the NFL you have to be on a laundry bag of the stuff." I remember, those were the words he used." He paused, thinking. "And Steve one time, that was three years ago …"

"Yes, Mr. Weathers?"

"Cocaine, as a matter of fact. He said it about cocaine."

"Yes?"

"That the investment world couldn't run without it."

"Unfortunately that may be true. What I don't understand is why are *they* doing this?"

"Run off with the coke? I can't figure it, unless they've got money problems."

"We're looking into that."

"Or maybe it seemed like a good idea at the start then turned out wrong and now they can't get out of it."

She cleared her throat. "So, tell me everything you can think of about these guys – I want addresses, phone numbers, bank accounts, any credit cards they used to book things, old stories, anything you can think of that will help us learn more about them..."

He was amazed how much he remembered. Stories they'd told him two years ago about the TV business, about what really goes on in Vegas and Wall Street. Girlfriends Zack had talked about – and now Monica Cruz, an emergency doc in LA.

What a horror, Curt had thought, *to be that.*

Half an hour later Whitney said goodbye and dialed Kenny Stauffenberg. "Curt's truck – what if they dumped it somewhere, rented something else?"

10 MILES FROM ASPEN Zack skidded across new-plowed ice and smacked sideways into a snowbank.

He gunned it back and forth several times making the tires howl but the Pathfinder was truly stuck, leaning way off the shoulder with the driver door facing up and the passenger door jammed into the snowbank. Favoring his broken arm he squirmed out the driver door and stumbled around the car to the front passenger tire, which was deep in snow. "Shit!" he screamed at himself. "I'll never get out!"

Barehanded he dug the snow out from around the tires and climbed back in, but the wheels still spun. He wondered should he hitch a ride to Wally's place – no that was stupid – with a Safeway bag full of coke?

He was punching in Wally's number when a green Mercedes wagon stopped on the road and backed up. A young guy got out, a kid really, thin-bearded, in a baseball cap that said *Boardpusher* across the front, T-shirt, jeans and sneakers. "You need a tow?" he called, coming up.

"Yeah, but..."

"Let's try it." The kid opened the rear hatch of the Mercedes and dragged out a tow chain that he hooked to a hitch on the back of the Mercedes. He dragged the other end under Zack's car and hooked it to the chassis. "Get in, turn it on and put it in drive. Don't accelerate till the car starts moving, then very slowly. Don't let your tires break contact with the ground." He turned back, the cap's brim shadowing his eyes. "That means don't spin."

The kid drove the Mercedes slowly till the chain was taut. For a moment there was nothing then the Pathfinder budged, lurched, and rambled forward with Zack steering and trying not to spin the wheels.

The kid backed up the Mercedes to slacken the chain, crawled under the Pathfinder and unhooked it from both cars.

"I can't thank you enough." Zack stuck out his hand.

"No bother."

"Can I pay you?"

The kid looked shocked, shook his head. "No need..."

"I've got a little coke – you want some?"

"No thanks, man." The kid edged away.

"Sorry, just a suggestion –"

The Mercedes was gone, the road black again, a deadly wind in the trees. The passenger side of the Pathfinder was dented, and dirty with snow.

Would the kid turn him in? How could he have been so stupid?

It's the painkillers. They're killing me.

IT WAS SO COLD. Steve realized he was shivering, then knew who he was. That the frozen grit against his body was the ground. And that this universe of stinging pain was his – his arms, legs, knees, face, ears, and toes all raw with it. Then realized he was naked, slid frozen fingers down his numb skin trying to remember what *it* was, what his fingers were.

He forced himself to lean up, then sat cross-legged, arms wrapped around his chest against the bitter wind.

He couldn't remember.

For a while he sat there. Then crawled, away from the wind but the wind was everywhere. Stumbled to his feet and fell, hands on sharp rocks. Pulled himself up again.

The searing cold under his soles was snow. Bitter aching cold through his skin and muscles, tendons and bones and up his legs.

He had to go somewhere or freeze. One way was downhill but that didn't seem right. How had he come here?

Brightness flashed across the knobby white landscape, died. Out of the darkness it flashed again, nearer, vanished then darted forward once more, swung away and he knew what it was.

A car's headlights. A car on a road.

He had come from that road.

The headlights swung nearer then away, following the road's curves, illuminated for a moment a parked white car and he remembered this was somehow his. It would be warm inside.

The door wouldn't open. Locked, he remembered. The keys had been thrown – who? Where?

He scrabbled in the snow near the car, remembered the flashing arc of the keys in the headlights – whose? There on the crusted snow a glint of plastic and steel. He picked it up and felt the rectangular plastic Avis tag and the two tethered keys.

He ran back to the car and pushed a key button. The trunk popped up.

Now he remembered. He'd been in this trunk. Naked. Then they got him out and threw the keys. And made him run after them. *Keep running till you're out of rifle range or we'll shoot you. We have night scopes and we won't miss.*

He'd been sure they would shoot him but they didn't. Or had they shot him, and this is what it's like to be dead?

It was even colder inside the car. He found the ignition and turned it on. After two minutes the car began to warm. He felt dizzy and wondered if it was carbon monoxide. Wanted just to lie there, sleep.

ZACK WAS 55 MINUTES late to Tamarack Way, an icy road on a steep slope, tall pines and tamaracks on both sides swathed in snow, glimpses of well-lit mansions filtering between the trees, pine smoke on the frigid air. He pulled to the shoulder and punched in Wally's number.

It rang and rang. He waited till ten rings then cut off and punched it again. Endless rings, no answer, no message. He checked the number – yes, it was the same that had worked before, punched it in again. No answer.

An hour and ten minutes late. He'd blown the whole deal.

He tried Emily's number but it didn't answer either. Fuck her, he decided. She set me up.

Driving back down the mountain he noticed headlights at a steady distance behind him. Halogens, bright, the height of an SUV. When he accelerated they seemed to drop back but before he turned onto I-70 toward Denver they reappeared.

"Lots of people take this highway," he told himself. "Calm down."

Passing through Vail he wondered if when he got to Denver he should put the ten kilos back in the storage unit. But it was suspicious to be doing so at night and it would take an extra half hour and even now he couldn't keep himself awake, the headlights of onrushing cars a kaleidoscope flittering through the sleet-sprayed windshield. *Where's the middle of the road?* he worried. *Where's my side?*

Too much morphine. Too much coke. Too much pain.

He made it over the Pass and through the Eisenhower Tunnel and all the way down to Littleton and The Rawhide Arms. Leaving the ten kilos in the Pathfinder, he took four morphine tabs with a tall vodka, called Steve's and Wally's phones without success, and tumbled into a sweaty pain-wracked sleep.

STEVE FOUND his clothes on the back seat of the Pathfinder and crawled into them. They stung with cold and he wanted to yank them off again. His feet wouldn't fit into his shoes so he put the shoes on the seat beside him and drove in his socks, with the heater full blast on them, headed toward Hermito Road, or where he thought it was.

He pulled over again, climbed into the back seat and raised it up. The twenty kilos were gone. He looked again and again, walked in cold soggy socks on the snowy shoulder to check again and again in the trunk.

No kilos.

How could that be?

He drove the road till it petered out in a gravel track. He turned around, found the map and saw that Hermito Road was only three miles away.

A quarter mile from the building he parked at the side of the road, squeezed on his shoes, took the Beretta, climbed a barbed wire fence and crossed a pasture till he was directly across the road from the building. There were no lights inside; the Mercedes and TRD were gone.

He crawled closer, trying to avoid piles of manure. At the road edge was a dilapidated fence of twisted barbed wire and inside it an electric line. It was live, a light stinging shock from a car battery delivered down hundreds of yards. It spooked livestock but a man could climb over it quickly and the shocks wouldn't be too bad.

For a long time he watched the building; nothing happened. The skinny moon dropped into the western hills, the cold redoubled, the handle of the Beretta too chilled to touch.

He drove till he found an abandoned road and turned up it, settled in the back seat with three floor mats over him, and waited for day.

"THEY'RE IN DENVER," Whitney said.

"Any news about my truck?" Curt said, cradling the phone against his ear.

"Not a sign."

"How'd you find them?"

"They turned off their phone locates but are still using a credit card linked to some charitable trust Zack has... We don't know where they're staying but they've rented two vehicles with that card and paid for food and other stuff... *And*," she added cheerfully, "we've mapped where they are by their purchases. The locus of all the places they've used that card."

He glanced at the sky. Still dark, that lovely time before the stars fade and the winter air has a special clean sting. The only time he felt hope – not for the world, but for God's glorious universe behind it. Hope like the winter wind. Revives you.

"Crazy. Wonder what they'll do next –"

"That's why we need you down here, Mr. Weathers. To help us find these guys. Before they get themselves in more trouble."

"That's hardly possible."

"There's a ticket to Denver at the Bozeman Frontier counter. And a Hertz Taurus at DIA."

"I want to get home. And I don't see why –"

"You know their background. Plus you're the best one to ID them. And," she said softly, "you *do* seem pissed off at them."

DEA

STEVE WOKE AT dawn, shivering, trying to understand what had happened. His mouth was brass, his body ached, his feet numb. He forced himself upright and threw off the floor mats, stumbled around outside till he found a patch of brush to shit, wiped his ass with snow. It made him feel no better.

At 8:05 he drove past the green aluminum-sided building. Two garage doors were up, with a Toyota on a rack inside, piles of tires beside it, a red rollaway of SnapOn tools along one side.

He turned around, came back and parked out front where the Mercedes and TRD had been, went in an open garage door. A mechanic in blue coveralls rolled out from under the Toyota. "What you want?"

"I'm looking for Radar."

The guy was big and unshaven and had a grease smear on his forehead. In his hand was a large socket wrench. "Ain't no Radar here. Maybe you should try the Air Force base. They got radar."

"Tony, then."

"Ain't no Tony either. You're in the wrong place."

Steve stepped past him into the office where Tony alias Radar and the girl Emerald had been. Just a large metal desk with car parts and work estimates and a coffee cup with cigar butts in it. "Hey," the guy came in behind him, wrench in hand. "Get outta here."

Steve stopped at the door. "Tell Tony or Radar or whoever he is I'm calling the cops."

The guy flipped the wrench in the air and it dropped back into his palm like a juggling trick. His hands were big and blackened.

He came closer, flexing the wrench. "Ain't nobody like that here. And no reason for you to call the cops. Get it?"

Steve got in the Pathfinder and drove away, grinned at the idea of calling the cops, "This guy stole my cocaine..."

Yeah, right.

"You betrayed me to some fuckups," he said when Roger answered his phone.

"I never betrayed anybody," Roger said. "I hardly ever spoke to you – check your phone. You're lucky I admit to even knowing you."

"How do you know me, Roger?"

"You're a lousy broker. And I'm changing my account. To Merrill Lynch."

"Buy some auction rate securities," Steve said, and cut off.

On his way back to the Rawhide Arms he stopped at a Safeway for Ziploc sandwich bags, Scotch tape, a roll of Happy Birthday wrapping paper, a card that said *So now you're forty – too old for sex?* and a box of *bounce* lavender dryer sheets. At checkout he scanned the magazine racks, settled on *5280*, a glossy Denver monthly that nobody could get back east.

When he got to the Rawhide Arms, Zack was still sleeping so he didn't have to tell him about the lost twenty kilos. Zack would yell at him, and Steve was moving too fast, getting things done, to put up with that. In any investment deal you sometimes lose a little before you make a lot. *See it like that*, he told himself. *Just another investment deal.*

He untaped the bag of coke they kept in the room and shook an ounce into a Ziploc bag, shoved a pinch up his nose for good luck, inhaled deeply and waited for the hit. "Oh lovely," he whispered. "Oh lovely *lovely*."

He taped the Ziploc shut and stuck it inside another, taping a lavender dryer sheet around each till they made a flat little package. Opening *5280* he cut out a square in the middle pages and taped the Ziplocs into it, wrapped the magazine in the birthday paper, wrote *Happy Birthday Jodie, here's a little reminder of home*, and taped it to the magazine.

"What's up?" Zack mumbled, waking up.

"Nothing, man. Headed back to New York."

Zack scratched his face with his good hand. "Nice."

"I can sell our stuff back there, know some fast lane folks."

"So what you going to do, drive it there?"

"Sending myself a sample." Steve held up the package. "Show it around, see who bites."

"You're the one's gonna get bit."

Steve sat on the other bed facing him. "Why are you always so *negative*?"

Zack pulled himself up, grimacing and holding his arm. "Because you got us into this. Because you lost my money. Because you got me kicked…" He scratched his whiskers. "Because you're a fuckin asshole."

Steve shook his head – how do I deal with someone like this? "I'll sell my half, you sell yours, however you like."

"Like I tell you, Vegas is easier…"

"You just like the hookers and all that false love." Steve leaned toward him. "If we sell it little at a time, this stuff would be like municipal bonds. Tax-free long-term income."

"Like what you shoulda put me into."

"But the problem is every small sale we're sticking our neck out, asking to get caught. It's riskier to make many small sales than one big one. But then again it's more likely the Feds will watch for the big ones, and the little ones slip under the radar…"

Zack swung his feet over the side of the bed. "Give me the money."

Steve grinned. "What money?"

"You sold those twenty kilos last night? Give me my half."

Steve was tossing stuff into his suitcase. "They didn't bite. I put the twenty kilos back in the storage unit. What about your deal in Aspen?"

"I was late," Zack sighed. "They never showed."

"Where's the ten kilos, then?"

"In my car."

From the bag of coke they kept in the room Steve shook about a hundred grams into a plastic bag and put it in his backpack, walked out to the Denali, tossed his things in the rear and drove away. Half a mile west of Rawhide Arms was a curving residential street of 1950s single-level tract homes. "Carrington," one mailbox said, "2785 Tomahawk". At the corner of Belleview and Zuni eight blocks away, he found a FedEx office, slid the *5280* magazine with the Ziploc of coke inside it into a FedEx envelope, addressed it to himself in New York with the Carringtons as Sender, checked First Overnight, paid cash, drove to DIA, parked in the covered garage, hid the Beretta, Winchester, four boxes of ammo and the hundred grams of coke under the Denali's rear seat, dropped off his other luggage, went through TSA Pre and took the underground train to Terminal B and United Airlines.

THE PHONE ERUPTED in Zack's ear. "Christ!" he yelled, knocked it on the floor. Pain from the broken bones hit like a train. He writhed on the bed gasping. It wouldn't go away, burning up and down his arm like lightning.

The pain lessened. The bedside clock said 1:47 in slanted red numbers. Light was coming through the blinds so it must be day. A woman was talking. Voice rising and falling faintly. In the next room maybe. Near but faraway. He sat up carefully, guarding the broken arm, decided to take the phone outside and throw it onto the freeway, realized he was naked, that it was cold outside.

His mouth tasted bad.

The woman was still talking. She was on the phone on the floor. Carefully he leaned over and picked it up. It was Siri. He must have hit her somehow when he shut off Rob's call. He shut Siri off.

It rang again. Rob O'Brien. He pushed the wrong button instead of shutting it off. "Zack," Rob kept saying, "are you there?"

He let it go to voicemail and fell back on the bed. No, he had to get up. To do what?

He dragged himself from the bed, sat on the can, flushed it, washed his face with cold water and stared at himself, unrecognizable. The sagging skin under the bloodshot eyes, the pouching cheeks and soft neck, the flecks of dandruff under the lackluster hair – what had happened?

"You're going to turn yourself around," he said. "You're going to win this thing."

THREE DEA AGENTS flanked Steve as he retrieved his suitcase at Newark. Two cops sauntered up behind them. "Please," one agent said, "come with us."

"What's up?" he said, as if not understanding.

"Right here, Sir." A steel door in a steel cubicle somewhere inside Customs. Steve felt his gut sink, and the cold foreknowledge of something horrible came up his throat.

There was a desk with four folding steel chairs and a side table. All was yellow and dusty under the flickering fluorescent light.

One agent swept a dead moth off the table with the side of his hand. "That your suitcase, Mr. Montclair?"

No way to deny it. "Of course."

"That's too bad."

He took the bait. Had to. "Why?"

"Cocaine, Mr. Montclair? We've caught you carrying cocaine across state lines."

Steve tried to remember – had there been any in the suitcase? Would they think to check FedEx, if he had any packages coming in? "That's ridiculous."

"What we want to know is where it comes from."

The Ragman's Daughter

"**B**ULLSHIT!**"** Trevor Hellman paced the room angrily, a large powerful white-bearded man in a five-thousand-dollar suit. "A little residue in a shirt pocket? *So what*? So maybe my client tucked some dollar bills in his shirt pocket – you *do* do that, don't you, Mr. Montclair? Sometimes stick dollar bills in your shirt pocket? Hell, we all do."

"Of course," Steve said, "like in a grocery store, a toll booth."

Hellman looked into the DEA inspector's eyes. "I bet even *you* do it."

The DEA agent wore what appeared to be an off-the-rack suit, and the weary expression of someone who's worked too hard too long for too little money. "Do what?"

"Stick loose bills in your shirt pocket sometimes." Hellman nodded, as if to himself. "And if one of those bills had coke residue on it, you could be pulled in for interstate transport, just like my client."

"This wasn't residue from dollar bills, Mr. Hellman. This was a packet of loose coke, something that spilled out…We're analyzing it now…"

Steve sat watching, hoping. Could Trevor Hellman get him out of this, the famed lawyer who got Wall Street guys off when they were caught with too much illegal stuff, other than the illegal financial instruments they peddled?

And if Hellman did get him off, how could he pay him?

Holy shit, would DEA now be watching his mail for incoming packages?

DIEGO GOT THE NEWS from María Christina that "our Harvard Stevie", as she called him, had been arrested at Newark.

Diego had never gone to Harvard. And was happy for it. Grew up till he was seven in the Basurero, the City of the Dump – Mexico City's vast ordure mountains where two million people live in tunnels burrowed into the festering trash. And survive on what they can dig out of it to eat or sell.

He was sometimes successful in not thinking about it.

"Where they going to put him?" he said, calculating how to make the hit if Harvard Stevie was in jail. How to get their stuff back.

"By the time we found out he'd posted bail."

"So he'll go home, no?"

"Seems he did."

"We should cover his place."

"We have."

Of course. María Christina never let anything slip through her hands. Tall, big-footed and stunning in an angular way, with slender breasts Diego longed to kiss, she was a tangled tawny blonde capable of great kindness and fiery wrath, and he loved and feared her with the same deep emotion.

As Diego saw it, María Christina might only be the daughter of El Trapero, the Ragman, but El Trapero was rich and dangerous, and she even richer and more dangerous than he. And it was El Trapero who had saved Diego from the Mexico City dump.

So there was nothing he would not do for her. Yet in his heart he feared he might somehow displease her without knowing. To him she was often kind, almost affectionate. Which made him love her even more. And determined to care for and protect her.

He had learned all he could about her. That she, like this guy Steve, had gone to Harvard. But whereas Steve had simply blundered through, all C's and D's, a rich man's son, María Christina had been Phi Beta Kappa, had gone on to a Yale MBA and returned to Miami to convert her father's cocaine wealth into an all-American empire of strip malls, housing developments, race tracks, chain restaurants and casinos.

Though the Ragman had grown up in the Mexico City dump, his family compound was now on the richest street in America, Indian Creek Island Road, on an island off Miami. Diego had been there once, waited his turn through the mob of security guards till María Christina herself came to fetch him in a green Maserati. The house big as the government palace in Mexico City, right on the gleaming blue-green water, her white yacht anchored offshore. A 250-acre island with an 18-hole golf club and only 30 homes, where eighty of America's richest people lived.

She was thirty-one, four years older than he. Still not married. Sometimes in black nights he imagined doing some impossibly heroic deed to save her, and she would fall in love with him. When a squad of killers surrounds the mansion he takes them down, one by one. He is wounded and she cares for him, heals him, learns who he really is.

But who am I, really? he wondered.

Although she was worth hundreds of millions of dollars, nothing enraged María Christina more than losing money. Even a tiny ten million in cocaine. She'd be like a hand grenade, ready to take everyone down unless the thieves were killed. And her property returned to her.

Whatever it took, Diego would make it happen.

Maybe someday she *could* love him.

STEVE GRABBED a cab home to East 76th and Madison. Nervous on the cab's worn slippery black seat, tapping fingers on his knees, feeling chilled, too hot, glancing around but seeing nothing, worrying what would go wrong next. When he got to the apartment, Eugenia the Salvadoran maid was leaving, jangling her keys. "Oh Missir Montclay," she looked up with dark open eyes. "How nice you home! The kids and Miss Montclay, they missing you."

"Thank you, Genie," he said, frustrated as ever by the enormous gap between them, thinking of her salary, this four-bedroom apartment, a dining room and salon, a kitchen so small two people had trouble working in it, twelve thousand a month rent plus fees, plus tips at Christmas, plus the kids' schools – eighty grand alone right there – the parking garage, Mercedes lease payments – maybe they should go down a step, get a Lexus – all the sorrows that come from living high on the hog in hog heaven...and now the money slipping away like water, investments going south...When the money ran out, where could they go?

Marcie in the living room on her cell phone, glanced up at him with a wide-eyed smile. "Right," she said, coming toward him, "but this kind of a deal, it doesn't happen every day...Yes, of course, I can find you something closer to downtown, the fifties, maybe? No, well let's keep in touch...if I see something special, not on the market maybe, I'll give you a –"

She shut off the phone and he took her in his arms, the sheer delight of her slim warm scented body against his making his heart soar. Her biceps were hard and strong around his shoulders. "You're here," she whispered. "Thank God you're here."

"Dad's here!" It was Jason running out from his room. "Dad! You're home early!"

He knelt to hug his son. "Yes!" he said laughing. "*Yes!*"

"Did you get one?" Jason said.

"An elk? Not yet." Steve tried to find words. "But I might go back. Get one then."

"You're going *again?*" It was Susanna, this magnificent contessa who was his daughter. Who like Marcie seemed to combine an ethereal, medieval Italian beauty with a total unawareness of it.

"Maybe, maybe just a couple days." It felt bad to say it. He hugged her, conscious of her newly adolescent need to retreat, scenting her lovely schoolgirl longhaired odor as if he'd never smell it again. "Okay," he smiled, pulling away, "what've *you* learned since *I* went away?"

"The periodic tables, five new elements every day – it's boring. But *can you believe* we've found a new habitable planet right nearby! Only *four light years* away –"

"So when do we go?"

She laughed and he snatched at his son who twisted away. *God I'm lucky*, he reminded himself for the ten-thousandth time, glanced up at Marcie smiling at them. *We'll make it*, he told her with his eyes. *Look what we have.*

"So, punk," he said to Jason, "What have *you* been up to?"

"That kid in third, Roscoe, I wanted to hit?"

Any enemy of Jason's was Steve's as well. "Yeah, that little asshole –"

"I still didn't hit him yet."

"Good. Or like I told you you'll get suspended."

Jason gave him an insider's smile. *Isn't that the idea, to* not *go to school?*

How true. Steve stood, knees hurting, his arm around Marcie's waist, feeling her ribs beneath the silky dress, a hand on Jason's shoulder, breathed in. *Peace.*

From a kitchen cabinet he took two short glasses, dropped an ice cube in each and filled them with Oban. Marcie came in and hugged him, chin nestled in his shoulder. "Honey what are we going to do?"

He wouldn't tell her about being arrested at Newark. "We'll figure it out."

"Can't we borrow on those securities?"

"The banks will buy them back at thirty cents on the dollar, but they won't lend on them."

"It's unfair; they said they were cash equivalent…"

He snuggled her. "If you're a bank you can say *any*thing, then do what*ever* you want."

She smiled up at him. "Maybe I'll find another hot client."

He loved her for it, this refusal to be dominated, destroyed. "I know you will…"

He went into Jason's room, sat on the bed. Jason turned away from Game of Thrones. "It's *super* you're back! You gonna stay aren't you Dad? I've got a game next week…"

Steve glanced at the screen, jostled Jason's shoulder. "I've missed you."

Jason shoved his shoulder into Steve's. "Cold, up there, huh?"

"Yeah." Steve shoved him back. "You'd love it."

"You rode horses?"

"In two more years you can come too."

"With Zack?"

"Sure. With Zack."

"You told him I watch all his games?"

"I did."

"So how come he can miss a game this week?"

"Every year his team has a bye week. That's when we go."

"I'm glad you're home."

"I have to leave again, but not tomorrow."

The boy faced away. "Okay Dad."

"How's your sister?"

"She's so snotty. Thinks she's special."

"Well, she is special."

"Yeah, but…"

Steve stood. "I'll go tell her to stop being snotty."

"Don't. That just makes her worse."

Susanna was sitting at her antique cherry school desk doing homework out of a workbook with drawings of trees and bushes.

He sat on the chair next to her. "Hey, Little Bear," her nickname since a vacation long ago in Yellowstone, the bear cub they'd seen. "I hear you're being snotty."

She laughed. "He should be so lucky."

He hugged her shoulders, delighting as always in sweet scent of her golden braids. "How's Latin?"

"*Agricola bona in tres partes divisa est.*"

He grinned. "That doesn't sound like fun."

"No, I love it, Dad. It's just we go too slow…"

He went into his and Marcie's bedroom and began making calls, to other guys he'd done coke with in the glory days… "Hey Pete, it's Steve Montclair, how you doing?"

"Yeah, fine. What's up?"

"Remember that wild party after the GE deal? We made six hundred and seventy-five million, and we spent a lot of it that night…"

"Yeah, so what? You doing something on GE, shorting them?"

"No, no, this is personal, Man. This is personal. Like how we spent all that money, that night. I've got a portfolio of it now, would like to offer investment…"

"Not me, Steve. Got to go –"

How many times would they turn him down before somebody called the cops? Somebody with a grudge? In this world of deals that could be anyone.

Always be ethical, his father used to say. *That way you'll come to no harm.*

Trouble is, these days, what the Hell is *ethical?*

The answer, Dad would have said, is *hurt no one.*

He stood in the living room as snow tumbled past the glass, the car headlights like tiny sea creatures far below, the windows on the towers all around him watching, waiting.

He shouldn't get down on himself. Daily life in the markets would drive anyone mad. Money as God, as if it could even overrule death. How many times had he told himself *I'm doing this for the kids, to give them the best life?* But would it?

Ten million from the coke would set things right. Five million, actually, when split with Zack.

Even with five million they could buy a boat and sail around the world. Show the kids what life is really like.

Who was it talked about lives of quiet desperation?

Fuck that.

IN THE MOTEL kitchenette Zack made a double instant coffee and poured in two Coffee-Mate non-dairy creamers. His cell rang.

Benny Silva, his producer, calling from LA. "When you coming back?"

"Tomorrow."

"When, tomorrow?"

"Don't know yet, getting a plane out of Bozeman … haven't got the ticket yet."

"You better get it fast. We need you down here … Tony's sicker'n a dog and asks can you do the whole game. It's an opportunity, Zack…"

"I'll be there." He stared out the window at the frigid black-white night. "I'll be there."

STEVE COULDN'T TAKE his eyes off Marcie. He'd wanted her every night up in elk camp, every night of that interminable drive with Zack from the Buffalo Horns to Denver. Wanted her the instant he'd come into the apartment today, the flash of her smile, her bright eyes, her hugs and kisses, her body warm and lustrous against his, the fragrance of her hair. If the kids hadn't been there he and she would have been doing it in minutes, like the old days.

And because of her each day felt sacred, every day they'd ever had, and he still wanted her like in high school in the back of Dad's new Buick, the seat cold and slithery beneath them in the bitter winter night.

He undressed and sat on the bed. She came out of the bathroom in black pajamas. Why, he occasionally asked her, do you put on pajamas when we're going to make love?

"How do I know we're going to make love? she'd teased.

"We make love almost every night."

She stood before him and slid the pajama top over her head. "Not when you're in hunting camp."

"You have beautiful breasts," he said. "You have perfect breasts."

She slipped off her pajama pants. "You are a Greek goddess," he said.

She straddled his thighs and kissed him, breasts against his chest, rubbing herself into him. "Let's do this forever, and not think about anything else."

"Like when we were kids –"

"Like when we were kids in high school and I was so hot for you I could look at you across six rows of seats in study hall and squeeze my legs together and come."

"You may be the hottest woman who's ever lived..." He rolled back onto the bed and she slipped down over him, surrounded him in golden hot wet darkness, her hair tumbling over him, her eyes half-closed, her lips apart as she rode up and down him.

Afterwards they lay holding each other, sweaty and sticky. Misery and fear and self-reproach came back on him. He lay there trying to think, but there could be no answer, no way out.

"All that counts," she said, sensing his tension, cuddled tighter, "is the kids and you and me. The rest is bullshit."

Liar's Paradox

"**A** DETECTIVE GOLDBERG here to see you." It was Casimir, the apartment concierge on the interphone.

Steve glanced at the clock on the stove. *8:17*. He'd just done ten miles on the treadmill, his t-shirt and shorts soaked. "What for?"

"He does not say."

He wasn't having him here, dressed like this, with Marcie in the shower and breakfast dishes in the sink. And Marcie didn't need to know. "Tell him I'll be right down."

He tugged on a shirt, jeans and running shoes, his North Face jacket, told Marcie he was going to the corner store and took the elevator to the lobby.

Guy standing there in a Mets jacket and a Miller Lite cap. About five-ten, athletic. A rugged face with a blunt boxer's nose. "Let's take a walk," he said.

They turned west on East 76th, the wind cutting into Steve's face. "What you want?" he said.

"I'm buying you a cup of coffee."

"I already had coffee. Get to the point, or I'm going back."

"Then I'll arrest you."

"For what? That bullshit at the airport? You heard my lawyer – I'm clean."

Goldberg smiled understandingly. "Nobody's clean, Mr. Montclair. Least of all you." He opened the door of Gloria Trattoria. "Indulge me."

They sat at a table in the corner under a stained glass window. Goldberg ordered a *doppio*; the waiter glanced at Steve.

He shook his head. "I'm good."

Goldberg glanced down at the table, as if remembering something, looked into Steve's eyes. His own were dark, unblinking. "We analyzed that coke in your shirt pocket and we know where it comes from. The Veracruz cartel. An old guy they call the Ragman, been shipping coke north for decades but we can never catch him. And now his daughter's built a financial empire out of it. They operate mostly in the western states where their major competition is the Sinaloa cartel. They also work in Florida, where the Ragman and the other top folks of the cartel live a very privileged life while they addict and poison hundreds of thousands of Americans..."

"What's this got to do with *me*, for Chrissake? Look, I got to go."

"You refused to provide a urine sample yesterday. Why?"

"My piss is my business. This isn't a police state. Not yet."

Goldberg reached out to touch Steve's arm. "Please, *listen* to me. We want to bring down the Veracruz cartel. You can help us. Just tell us where that coke came from. Where *exactly* you got it."

"I never *got* it, Mr. Goldberg –"

Goldberg waved a hand: *Of course you did.* "We won't ever prosecute you. We want the Ragman and his crooked daughter."

Steve stood and slid his chair to the table. "If I knew what you were talking about I'd be scared to death. I'm far too much of a coward to even *mess* with stuff like that."

Goldberg shrugged. "But if you don't help us, we're going to throw the book at you."

Steve looked down at him. "How many Americans die from cocaine every year?"

Goldberg looked surprised. "About five thousand."

"What's the budget of your anti-cocaine war?"

"The DEA budget all together is about three billion. Local and state budgets add another seven billion, more or less. But that includes heroin, other drugs too..."

"That's two million dollars per death. At the same time, about thirty-three thousand Americans die every year from vehicles, another half million handicapped for life. The national highway safety budget is about nine hundred million, as I remember, so by comparison that's only twenty-five grand per death – barely one percent of your holy cocaine budget... And what about the half million Americans who die every year from cigarettes? You know what the budget to fight that is? Almost nonexistent."

Goldberg stood. "I'm not here to argue statistics."

"You want to get rid of these damn cartels, Detective? *Legalize* the stuff. *All* of it. Let the people who want it buy it at market cost, grown legally, brought in legally. It'll kill the cartels overnight. But you guys'll never do that. Because the cartels are your bread and butter. Without the cartels, you wouldn't even have a job."

Goldberg walked beside Steve back to the apartment building as if he were an old friend unwilling to part. "There's always a way to validate one's actions, isn't there? No matter how crooked they are?"

"You read any Victorian novels, Detective? The English empire, the greatest in history, was driven by cocaine and opium... you know that? And there wouldn't have been an IT revolution without cocaine, nor Sigmund Freud, or modern medicine –" He was going too far, Steve knew, but couldn't stop – "or how about the greatest music of the last century? Most of it wouldn't have happened without cocaine."

In the No Parking zone in front of Steve's building a FedEx truck was idling, exhaust rising from its tailpipe, its uniformed driver carrying a package through the front door.

Steve halted, turned. "Long as I'm out here, might as well get *The Times.*"

Goldberg's eyes widened. "Smart guy like you, you don't have a subscription?"

"From now on," Steve nodded goodbye, "talk to Trevor Hellman."

"I'm sure we will."

Steve watched Goldberg walk away, then made as if going to the corner store. Without a penny in his pocket how was he going to buy the *Times*? Who'd want the damn thing anyway?

Goldberg had vanished. Steve went home. "FedEx for you, Steve," Casimir said in the lobby, holding it out, a gift.

CURT DIDN'T LIKE DENVER. Never had. Not in all three times he'd been there before. And he didn't like it now.

It went on for miles and miles, Denver. One freeway exit after another, shopping malls, fast food and big box stores, hills and valleys of subdivisions then the stark downtown highrises and sports domes then miles and miles more freeways, subdivisions and malls.

All choked with traffic, under a polluted cloud.

Amazing it had only taken a hundred fifty years to turn a paradise of prairies, rivers, streams and hills teeming with wild animals into this.

The DEA office was on East Easter Avenue, out in the flatlands, and he didn't like that either, but at least they were trying to find his two dudes. Whitney wasn't there but Duane McCord said that Steve and Zack had disabled the GPS beacons on their two rental cars, or the beacons were defective, who knew... But their credit card use, the one card belonging to Zack that they both seemed to use, indicated an area in South Denver surrounding Santa Fe Boulevard.

"But we don't have the faintest idea where your truck is," Duane said. "We've had an APB on it for three days and haven't heard a thing."

"Since they've rented two vehicles," Curt said, "maybe they don't have it anymore."

"Or they're hiding it? So they can use it again?"

"THE DEA," María Christina said, "they have put someone on this. A woman."

"A woman?"

"*Sí.* A black woman. It appears she may be very dangerous."

"*Como?*"

"She is using this little matter of the two guys to try and take us down, Diego."

"This must not happen."

"It is not just our mail that is endangered. It is us."

"*Nosotros.*"

"*Sí, nosotros.* She has already been causing trouble for us. For others."

"Shall I fix this?"

"Not yet. But you will know, when it is time."

THE WALDORF ASTORIA had always been for Steve a personal place, one everyone knows about but few know, where every US President since Hoover has stayed, where many other politicos have lived or visited, sometimes for an hour or so with a young lady, sometimes for a campaign tour, sometimes just to stay in the city for a few days, see some shows and do a deal or two. A grand old tower reeking of judicious wealth and conservative ostentation, 1930s art deco design, and unpublicized meetings where railroad barons, bankers, politicians and others of that ilk bought and sold the future of the nation.

Steve felt at home here. When he was little his Dad brought him here for a root beer after a trip to the top of Rockefeller Center or the Empire State Building or a wander in Central Park, and Steve, already a young gentleman, reveled in it in his own understated way.

Now here he was again. With a teaspoon of cocaine in a yellow plastic vial in his pocket. Checking emails on his phone in a quiet booth at the back of the bar, all gloss and dark leather, where prosperous young men took their dates to impress them, and tired older gentlemen kept in touch with each other and arranged things how they wanted.

Ibrahim Al Kahtani slipped into the seat across from him, just another investment banker in an expensive suit, a fund manager maybe, call it what you want. In Manhattan you could never have enough money, and you got it however you could.

Ibrahim ordered a Lagavulin and stared out the window where fat flakes of dirty snow tumbled out of the gray sky, glanced at a girl walking by, wiped a napkin at the damp spot on the table where his glass had sat. Steve took the orange pharmacy vial from his suit pocket and handed it to him. With a smile Ibrahim took it in his lap, popped the cover, licked his finger and dipped it in the vial, ran it under his nose, rubbed it on his gums.

"Holy shit." he leaned back, eyes on the ceiling.

"Didn't I tell you?"

Ibrahim sipped his Lagavulin reflectively. "So you really *have* this stuff?"

Steve chuckled, a little forced. "Have I ever lied to you?"

Ibrahim shrugged. "Probably many times. I don't remember."

"I haven't. And I'm not lying now. Question is, how much you want?"

For a while Ibrahim didn't speak. "If it's all like this –"

"Never will you find shit like this. Not ever again..."

"Okay okay." Ibrahim waved a hand. "As you know, there's an endless market downtown. Endless." He sipped more Lagavulin, inhaling its ether up his nose, across his sinuses, into his brain. "We both know this."

"I've got other options. Came to you first."

Ibrahim grinned. "So you *do* lie to me."

"Who was it said, *Everything I say is a lie?*"

"The liar's paradox. Some Greek, long ago." Ibrahim turned up his nose, the ancient Arab disdain for Greeks. "We work on the basis of a purchase option. You bring it to me, I check it out. If it's what you say it is, I'll take three."

"Three kilos?" Steve sat back, trying to keep the hardness out of his voice. "For all this hassle and all you want is *three* kilos?"

"No no, you silly infidel," Ibrahim smiled. "Three million *dollars*. 120 kilos."

"I'll sell it in DC before that."

"Look, look, you know what it's worth on the street. You want to stand on a corner on Wall Street, little sign around your neck, *Buy your coke here?*"

Steve snickered, wanting some now.

"Look," Ibrahim said again. "If it's this good, I'll give you top dollar, which as you know is twenty-five grand a key...because if it's all this good I can share it out for top dollar." He shrugged his shoulders, tugged his collar up around his neck. "We got a purchase option going. We know each other. We don't back out."

"I'll want the funds wired simultaneously…"

"Okay okay no problem. You bring me the stuff, I do the wire." He tossed off his Lagavulin, stood. "I'll have bulletproof backup. You should too."

Steve looked up at him, refusing to rise and shake hands. "Three days."

"Three days." Ibrahim went out the door into the falling snow.

Steve stood, feeling tired and old, fear like acid reflux in his gut. Bulletproof backup – where was he going to find that?

GRACE

THE GNOCCHI were beginning to float on the boiling water so they were nearly done. Steve slid them to a back burner, shook the stainless steel skillet to refresh the green beans and almond slices in the olive oil and tarragon and moved that to a back burner too. He ducked out onto the balcony, turned off the Weber and forked the four filet mignons onto a plate, dashed into the dining room and set the platter on the table, ran back to the kitchen, dumped the gnocchi and green beans into two bowls and set them on the table. "Dinner!" he called. "Come and get it!"

Marcie came over and put her cell phone on the kitchen counter. She let out a long sigh. "I'm so worked up I'm not even hungry."

He slipped his arm around her waist. "More and more I'm realizing what you said is true. All that matters is us. The four of us. We can go through Hell, if we have to –"

"And come out fine."

He poured the St. Emilion. They sat there a moment in silence, the food and wine giving the room the entrancing fragrance of a Siena sidewalk café, the snowfall beyond the windows softening the city sounds. *This little island of ours*, Steve thought. *This beautiful little island.* Not knowing why, he said the old grace, *Bless us O Lord for these thy gifts,* as they had at the dinner table in Glen Cove when he was a kid and Mom and Dad were still alive and there was a constant awareness that what you had came from God, and so you didn't mind thanking God for these gifts.

"Thank you, Darling." Marcie squeezed his wrist.

"I have to leave in the morning. But when I get back we're going to eat dinner together every night –"

"Really?" Jason said. "You're not going to be always working late?"

Marcie smiled: *these children of ours*. Steve felt a flush of sudden hope, took a breath. It felt good, as if saying grace could change him. Is this what it *is*? he wondered, not knowing what he meant. "What would you guys think," he looked at the kids, "about taking a year off?"

Marcie looked at him wide-eyed. "How?"

"I've been thinking, what if at the end of the school year in June we go someplace, the Caribbean, the coast of Spain – it's called the Costa Brava, the brave coast – what if we buy a big sailboat and sail around the world?"

"Dad," Jason said. "What about school?"

Steve looked at him. "Think you could survive a year without it?"

"With what," Marcie looked at him steadily, "do you intend to buy a boat? Or take time off? Or do anything?"

Steve nodded: this horrible hamster wheel of debt, of never enough, of trying to show you're fine when you're drowning, what if it all went away? He imagined being a farmer, living off the fruit of the land, not giving a damn what anybody thought.

"It's just possible," he said, "when I come back from Denver, if this deal works out, we'll have some funds to enjoy life for a while instead of running this rat race..."

"It's not a rat race," Susanna watched him. "I *like* my life."

Marcie patted her daughter's hand. "Let's see what Dad comes up with, before we criticize."

"Maybe the rat race," Jason added, "is when you grow up."

Marcie turned to Steve, again her unerring look, saying nothing, that reminded him of when he and she were kids back in the fourth grade in Glen Cove, and he'd said to her, full of boyish self-importance, "what if when we grow up we get married?"

"Why don't we wait to decide," she'd answered after a moment, tugging at a long auburn pigtail, "Till we grow up?"

"HOW ARE YOU?" María Christina said with a catch in her breath that meant she cared for him and nothing was going to stop her saying it.

"Of course I'm fine," Diego reassured her. "I'm always fine."

"These friends of yours, they're in Denver for sure."

"How you know?" It was okay to challenge her, to show he loved her.

"The police, they have the license plates, I'll give them to you. These two guys, they shut off their GPS –"

"They are idiots. That will not protect them."

"This other truck, the Ford, is still disappeared."

"*Todo lo major.*"

"You are not afraid of anything. Are you?"

"Yes I am. I am afraid of you."

"Good," she said, warm and friendly. "Let's keep it like that."

"I don't want to be afraid of you – I want –"

"So you drive around Denver, the motels, the parking lots? Looking for these two license plate numbers I will give you…"

"YOU DON'T ANSWER your phone," Zack said. "Twice I left you messages."

"I been busy," Steve said. "Finding us a solution."

"You got one?"

"Not yet. Like I said, working on it."

"When you coming back?"

"Tomorrow, by noon."

This reminded Zack he was supposed to be in LA for the pre-show run-through. Had to call Rob O'Brien, Benny Silva. Tell them he couldn't make the pre-show run-through today. *Be there tomorrow.*

How could he be there tomorrow? That meant when Steve arrived tomorrow at DIA he could take all the coke. While Zack was in LA.

What was he going to tell Benny?

Would they dump him? Would Rob dump him too?

In the next three years he could make five-fifty a year from Benny, or maybe only four-fifty for one year. Rob wasn't finding him other deals. So if it all went to pieces he'd only have his NFL retirement. With that he'd never pay off the Vegas debts.

Fuck TV football. Sell the coke. Live your life. Be with Monica.

"There was a problem in Newark," Steve said. "I was going to tell you."

Zack came out of his reverie. "*What* problem?"

"DEA says they found residue in my pocket. A shirt. Have not the faintest idea –"

"*Wait* a minute – they found *what?*"

"A little powder, that's all. Don't know where it came from. I have the best attorney in town. He says it could be from putting dollar change in your shirt pocket. Tainted money."

"You unbelievably stupid fuck –"

"They picked up traces, that's all."

"So how'd you get out?"

"Fifty thousand bond –"

"But you don't *have* that, you've already told me."

"I securitized it."

"You *what?*"

"I gave the bondsman first call on some securities … He didn't know he couldn't call on them."

"Which securities?"

"Those auction rate ones. Look, man, don't worry –"

"*My* auction rate ones?"

"Mine …"

"You said they're *worthless!* So when that bondsman finds out, he's gonna send people after you. I hope he does."

"Zack, you worry too much. Let's just do this and make our millions."

"Okay, let's talk about that. You gonna unload some?"

"They're going to be watching me, because of the airport thing … hard to do deals …"

"So what's that mean?"

"I'm trying, but we might have to do it your way."

"Vegas?"

"That's what I said."

Zack thought a moment, lining it all up in his head. "So you *start* this whole thing, *steal* this stuff, get me involved when I don't *want* to, then you say *Oh it's too hot for me, you take it.* Is *that* what you're saying?"

"Look, it's not my fault –"

In a football game a linebacker can go easy on a receiver or running back for a while, then hit him when he least expects it. Take him right out of the game. "If I sell it all," Zack said, "the money's all mine." He killed his phone, went into the bathroom and washed his face in icy water. If DEA had arrested Steve, how long before they found the stash at Maxi Self-Rent on Santa Fe Boulevard?

Whatever Steve did would be stupider than you could imagine. Like losing Zack's money with these auction rate securities. Like stealing the coke from the plane. Like spooking the horses so Zack got kicked. Like losing twenty kilos in some double cross in Fountain. Or did Steve lie about that? Hide it somewhere?

Like getting caught at Newark with coke in your pocket. What next?

"Come here, honey," Lady Coke whispered. She was so gorgeous naked under that filmy black negligée. "You're a little jazzed, honey. Let's have some fun, get your head around this."

He cut an edge off one of the kilos he'd brought back from Aspen and took a hit.

Lady Coke was right. Zack was *on*. Steve could come back any time he wanted, but the coke would no longer be at Santa Fe Maxi Self-Rent. And Steve would be just SOL.

Nine Million Easy

STEVE HAD TWO JAMISONS before the cabin attendant closed the door. She was short and fat and her hair was tangled but her smile was sweet, and he tried not to look nervous and hurried. He'd feared that Visa would refuse the charge for the plane ticket but it had gone through. Though he doubted he could use the card by the time he landed, he had to have gas for the Denali, money for food, a room somewhere.

But soon as he got the coke he could sell some, somehow. Have money then.

Ibrahim was hot for it. More people would be, once the news got around.

Nine million easy. Maybe more.

Success is measured by how much you dare.

Four hours to Denver but really only two because of the time change. He could get to the Santa Fe self-storage by two-thirty. Load the coke in the Denali and twenty hours later it's in another storage unit in New Jersey. Or maybe up in Westport, someplace tony like that. Where they don't expect you to store nine million of cocaine in their unit.

To be a good crook, he reflected, is like a casino. Like a banker, a broker. Like politics.

Success is in the details.

ZACK LOADED THE TEN KILOS he'd brought back from Aspen into the Pathfinder, packed his suitcase and the Winchester and drove to the Maxi Self-Rent storage unit on Santa Fe Boulevard.

His phone said it was eighty-three degrees in Malibu, but according to the Pathfinder's dash display only eleven in Littleton. It felt even colder, made his arm throb.

The problem was should he drive the coke to Vegas or leave it somewhere else in Denver? If he just took samples to Vegas and people liked them (of course they would, they'd never had snow this good), they'd want to buy. So then he'd have to drive back to Denver, pick up the kilos and drive them to Vegas. Either way, he'd have the dangerous drive from Denver to Vegas with hundreds of kilos. Which meant a life sentence if he got caught. Or he'd get shot. Or he'd be eighty if he ever got out.

But if he couldn't do a deal in Vegas it was better that the coke stay in Denver. So if it sold in New York he wouldn't have to drive it from Vegas back to Denver first. Anyway it was crazy to be driving anywhere you didn't have to with all these kilos, especially when the cops were maybe looking for you.

Best to leave the coke somewhere new in Denver and just take samples to Vegas.

"THIS MRS. MONTCLAIR?" the definitely Hispanic voice said on the telephone. "I am a friend of Steve, your husband."

"He's not here."

"I am trying to find him, I work for Curt, the guide, we were on an elk hunt together. I've got Steve's jacket."

"Oh my. The North Face?"

"Yes, that one."

"I thought he brought it back, to New York –"

"Even now, he is there?"

"He's gone back to Colorado. He didn't tell you?"

"Yes, but I thought it was for tomorrow."

"He should be there now."

"Where, do you know?"

"He didn't say – don't you know?"

"Tell me your address, I will send the coat there…"

"Never mind –" Something made her fear, she didn't know what. "I've got to go –"

"I have it as 29 East Seventy-Six Street, yes? In Manhattan?"

"Goodbye."

"Tell Steve I called. And that I may drop in, visit you and the kids. Maybe me, maybe with some of my friends. You tell him that, okay?"

ZACK BACKED the Pathfinder up to the storage unit door, stashed all the kilos in it, covered them with the blue tarp, and drove to Santa Fe Boulevard wondering where to go next.

Tiny windborne icicles glittered against the hard sky. The sun was pure white, halfway up, but gave no heat. Traffic was thin, the malls, bars, railroad sidings, and trailer parks sliding by like dioramas on both sides.

He pulled over to take a hit from the coke container in his pocket. Jesus this feels good. Makes your pecker hard and your body warm and you can take on anything and win. *Jesus good.*

Coal train after coal train passed trailing clouds of cindery dust, two hundred tons of coal per car, two hundred cars per train. Warren Buffet's Santa Fe and Burlington Northern Railroad strip mining the American people's public lands in Wyoming and doing what it could to increase global warming.

Was this the ugliest road in America?

He was depressed, already needed another hit. To buoy his spirits, ease the pain, put him back in the fighting mode.

He drove south on Santa Fe toward Highlands Ranch, the vast subdivision that was neither ranch nor highlands, just another unending suburb of cookie-cutter houses, churches, chain restaurants, malls, and more churches. A great place to store nine million in coke.

Any self-storage would do. Someplace Steve couldn't find.

He found the perfect place off Highlands Ranch Boulevard – who would suspect? Good News Self-Storage; it even had a little fish on the billboard, letting everybody know it was a Christian place. A bit pricier to be sure, but of course it cost extra to have God keep an eye on it.

Number 409 in the second row, the kilos would go in nicely. In the next row a family was unloading furniture into another unit – a frilly lamp, a Barcalounger.

He moved the bricks one-handed, swearing at the pain in the other arm, locked the unit and drove north on Santa Fe then west on I-70, ten baggies of coke secreted under the back carpet, a pill vial under the front seat to keep him company on the road west. I-70, the same highway he'd driven to meet Wally in Aspen but Wally hadn't been there when he'd been late, and Emily hadn't answered her phone.

Driving one-handed he took out his iPhone with the other hand, wincing at the pain, and tried Emily. She'd always loved coke, knew people who sold it, maybe she could help.

She didn't answer but five minutes later called back. "Wally said you never showed."

"I had an accident, was late. He didn't answer when I called him. You didn't either. Is he still interested?"

"Maybe, but he's gone for five days. Where are you?"

He glanced at the eroded snowy slopes rising on both sides of the highway. "Almost to Idaho Springs... And, I have a present for you."

"What about your cute little Monica? The one you tossed me over for?"

"Don't talk crap, Emily. Besides, I need you to help me figure what to do with this stuff."

"Whyn't you come up here?"

"It's way out of my way. I'm in a rush."

"Where to?"

"Do me a favor?"

"Uh-uhh."

"Rent us a room at the Hotel Colorado in Glenwood. In your name only. I'll pay you back, cash."

"This doesn't sound good, sweetie –"

"Please? I'll explain when I see you."

WHEN STEVE drove the Denali back to the Rawhide Arms Motel there were three hookers in his and Zack's former room offering a trio for $99.

"We just came this afternoon," one said. "We don't know anything about some guy was here before."

He drove west to Maxi Self-Rent, the sun sinking like muddy blood through the gray smog between the snowy mountains.

When he got to the unit the lock and chain were gone.

There was nothing inside.

Three times he called Zack but it just went to voice mail. He sat in the Denali watching the night fall and trying to figure where Zack might have gone with the coke.

It had to be Vegas. Zack had never considered selling his share in LA, said why drive all that way? "I'll take my half and go to Vegas, try people there..." That's what he'd said. Was he lying? Was planning all along to do LA?

Liar's paradox. Crazy motherfucker up to his ears in casino debt but thought Steve didn't know. Why lie to your broker? He always knows.

Steve drove north on Santa Fe and took I-70 through the Denver's ragged western suburbs, this city growing like melanoma, eating across the prairies and wooded foothills.

I-70 climbed and twisted through miles of tree-thick steepening ridges toward the Eisenhower Tunnel, then down the other side toward Vail, that city also now spreading in all directions over what fifty years ago were deep forest, and toward the bouldered canyon of the Colorado River. What do you do, Steve wondered, if you're Zack and you're trying to sell nine million in pure cocaine?

How do you find him, one out of two million people in Vegas?

And if Zack wasn't in Vegas, what then?

IT WAS DARK when Zack reached Glenwood Springs. His arm ached and his eyes felt gravelly from the drive, his stomach burning from too many Big Macs. He called Emily. "Room 229," she said. "You owe me a hundred eighty bucks."

In the parking lot he saw her yellow 500 SL parked under a Colorado spruce by itself where nobody could ding it. He shouldered his backpack and hiked up to the room. She came to the door, her face fresh and desirous, alive and ironic, her kiss like a dive into uncertain depths.

"Wow," she said, "I've missed you." Dressed in a purple scarf, purple jacket, short white skirt and leather boots, she was so lovely it made his chest ache. She took his backpack and dropped it on the spare bed, gave him another long kiss and sat on the other bed beside him. "So what's this?" she said, nodding at his cast.

"Slipped on some stairs ..."

"You, the guy who never went down?"

"I never tossed you over, Emily."

"What – you mean what I said on the phone?" She had a classical yet vivacious face, purposeful mouth, bright green eyes and glowing chestnut hair that made you want to sink your fingers in its folds. "I said that to piss you off."

"Like always."

She grinned, jounced the mattress. "Eat yet?"

"Not hungry."

She glanced at his cast. "On painkillers?"

"Was on oxycodone but it does nothing." He stood and opened his backpack, pulled out a baggie of coke. "This is better."

She looked at it. "Holy crow. *That's* what you wanted to sell Wally?"

"That and more."

"You're way out of his league, honey." She gave him a worried smile. "Where'd you *get* this?"

He shook his head. "No questions. I just need to unload it."

"You've gone big time. Big money and big jail time if they catch you."

He shrugged, not believing his own insouciance, shook a little coke on the Gideon Bible and handed it to her. "You've never had anything this good."

She sniffed it in, ran a finger under her nose, licked it. "Wow." She lay back on the bed, white skirt up around her thighs. "Holy crow."

His phone rang; Steve. He clicked it off, took a hit on the Bible and sat down beside her, leaned over and kissed her nose, smiled into the depths of her sea-green eyes. It came to him all at once, what they'd had, what they'd lost, and why. He caressed her cheek softly with his good hand, feeling its roughness against her silky skin. "Wish we'd ..." He couldn't say it, didn't know what he wanted to say, thought of Monica.

"Wow," she said, eyes faraway. "*This* is *fan*tastic." She leaned up on one arm, grinned. "Let's keep it and go off together and do nothing else."

He thought of Monica again. "Wally wouldn't like that."

"Fuck Wally."

"You really deep with him?"

She made a *moue* – who knows? "I'm his home girl. When he's on trips he fucks other girls but won't admit it."

"So why you with him?"

She raised her head to stare at him. "What else should I do?"

"Go back to work?"

"I got a beautiful house, nice car, all the money I want, can ski all winter and hike all summer. It's a good life. Who wants to hire a thirty-three-year old model anyway?"

"Get yourself some TV roles, a movie –"

"And move back to LA? I'm done with that."

He shook out some more coke on the Bible. His phone buzzed. Steve again. There were three messages, the first two from Steve. *I'm at the storage unit*, the first said. *Where's our stuff? Where are you?*

I will find you, the second message said. *No matter where, I will find you.*

The third was from Sheriff Stauffenberg. *Turn yourself in now. It'll make it easier on you later.*

He unbuttoned her blouse, as always no bra, the little breasts rising and falling with her quickened breath, the cute belly button he'd loved to kiss, unzipped her skirt and pulled it down. She sat up, kissed him quickly, tugged off her underpants and lay back naked, a magnificent beauty, the source of life.

"It's going to be so lovely," she said, "to do this again."

Afterwards they went to the Hotel's Baron's Restaurant for dinner. He had a double vodka martini and she had a Cassis *kir* and then they had a bottle of Malbec and the lights were low, the food exciting, the room full of diners bathed in a warm, friendly haze. It's so good, this life, he told himself. I can do this deal.

His phone buzzed: Monica. He sent it to voicemail, ordered more wine.

"I can't believe we didn't work out." Emily twirled her glass by the stem, the wine shimmering like rubies. "Maybe your Vegas trips – I got tired of them…"

"That's where I'm going now."

She gave him a sharp look. "Vegas?"

"Just for a couple days." He laid his hand on hers. "Why don't you come with me?"

INTELLIGENCE

"**Y**OUR BOYS are on the move," Whitney said.

Curt stood, phone at his ear. "Where to?"

"Zack just paid for gas in Idaho Springs with that fancy credit card."

"So he's headed west –"

"Seems so. Could be to anywhere – Seattle, San Francisco, LA."

"Vegas," Curt said. "He spends lots of time in Vegas."

"He does?"

"He used to talk about it. About the people throwing their money away, the girls, the wild parties. I think it excited him, but disgusted him too –"

"Mr. Weathers, you *want* these boys?"

Curt thought of his truck, the horse Tom with the broken leg. The broken faith. "I sure do."

"We want them even more than you do." She paused for a moment. "Where are you, right now?"

"At this motel you put me in."

"Why don't you jump in that Ford Taurus and get yourself on I-70 heading west. I'll meet you in Glenwood Springs, at the Hotel Colorado."

"Hell, that's a three-hour drive."

"Then you better get going."

IF HE KEPT DRIVING FAST Steve figured he could maybe make Green River, Utah by midnight. Straight west on I-70 up the steep black mountains toward A-Basin, Eisenhower Tunnel, then Vail with its dreadlocks of ski runs.

The unending streams of trucks and cars made him think of the poisons they spewed into the bitter winter air, tried to imagine all the vehicles in the world belching toxins in a catatonic cacophonic frenzy from place to place like maddened wasps. He'd always figured it was world suicide: if you want to die just drive into your garage, shut the door, and turn the engine on. And the atmosphere was one big closed garage.

So what do you do if the world's committing suicide and you're part of it?

You protect the people the you love. And try to protect everybody else. The best you can.

All the times he'd thought about this, driving place to place, Albuquerque to LA, Baltimore to DC, anywhere to anywhere in concrete America. You just shut your heart to it, the desolation of the natural world, its long slow death.

Idaho Springs flashed past, the slopes barren from hydromining – did humans really *need* all that silver? Was it worth destroying every river in the west?

What if what he'd been doing was the same?

The road glistened in the oncoming headlights. So easy to die here. So dangerous.

If he could change his life. If they got this money, took time off, he could find a new job, a new profession ...

He'd always tried to do right, got blindsided by those auction rate securities. He'd never tried to cheat anyone ...

That's true, he told himself. Don't put yourself down. You never tried to cheat anyone. So why do you feel guilty, as if you had?

The road flattened out after the hill down from Vail then through Rifle to Glenwood Springs. And there was the Hotel Colorado on his right, a Medieval chateau with two tall towers, buttressed walls of pink stone, and Renaissance windows.

He was so damn tired, should stop here. But no, in three more hours maybe Green River. No, should stop here, eyes grainy, nodding off and waking at the shudder of the rumble strip, swerving back on the road ... Too long a day, all the way from making love again at dawn with Marcie, how wonderful, then ten miles on the treadmill then getting the kids off to school...that cop Goldberg with his boxer's face and sarcastic smile, promising to throw the book at him if he didn't come across.

He sped up, past the sign that said Silt 19 miles, Rifle 27, Grand Junction 88. Green River 187 miles: no way he could make that. But he had to get ahead of Zack, get to Vegas first. No resting, no stopping.

9:21 on the dashboard clock, plenty of time to call Marcie and the kids. *No,* he suddenly realized, this is Mountain Time. It's almost eleven-thirty back there.

They would all be asleep.

Brakes screamed as a car flashed past honking spinning half-sideways then swinging straight. "What the fuck!" Steve screamed, then realized he'd strayed across the solid line, falling asleep, the other car had almost hit him.

Would have taken him out. And them too.

He took the next exit back to the Hotel Colorado, got Room 301 for $149, and tumbled into exhausted sleep.

WHEN CURT'S PHONE BUZZED he grabbed it thinking it was Whitney again but it was a man with a thick Mexican accent. "So I think I give you a call."

"You got the wrong number –"

"This is Mr. Curt Weathers, yes?"

Curt slowed down and moved to the right lane. "Yes."

"Then I don't have the wrong number."

"What you want?"

"Look, I know what happen."

Curt didn't like the guy's accent, his grammar. "*What happened?*"

"How those guys steal your truck, take your horses. One horse, he's hurt, you know?"

"Who the Hell are you?"

"You hear that they are not in Denver any more, these guys? That they are driving west?"

"Who says?"

"Look, I am law enforcement. We are trying to catch these guys."

"You're DEA?"

"And like you I'm going wherever these guys are going. So you and me, we should get together – maybe I can help you find them. Or you can help me ..."

Curt felt hemmed in, a presentiment of evil. "Look, Mr...."

"Paco. Like I said. I can't believe what they done, those guys. Maybe you want to get even?"

"Look, Paco, I don't need you to get even."

"How much they owe you, the horses, takin your truck – all that?"

"That's my problem."

"You want to go your own way, fine. You decide instead you want these guys, I can help you find them."

"So who are you?"

"Just think intelligence ... you don't need to know who I am, just that I can help you."

"What for? Why do you want to help me?"

"In the morning we can meet in Glendale Springs, since you're going that way. At the Tower of Pancakes, it's right off the freeway. How about nine o'clock? They have good breakfast, you know, pancakes with blueberry syrup, sausage and bacon."

"Who are you?"

"Like I said, intelligence. Just keep it to yourself. Now, you want to work together, find these guys? Or maybe you're a little afraid? Don't want to get too close?"

CURT PULLED INTO the Hotel Colorado at ten to eleven and went up to the room Whitney had reserved for him. He lay on the bed with his boots hanging over the end and closed his eyes, head spinning. Weary. Gritty eyes that stung when he opened them, weary face, weary shoulders slumping down into a tired body.

But his two dudes somewhere near. As if he could smell them, feel them, they were so close. Nah, he reminded himself, that's superstition, from *the ancestors.* That you can sometimes sense your enemies when they're near. If you've lived a good life.

Have I lived a good life? he wondered. Would *the ancestors* think so?"

He dug his phone from his pocket and called Whitney. "How about the Polo Wine and Martini Lounge, downstairs?" she said. "In fifteen minutes? We can get something to eat and have a chat."

SHE WAS 28 maybe, slender, tall and radiant, with a beauty that is completely unaware of itself. Or, more likely, that doesn't give a damn. She wore a red jacket with faded jeans and black running shoes, long curly hair like an ebony cascade down her back. She tucked aside her holstered Sig Sauer and slid into the seat opposite him, stuck out a hand.

She had a grip that would kill a rhinoceros. Her eyes gleamed with a flame that seemed to light the whole room. "We found your damn truck."

"Where?"

"You know Bridger Canyon?"

"There's a ski resort up there."

"Your truck was off a logging road, pretty banged up."

Curt glanced down. That they could *do* this. He'd been a good guide, they'd always got their elk. He'd fed them well, kept them safe, told them good stories, shared life with them and liked them. Had thought they liked him too.

"What are the chances," he said after a moment, "we can get them?"

"Depends if they do a deal, make the money, maybe disappear? Unlikely. But if they're just driving out west somewhere, we can hardly arrest them for that."

"Well they stole my truck, they moved all that cocaine –"

"Unfortunately we didn't find any cocaine in your truck. They must have covered it well, or the snow in the truck bed washed out any remains." She smiled. "Or maybe they didn't have it."

"So all we can really get them for is stealing my truck?"

"That's no small thing. Grand auto theft can get them a few years. But without the cocaine connection we bow out of this –"

"DEA does?"

"You said it."

"By the way," he said, "you got somebody tracking me?"

Her eyes widened an instant. "Uh-uh. Just me. And I'm not really tracking you, just staying in touch. And of course Duane, but he's in the office."

"He an office guy?"

"He's got twenty cases on his mind. He gives me rope, lets me make my own mistakes."

"So you don't have anybody following me?"

She folded her fingers in under her chin, stared him in the eyes. "I just told you that."

"You want another whiskey?"

"Hell yes."

When the waitress glanced at them he held up two fingers. She smiled and waved back. "A guy, says his name is Paco, called me on the way here."

"Paco? Such a nice name. What'd he say?"

"Said he's intelligence, he's tracking these guys too, wants me to help him."

She didn't answer, stared at the room, back to him. "Nobody on *my* team."

"I'm supposed to meet him tomorrow, here in Glenwood, Tower of Pancakes."

"It's right down the road."

"His English was a little rough, he didn't sound like a law officer," Curt shrugged. "Maybe he's got something to do with the plane?"

She clasped her hands as if pleased with his acumen. "You should meet him tomorrow at Tower of Pancakes. I'll record you and be there undercover, as backup if you need me."

"Need you?"

"Like if he pulls a gun, or some other damn foolishness."

BACK IN THE GAME

ZACK WOKE TO intense pain in his right arm. It hurt so bad maybe he'd fractured it again, but how? He'd loaded the kilos left-handed, driven to Glenwood with his right arm slung in his lap. Even making love with Emily he'd laid on his back with her atop him. The way she liked.

No way he could've broken it again. But the sharp ends of both bones throbbed with each pulse, fired jagged pain into his brain with every shift of weight or posture, every ripple in the carpet when he walked or bent over the sink, and now with the elevator's quick drop from the third floor to the lobby.

"Sweetie you're gonna be okay," Emily hooked her arm in his good one as they entered the restaurant's smells of coffee and bacon, and for a moment he banished the pain. They found a small booth at the back where he swallowed two 15 mg morphines and ordered a double vodka and black coffee.

"My, *my*," Emily shook her head, "you *are* up to your old ways again."

"It's just this damn pain, got me back on the pills – I'll get off them again, once it goes away."

At the next table a thin balding man in a red-striped dress shirt and red suspenders was reading *The Denver Post* folded to a story about a crashed plane in Montana and a drug trail that had led to Denver then disappeared.

"So tell me, Zack," she caressed his good forearm, "why are you planning to drive all the way to Vegas, in pain like this?"

He eased back in the booth, waiting for the vodka. "That stuff we been doing? I've got lots. Going to sell it there."

Emily sat back, considered. "Well, Vegas is the best place. An endless black hole for it."

"So I have to get there, make the deals, go back, get the stuff and deliver."

The waitress brought the coffees and vodkas. "Go back *where?*" Emily said, sipping her latte after the waitress left.

"Somewhere back east," he answered quickly, feeling weird for the lie.

"Then what?"

"Then what? I'll be liquid again. Back in the game."

She tucked a lock of hair under her chin. "Your game or ours?" She turned to watch the customers coming into the restaurant, all smiling with anticipation of the food and happy to be able to ask for it and it would magically appear.

He studied the strong line of her jaw, the tumble of lovely dark hair down her high cheekbones, the scalloped unpierced ear, her skin natural as the rest of her, no mascara – the Spanish word for *mask*, no reddened lips with their genital connotation, just Emily as she was. Who wouldn't pretend, wouldn't lie, and wouldn't change.

"Oh Jesus Emily. I wish I knew." It was coke that had driven them apart, really. The Vegas parties, seeing millions vanish on the tables and pretending to laugh, to prove you were so rich you didn't care. The jocks on their last legs, the old starlets, the sour side of morning.

She'd had enough, went to Wally with his steady income and affectionate disinterest. Who just wanted a fuck when he felt like it, and a beautiful smart woman on his arm. But who came home from his trips and talked to her for hours. Because in his own obdurate way he loved her.

"Let me do *that!*" she snapped, scraping the lime marmalade from Zack's placemat where he'd dropped it, one-handed. She put it on his toast.

"I can do fine for myself." He glanced away from the passing strangers. "I don't need your help, dammit." His tone softened. "I just love to be with you."

"Me too," she grinned. "Wally's gone for four more days. Let's do Vegas."

TOWER OF PANCAKES was an old square white clapboard building with a huge yellow sign on its flat roof. Curt parked and crossed the mushy cold parking lot past the truckers smoking, the mechanics and laborers and carpenters and all the others trying to wake up before heading to the jobsite.

As he entered he saw Whitney at the far counter, where she could watch the whole room and not be noticed.

A slender dark-haired man at the third booth on the right raised a hand. Curt went over and the man stuck out his hand. "Howya doin Curt?"

His grip was hard and cold, and he held a moment too long. Curt ignored a desire to leave, and slid onto the other bench. The man waved at the waitress. "Coffee?" he said to Curt.

Curt turned to the waitress. "Black."

The man shoved aside a half-eaten plate of steak, fries and eggs. "I don't have much time, so here's the deal: Your boys have been in Denver, but we think they're heading west, maybe on I-70, can't be sure. Probably to Las Vegas."

"What makes you think that?"

The man shrugged: *I can't tell you.* "One of them went to New York but maybe he's back. The other, we don't know. How you can help us is background: everything you can remember about these guys."

"I already told Kenny..."

"What Kenny?"

"My wife's cousin, the Gallatin County Sheriff...You're a cop? You should know all this."

"I'm Denver PD," Paco said. "These country cops..." he turned his palms up – *what can I do?* "They don't share with us. And DEA, they want these two guys real bad, but the country cops want to make the hit themself. I don't care who, I just want to get these guys."

Curt sipped his coffee, burning his tongue. "So what you need from me?"

"Background. How long you know these guys, everything you can remember." Diego took out a pocket notebook that said *Homicide Section* in small letters across the top.

Curt nodded at the notebook. "Thought you said you were Narcotics?"

"What, this?" Diego held up the notepad. "In the cop business these days you take what you find. Narcotics has been out of note-pads since I been there, thirteen years ago."

"I just explained all this to the Gallatin Sheriff, like I told you. My wife's cousin."

"An' what I just tell *you?*" Diego shook his head as if in wonder that anyone could be so naive. "Country cops don't share. Want to make the case themself. But down here, Colorado, they don't stand a chance. Your two guys going to get away."

Curt put two ice cubes from his water glass in his coffee and sipped again. Better, but his tongue still stung. "Four years now I've guided these guys hunting. They're both…complicated. Sometimes they act like city hotshots, but they're real smart, both of them, and most of the time good guys, but they went crazy, broke my horse's leg, stole my truck, seems they stole the cocaine in that plane – that's why they took my truck –"

"They tough, these guys?"

"You know the football player, Zack. He's damn tough. Not like three years ago, when he retired, before he started this announcer thing, but still he's damn tough. I can't imagine anyone could beat him."

"And the New York one?"

"He's just as tough. Runs these triathlon things – bicycling, swimming, running – crazy. Don't know when he finds the time, with all the other things he does."

"Some people are like that." The man called Paco tugged at his collar. "How about you, Mr. Weathers, are you like that?"

"Me? Hell no."

"So why are you in Denver? And not home with your wife up in Judith Basin?"

Curt's muscles hardened. "Why you say that?"

"For a moment, early on, you were even on our list of suspects." Paco smiled. "My apologies."

Curt sat back, looked him over. "How so?"

"We weren't sure if you seen something in that plane and went back for it later. It made no sense though. And then your truck got stole, and all these other things." Paco leaned forward, hands clasped. "We know why you're here, Mr. Weathers. You have a grudge against these guys. Denver PD does too, and we can put some muscle on this."

He unclasped his hands palms up, a questioning gesture. "So let's work together?"

"WHAT NEXT?" Curt said when Whitney returned from following Paco outside to take more pictures.

"Never seen him before." She was punching his license number into her phone. "2017 Range Rover Sport, Hertz from DIA." She punched in more numbers. "Rented by a property management company in Orlando."

"You can't arrest him?"

"For what? Pretending to impersonate an officer? It's your word against his."

"So what do we do?"

She shrugged. "Let's go to Vegas? Along with everybody else?"

"How does he know where these guys are? Where they're going?"

"Good guess work? Unlikely." She thought a moment. "So is he the guy up there on the blue snowmobile, when you were at the cave?"

"I never met him up there, can't tell. But he seems to know everything you do."

She looked at the room, past it, a thousand-yard stare. "See if you can find out more about *what* he knows, *where* it comes from. Challenge him, say he's lying, make him prove it to you... We'll make it worth your time –"

"Fine, I can do that. But really all I want is what I'm owed for a ruined horse and wrecked truck."

"That's what we all want, isn't it? What we think we're owed?" She twirled her water glass making the ice sparkle. "So help us with Diego, and we'll help with what you're owed."

CURT CALLED Diana and again there was no answer and he figured she was outside somewhere, didn't matter that it was twenty below, she loved that kind of weather. Said it made her *breathe*. In the old days the Cheyenne would go around half-naked at twenty below and not even notice. When they were sleepy they'd snuggle up in the snow quite happily. And once the Spanish horses came they made bigger lodges with buffalo robes to sleep in, all things the horses could travois, so you didn't have to travel with everything you owned on your back.

Like our ancestors had for millions of years.

Were we better off then?

I wish I knew.

IN THE GLENWOOD *POST-INDEPENDENT* among four hundred vehicle ads Steve found a *"2002 EDDIE BAUER Ford Expedition, FULLY LOADED!!! 4WD, New tires, new oil change. Ready to GO! 122K. Great deal! $5,900."*

From his wallet he pulled a red Master Card, the one for emergencies…But if this wasn't an emergency what was? It was in the name of an investment machine he'd invented, domiciled in Dominica and debited in Switzerland and which fed off certain transactions of the bank he'd worked in at the time. In which he had a borrowing limit of thirty-one grand.

He drove to the Bank of Colorado on Grand Avenue and took out nine thousand dollars on the Swiss card. He'd have liked more but the Feds traced cash transactions over ten grand. From a pay phone he called the Eddie Bauer's owner and got the address on Beaver Place.

The owner, a short man with a large belly in a yellow cardigan, rode with him on the test drive. The steering was loose, the shocks worthless, it nosed constantly to the left like a barn-sour horse trying to turn home. The driver's visor wouldn't stay up, the dashboard jiggled, the driver's seat was concave with use and the tires weren't really new, but the oil was clean and the engine ran fairly steady.

"All I want to know," Steve said, "is will it get me to Chicago."

"Chicago?" The man raised little chubby hands. "It will get you there easy. No problem."

"If it doesn't get me to Chicago I'm coming back." Steve eyed him. "To have a serious talk with you. So if you don't think it'll reach Chicago, tell me now."

"Sure, sure." The man glanced around. "No problem."

Steve gave him fifty-five hundred in cash and the little man signed the registration over to him. Steve now had thirty days under Colorado law when he could drive the car in the little man's name, so no one could ID him by it. And when it was time to move the coke the vehicle had plenty of room inside to do it.

He moved his backpack, Winchester, Beretta, ammo and the hundred mg of coke from the Denali to the Eddie Bauer, left the Denali in long-term parking at the Glenwood Springs Airport, grabbed a cab back to the little man's house, drove the Eddie Bauer back to the hotel, packed his bag and checked out using the Swiss Bank card. On the way down to the desk he saw a man who looked like Curt from the back, with a tall black woman, but when he glanced toward them they were gone.

Curt's in Bozeman for God's sake, he told himself. *I'm seeing phantoms. Could use a taste of Lady Coke.*

He took a good hit and felt wonderful. Lady Coke, the perfect traveling companion.

And soon he'd be in Vegas. Lady Coke's home town.

He filled the Eddie Bauer at the Kum & Go across from the Hotel and bought two liters of Fiji Spring Water and three double Baby Ruths with the Swiss bank card.

"Find me now!" he told them – whoever *they* were – as he took the on-ramp for Grand Junction and West, noticing for the first time that the Eddie Bauer's left turn signal didn't work.

"So what the fuck," he laughed. "The day is young."

ONLY HUMAN

EIGHT HOURS FROM Glenwood to Vegas across the bitter windy wasteland of Utah. Towns two hours apart, each with a hideous restaurant featuring greasy burgers, deadly meatloaf and not a glass of wine, not a beer, let alone gin. The people dour as if shackled there by fate.

Steve hated it, felt sorry for them, looked out at the wind-scoured desert and remembered the photos tacked on restaurant walls of the old days of bounteous prairies with grass up to the horses' withers, sparkling streams. Before the cattle came.

He kept trying to fight off a heart-plunging despair, a knowledge of the world going to hell and sorrow and all he could do was carve out his moment of peace, make the money he needed to get his family away from it all.

But was there anywhere, any more, away from it all?

All he had to do was find Zack and get the coke back.

DUSK WAS FALLING across the Nevada jackrabbit desert of stunted sage, tumbleweed, and arid ridges, last sunlight fading in dusty reds and yellows under the pallid clouds, and above them the darkness that reminded Zack of death, of the endless restless universe out there.

After the Nevada border the desert began to change from barren wasteland rimmed by naked mountains to mines and factories dug into the raw rocky cliffs, dirt roads heading nowhere, highway signs quivering in the ferocious wind, truck stops of slot machines, hookers, booze, and uppers, parking lots with tumbleweed cantering across them, the first furtive subdivisions tacked against the desert, a prison making his stomach roil with fear at the high triple walls topped with concertina wire.

Whispering Meadows Industrial Park, Nellis Air Force Base, then truck lots, used cars, dusty little casinos preying on the folks who came there for cheap gas, cell phone towers, more mines – potash, maybe – highways crisscrossing the desert, strips malls and strippers – everything you could imagine you wanted except the quiet and peace of the desert.

The desert, he could imagine it was still there, absolutely and purely silent but for the touch of a breeze on your face, the whisper of a crow's wings echoing through canyons a half mile away. What the world was like.

You could see Vegas for fifty miles before you got there, the ghoulish glow, then the wide boulevards crowded with people seeking fun at any cost, the neon stars and bright lights, the family men with smiling hookers, the gleaming towers arisen from the desert like ravaging aliens, the ragtag disinherited and dispossessed stumbling down back alleys, the dumpster divers and hungry rich, the fast cars and beat-up junkers, all the sorrow and ersatz laughter of the world distilled in one place.

Zack blinked his eyes against the scintillating lights, the driving fatigue, the ache that snaked from his broken arm through the shoulder and neck into his brain.

"I can't believe we used to love this place," Emily said.

CURT WIPED MIST off the inside of his windshield with the backs of his fingers, his wedding ring scraping the glass and making him think was it right to be leaving Diana up in Montana at the start of winter just because he had a grudge against these two guys?

Wasatch Pass rose above him like a door in a mirror one could pass through to a different world. At nearly 8,000 feet, sleeting now, cold and dangerous, easy to slide off the highway and roll over.

He imagined smashing headlong into a semi – the huge crash and noise and crushing obliteration, his blood and guts ground into the highway. Foolish, really, to be chasing these dudes when they were already being hunted by DEA and that smiling, dangerous Mexican called Paco who pretended he was Denver PD. And by the Colorado state cops too, no doubt.

But did these two dudes even *have* the cocaine? The Mexican thought they did. And he would know.

Or was he, Curt, just chasing the two of them because he was pissed off they stole his truck and hurt his horse? And because they'd lied?

He realized with a weird frustration that he was also doing what he'd always done: trying to keep them safe.

ZACK NOW HATED VEGAS but it wouldn't let him go, a place that never should have been, neither for himself or the world. A test study of consumerist insanity and the bloodthirsty grip of marketing. Of people wanting something for nothing and not being who they are.

He'd read somewhere that before the Europeans came Nevada'd been a dry yet verdant plateau, well-watered by springs and creeks lined with cottonwoods and willows, populated by people who lived there with gratitude and comprehension, where the wind-waving grass came up to the saddles of the first white men to ride through.

Then more white men came, killed the people, brought the cattle and sheep that denuded the land, then cut the forests so the streams eroded onto the lowlands and everything turned to desert. And once the land was bare and eroded, the rains vanished. The days grew hotter, the sun more relentless.

By a century ago Vegas was a railroad town, a brief stop on the Mormon Highway between southern California and Salt Lake. But once Prohibition began, a sea of illegal money started looking for a legal home, and a lot of that sea floated to the desert sands of *las Vegas*, the Spanish word for the lowlands between the surrounding mountains. It became a place folks drove to from Hollywood, which was little then too. Nobody would have imagined that Vegas would ever be anything but a sleepy wide place in a dusty road with lots of cactus, rattlesnakes and sand. The water tasted of arsenic and the electricity often went out. It was blazing in summer and bitter in winter.

But there were lots of bars and brothels. The bars were fun and wild, the drinks sometimes poisonous. A place to lose your money, find some more money somewhere, come back and lose that too. Where by doing what you thought you wanted you imagined you were free.

Like all aggressive cancers it grew. As more and more people flocked there to lose their savings, it became financially more powerful. And the people who ran it started to think about how best to use the government to promote and protect it.

They spent countless millions purchasing politicians at all levels, and those millions were repaid a hundred times over. The Vegas rich grew even richer, the city sucked in workers by the thousands – dealers, hookers, con men, waitresses, pastors, valets, cooks, dishwashers, maids, doctors, carpenters, teachers, policemen, therapists, firemen, nurses, bureaucrats and more and more politicians. Unions, public offices, public projects, roads, utilities, airports, sewers and schools – they all grew like mushrooms, cancers inside cancers. Lobbying outfits were created to represent the casinos – the Nevada Gaming Commission, whose Director, Harry Reid, became U.S. Senate Majority Leader and controlled the other Democratic Senators and told them how best to protect and enhance the casinos on the national stage, and how to collect their own casino contributions too.

More and more people came to sacrifice their savings at the altar of Vegas. You could walk into restaurants at dawn and see couples in booths staring speechless at the street, having lost everything they'd had – the car, the house, the savings account. The sorrow of it made him hate Las Vegas, but by now he'd had little choice but be there.

Was it because of Monica he'd come to hate it? She scorned Vegas, TV sports, cocaine, the stock market. She cared about helping people, healing them. And from the first time he'd met her he'd begun to feel the same. As if she were the first rays of the sun to someone who'd only known clouds.

So why was he betraying her with Emily? He didn't know. Only that he'd called Emily to see if Wally would buy some of this evil coke. And he was in so much pain from the broken arm, so near to collapse, that he *needed* her, to save him from this fatigue and pain. And she'd sensed it, wanted to help him.

And the fucking. Oh Jesus the fucking. Made his body feel alive again. Fucking a beautiful woman you care about while you're both high on cocaine is about as good as it gets.

Two years ago Zack's agent Rob had called to say that the manager of The Cavalcade Casino, Lou Haney – Haney the Rat – had invited Zack as a special guest one weekend at the high tables. "You don't have to play you don't want," Haney the Rat had said. "Ten grand a weekend plus everything comped and all the girls you want."

"Christ, Lou," he'd answered, loving the girl part already. "I'm only human."

They'd even comped him the tuxedo and of course the special girl on his arm, a Chanel model temporarily out of work, and he'd shaken hands and listened to football stories and mucky praise and genial yet disrespectful joshing, but all that wasn't so bad, and the girls were fantastic. Sometimes three at a time, even better than back in his football days.

And making love with three beautiful women is even better than it gets.

"I CAN DOUBLE YOU THIS," Haney the Rat said one night as he handed Zack his $10,000 check. "Lemme buy you some shekels and you have twenty grand in an hour."

So he gave Haney the $10K and an hour later it was $31,430, by the end of the night nearly $47,000. He'd given fifteen of that to the three girls he spent the night with, and used the rest for a down payment on a Lamborghini Huracán LP 580 that Haney always let him park in front of the hotel when he was there.

Another time after a long night of wins he was having coffee in the Cavalcade café and noticed a couple at the next table. They were silent, nearly immovable. Then the woman, round and rolly like the Pillsbury doughboy, with gray hair, a soft kindly mouth and wide bosom, wearing oval glasses that made her look like a surprised child, picked up her cellphone and called someone named Roddy.

"Can you come down here and get us?" she said. "Las Vegas. We're in Las Vegas. No, I can't explain now. No, we lost the truck... No, we can't take the bus, we lost our money. I know it's a long way but can you come get us?"

She broke off, turned to the man. "Roddy says he can't, it's too far."

"How much you lose?" Zack said, across the table.

The man turned to him, old and pale, skin like paste, took a folded sheet of paper from his pocket. "I added it up. Twenty-two thousand five hundred and eight-nine, that's what they gave us for the deed on our house trailer. Then there was seven hundred forty-nine dollars on our truck, after you subtracted what we owed..."

Zack had won over a hundred thousand that night. It made him feel good to peel twenty thousand off his roll and give it to the man and woman, who stared at him with astonished guileless eyes.

"You head home, now," Zack said. "And don't come back." Only to see them, later that morning side by side at a poker table, highball glasses in their hands.

In the next three months he made over two million at the tables, and then his luck began to slide. Lost a hundred grand one night, got seventeen back, then lost three hundred. Didn't matter, he was still way ahead.

"You got to meet and greet more," Haney the Rat told him. "We're paying you all this money..."

"Fuck, most of it you're getting right back."

"You've just had a bad run. It'll change," Haney patted Zack's shoulder. "Or are you just playin stupid?"

The idea angered him. "Maybe I am. Maybe I should stay away from the tables."

"Just mix and greet, Zack. That's all I ask. And you're running a big debt, we need it paid down. Bring some money to the table."

He lost more. And then more. But for some crazy reason couldn't stop. It was like trying to stop in the middle of fucking, he told himself. Finally he'd cashed out of his last money market but didn't worry because he still had the twelve million Steve had put in auction rate securities. And maybe his luck at the tables would change, like Haney'd said.

And it was costing barely twenty grand a month for the incredible bliss of Lady Coke. Like fucking, impossible to stop. And when you need it to make money, to have that relaxed TV anchorman high, the genial smile and the view that things work out, finally, in everybody's favor.

As if that were true.

But now he was a sleepy two million down, plus change. With no auction rate securities and maybe no job. And Haney's hoods were coming after him.

"YOU'RE ONLY GONE two days," Marcie said, "but it seems like forever."

"Yeah, Dad," Jason said.

"Where are you, anyway?" Susanna said.

"Out west." He didn't want to lie to her, couldn't. "Utah."

"Utah?" Marcie said.

"Part of this deal I'm working on." It bothered him, to say it like this.

"So we can buy a boat?" Jason put in.

"I get seasick," Susanna said. "Remember?"

"Are you driving?" Marcie said. "We shouldn't be talking if you're driving."

Steve looked through the windshield at the empty, wind-scoured highway. "It's safe."

"You'll still be back," Jason said, "for my basketball game?"

"When is it?"

"Next Tuesday. I told you, Dad."

"Yeah, Dad," Susanna chided.

"Anything new in the office?" Steve asked Marcie. Meaning *are any possible new deals coming in?*

"Quiet as a church mouse."

"Do you really mean," Susanna said, "we might take a year off? Then I'd be a year older than anyone in my class."

"We can take books, home school you that year. You won't fall behind."

"Not home school," Jason said. "*Boat* school."

ZACK PARKED the Pathfinder in the Cavalcade garage, left the rifle hidden in the back. He and Emily checked in at the Members' Only desk and took the elevator to his old suite on the 49th floor. There was a bottle of Beluga vodka in the freezer, a Pouilly-Fuissé in the reefer and a 2007 Châteauneuf on the granite counter. He poured Emily a white, dumped three ice cubes in a glass and filled it with vodka, drank it down with two morphine tabs, and took the elevator down to the long narrow room stinking of cigar smoke, liquor and old coffee where Haney the Rat sat overlooking his main floor casino.

"What, you suddenly got money on you?" Haney looked up at him from a desk strewn with spreadsheets, mug shots, purchase orders, nude photos and printouts.

"I came to settle up." Zack tossed one of the Ziplocs of coke on Haney's desk. "Give this a try, spread it around, see what folks say."

Haney eyed him. "What, you're in the drug business now? The superstar TV jock hustling cocaine?"

"It's from a friend. He'd like to unload some."

A grimace that passed for a smile. "This ain't like you."

"You want me to come even? Or you going to keep sending your thugs after me?"

Haney shook his head in wonder. "Your call."

"Since we're doing this other business –"

"I didn't say yes."

"– you want to front me a few chips? I'll be good for it."

"Zack…"

"Yeah, what?"

A moment of silence, Haney making up his mind. "Come up to the high tables, we'll front you twenty."

"Twenty grand?"

"That's what I said."

THEY HIT the open bar in the Casino and Zack had a double vodka martini and Emily another white wine. Then to Mon Ami Gabi, where, she remembered, the *steak frites* are nearly as good as France, and you can get actual French wine.

Though the Eiffel Tower of course was fake, and even worse, the Arc de Triomphe, as were the trucks driving up and down the Strip with pictures of naked women and phone numbers pasted to their sides, the touts at the corners with cards of naked girls with their numbers, $49 Special for Jade, the Asian Princess, or only $99 for Priscilla and Jane, a night you'll never forget, and across the Strip in the false lake of the Bellagio its many fountains exploded high into the sky and misted away on the desert air.

"Where do they get all that water?" she said.

"Who knows," he said, feeling agreeable and a little high, the pain in his arm having subsided to a comforting ache. "They keep damming the Grand Canyon – maybe from there?"

"And the electricity...all these lights, the neon, the air conditioning in summer, those silly fountains?"

"Don't ask, don't tell."

"What a crime," she said after a minute. "And we got sucked into it."

"Crime always sucks you in," he said, still being agreeable. "Otherwise no one'd do it."

Up and down the Strip paraded the hookers' trucks and sleek Mercedes, the battered vehicles of the poor, while expensive girls strolled past and bums excavated the trash cans, gawkers gawked, college boys laughed drunkenly, and families from Idaho and Iowa stared in all directions, grinning.

"And the endless country music," she said. "I think it preys on people. Some guy from New Jersey puts on a cowboy hat and snake-skin boots and yodels about how bad his life sucks and he can't get a relationship and geez can he have another drink..."

He lay a palm on her forearm. "Calm down, Emily."

"I shouldn't've come." She looked at him. "I'm sorry."

"We're here now."

"So get it done, whatever it is."

"And then?" Suddenly he feared she'd reject him. That he'd betrayed Monica with Emily and now might lose Emily too.

"We'll see."

They crossed the casino with hundreds of beeping machines in endless rows, with names like *Gypsy Eyes, Double Diablo, Let it Ride, Lil Lady, Champagne Slots* and *Pharaoh's Fortune*, countless people hunched over them, feeding them money, begging them, praying to them. The names were wanton, enticing, life on the wild side. To talk you into giving up what you have. It seemed suddenly nefarious, that someone had actually *created* these names, solely to hook people, to take their money.

"You were going to take me to dinner," a pretty blonde woman with torn knees in her jeans was saying to her bearded partner. "Now we've spent hours here –"

"I'll get it back," he said. "Then we'll do dinner."

"Lost Wages," Emily said, "what we always call this place, but it's worse. It's Lost Life, lost spirit, lost soul. Look at all the electric wheelchairs and tobacco smoke? There's a link between obesity, smoking and gambling – has to be."

Zack wanted to lie down, make the pain go away. "Like the link between a self-defeating lifestyle and country music?"

"It's sad, that's all." She walked on ahead, past the ersatz French café and bistro and news store to the stack of elevators for the top floor suites. "I'm not going with you tonight," she said, "you do your Greet and Meet. I'll be in the room when you get back."

"Maybe I won't go. Fuck them."

She looked at him. "You have to. Or Haney won't find you a buyer." She squeezed his good arm. "But please, sweetie, stay out of the game."

MARÍA CHRISTINA did not allow failure. Though he didn't put it in so many words, Diego knew that either he found the coke or didn't return to Miami. Not that you could vanish for long if she was looking for you.

To steal from María Christina was to steal from him. Didn't matter that he'd stolen for most of his life, you didn't steal *from* him. Most of all, you didn't steal from *her.* Unless you wanted to die.

"This talk of legalizing drugs," he'd said to her one time, "it makes me angry. It will not be good for us."

"Not to worry," she'd answered. "That is why we hire politicians."

But what angered him now, as he drove his rented Range Rover past Mesquite and the Utah-Nevada border, seventy miles from Vegas, was that he still didn't know where these guys were, had no clues to track them down.

But if they were stupid enough to go to Vegas they were like mice climbing into the cat's mouth.

And thanks to María Christina's friends in DEA he would soon have their photos and everything else he needed to find them. And thanks to her friends in Vegas he might soon be able to track them down. And the guy named Steve had a nice family, Diego could make them pay, do anything to make Steve see the light.

Before he died.

BREAD AND CIRCUSES

IT WAS 8:45 in Vegas when Steve booked into the Mirage. But nearly midnight in Manhattan, too late to call home.

When he was away from Marcie and the kids he always wanted to be with them, and when he was with them he never wanted to leave. Did he love her too much? Was he too emotionally tied to the kids? Did all guys love their wives like this? Their kids?

The problem with being a guy was that other guys never tell you what they really feel.

Didn't matter now. He'd find Zack, take back the coke and sell it in New York. Not just to Ibrahim but other guys... With how many guys at the big banks had he inhaled how many thousands of dollars back in the glory days? Before the markets tanked again and everybody pulled his dick out of the ringer except the little guys who as usual got whacked?

Can't solve that, he reflected. The little guys always got whacked, that was their job, their role in life. They'd soon be back, salivating to get whacked again.

Like the time he and Marcie drove to Vermont where the locals were hustling maple syrup, cheddar and pastoral trinkets to city folks hungry for authenticity. As one local chuckled, "We bring in the sheep, we shear them and we send them home."

The markets, cocaine, TV, the NFL, politics, Vegas – all shearing the sheep. Coke was Wall Street was Vegas was idolizing money was religion. Had anything ever changed?

And every eight years the markets tank and the little guys get sheared. The sucking sound of money rising to the top.

Where the people at the top believe it belongs.

Too long he'd hated being in that world. But told himself *Do this a few years,* make a lot of money and get out. Buy a boat, go somewhere. Live.

Enslave yourself now to become free later.

But after all these years he still had no money and was still working like a slave.

Maybe losing these auction rate securities was telling him something. If the banks can steal billions from people with these securities, what did it matter if he sold a few million in coke? Was anything illegal anymore?

Funny that the real Coca Cola had just been caught paying off a bunch of scientists to say the sugar in Coke doesn't cause obesity... Are we *truly* as stupid as they think? Maybe we are...

Football on the box, smiling TV talkers like Zack full of exciting semi-articulate rap about absolutely nothing – as if the latest attempt by some guy to run into other guys for money was really as important as another thousand murdered children in Syria, a new way to defeat cancer or discovering water on Mars... Or that the United States was now twenty trillion dollars in debt. Not to worry, the politicians kept saying as they created more and more debt to pay back their corporate contributors...

Not to worry.

True, Zack had been a friend. Someone you love and take care of. But a real friend would have understood about the auction rate securities, wouldn't pull Steve's chain like this.

Would never have stolen the coke from the storage unit.

Not to worry.

That's what Lady Coke teaches, isn't it? Not to worry?

Maybe Lady Coke was right: *Just stay high? On top of it?*

Was there anything he believed in anymore?

Was freedom truly an illusion?

One thing he believed in: finding Zack.

AT A PRIVATE CAVALCADE TABLE sat a florid old man, balding and fleshily overflowing his hand-tailored silk suit. He had a snifter of 1937 Rémy Martin by his right hand, a saucer of coke by his left, an oxygen tube in his nose, a Cuban cigar between his teeth and a hooker's red panties stretched over his head, the half-naked hooker standing behind him as he slid ten-thousand-dollar markers toward the rake, again and again.

"Who is that little fuck?" Zack whispered to Cruikshank, the dealer.

"That? That's the largest publisher of parochial school text-books in Mexico. He lost eight million last night and he's back tonight. He's a good client, we take care of him."

A table with a twenty-thousand minimum buy-in, two actors he recognized, the parochial publisher, an old crone in a black dress and too many diamonds, a couple of New York hedge fund types, and two silent Chinese guys in their thirties checking the odds of each move on their cellphones, all willing to lose multiple million dollars in the hope of winning some, loving the adrenaline, the sweat, the dominance and domination. The sex and cocaine after-wards. As if life were a fuse and you could burn it real fast but it never blew.

How could you not want to?

"It does people good to see you out there, Zack, gives them con-fidence, legitimizes us," Haney had repeated. "They go home and tell everyone *Guess what, I met Zack Wilson, shook his hand…* Makes them feel important. So maybe they lose money, but they feel they had a good time. So they come back."

And lose more money, Zack finished the sentence. Wasn't mak-ing people feel good for no reason what he *did* anyway? Talking on TV, making people feel good about wasting three and a half hours watching tiny electric signals race back and forth on their TV screens? In which there was less than ten minutes of actual football play. The other three hours and twenty minutes was advertising, talk talk, half time, and time the players spent milling around the field.

Bread and circuses. What brought down Rome.

One night in Lost Angeles he'd spun out the Lamborghini and ended up at the Good Samaritan ER needing forty stitches. Monica was an Emergency Room MD, one of those people who tried to save the bludgeoned wrecks of car crashes, the knifed and shot victims of many crimes, the maimed and innocent.

He'd lain on the gurney with that TV smile waiting for her to recognize him, so he could go through all the bullshit he'd grown so tired of repeating, but to her he was just another casualty, someone to repair before the next came through the swinging doors.

Monica could have cared less he was a TV sports star. She didn't have time to bullshit or go to Vegas. She didn't watch TV football. "It's senseless," she'd said, "all that silly violence. Just so millions of wannabees can get their rocks off imagining they're as tough as you."

Sports porn, she'd called it, *people watching others do what they'd like to do themselves.*

And he the provider, the portrayer of false enthusiasm.

"All that Vegas is," she'd said, "is gambling, fakery and whoring. Stealing from the poor, false experiences, and false love. Paris Las Vegas is not Paris, the Venetian isn't Venice, Caesar's Palace is nothing like Rome ... a pretense to make money that steals your money, a whore who doesn't love you, no matter how much she moans ..."

When he realized she was right he'd dropped cocaine and fast nights in Vegas. And decided to spend a couple more years as a sportscaster to make as much as he could, then do something valid with his life. Teach kids or write the truth about football or hike the Colorado Trail. He had the money, didn't need more. Just to be with Monica would be happiness enough.

But now he didn't have the money any more.

Thanks to Steve.

And Lady Coke had him by the balls again.

Thanks to Steve.

And fucking Emily for hours on a cocaine high felt better than sitting around the apartment waiting for Monica to get home, exhausted, from the ER.

Isn't this, Lady Coke whispered, *what you really want?*

"WE'RE PICKING UP all his calls," Whitney said.

"The Mexican?" Curt said.

"Yeah, him. Diego Iglesias. He's an enforcer for the Veracruz cocaine cartel. We want him but haven't found a way to touch him. Until now."

She'd booked them two rooms at the Super 8 on Fremont and now they were at Denny's down the road, just a few blocks from the gambling towers and the Strip. At least at the Super 8, she'd said, there was plenty of space for his Taurus and her undercover Camaro with chrome wheel spinners and black tinted windows.

"He said you didn't know where these two guys are," he said. "That all you have are a credit card and two license plate numbers. And that any fool could get those."

"Hm." She chewed an ice cube. "Maybe we *should* arrest him."

He couldn't resist: "For being smarter than you?"

"We *need* to take these people down!" She reached across the table to grip Curt's wrists. "You were a Marine, Mr. Weathers, *you* protected our country…We've got tons of faults, the good old United States, governed by crooks, educated by fools, preached to by the viperous…" She squeezed hard, making his wrists throb "…but we're still the best damn country on earth."

"I'm not sure we're so bad as all that. But I agree, about being the best…"

"So helping us take down these bastards – is caring for the country we love."

"You don't have to tell me about cocaine, heroin, all that."

She let go his wrists. "Up in Judith Basin, Montana, there can't be much of that."

He waited a moment. "Let me tell you about my daughter."

She sat back. "Tell me."

"Serena. After her Diana couldn't have any more. Maybe if you have perfection, no need to try again. Valedictorian of her high school class, won an MIT high school prize in plasma physics – imagine that, coming from White Sulfur Springs High, with a total of sixty-one students …"

"Hell, in black schools in Denver we had more than that in one classroom."

"When she was little one of our neighbors fell off his barn roof and got paralyzed from the waist down. That's where she decided to become a neurosurgeon. She was ten when she described how you could use stem cells to repair the spine …"

She took his hands, softer now. "Please, Curt, *please* no."

"Oh, and her senior year won state title in the two-hundred-meter high hurdles."

Whitney turned from him to face the wall, anything to get away.

"Her second year at MSU some drunk on crystal meth ran the red light at Seventh and Main. You know the place."

Tears were streaming down her cheeks. "I'm so so sorry, Curt." She wiped at them. "Oh my God I'm sorry –"

His eyes were stinging too and it pissed him off. "So anyway," he said, meaning nothing except to break this chain of memories. "So I don't like drugs. Of course I don't mind that marijuana stuff, heck I've smoked it a few times, it was fun. Does no harm. Helps you to see how beautiful the world is."

"Yeah?" She tried to breathe through the tears in her throat, wiped at her eyes.

"But I hate these bad drugs. Like the ones that killed Serena."

She swallowed, lips tight. He had a sudden fear that people in the restaurant would assume a scene. Between this beautiful young black woman and this wiry Montana rancher.

"My Momma," she said, "named me for Whitney Houston, one of the greatest singers of all time, and now she's dead from cocaine, and her daughter Bobbi too, morphine and other evil shit."

Curt nodded, looked down at his roughened hands, as if to find an answer there.

"My Daddy," she added, "died from heroin. We lived in Five Points, Denver's worst ghetto. He was a good man. He loved us... It took him a long time to die... It's not right."

"The great gift of life."

She looked around the restaurant, the world, back at him. "So we do what we can do."

RAISE YOU

NEEDLE IN A HAY PILE – wasn't that what the *norteamericanos* called it, an impossible search? But no, Diego told himself, it isn't really that hard. If you know there is a needle in that hay pile, you just take it apart, one stick of hay at a time. Till you find the needle.

He parked the Range Rover in the underground lot at the Forum and rode the elevator to a top floor suite. All leather, chrome, Orientals and walls of glass overlooking the reflecting pools, silly statues of Julius Caesar and all those other guys from long ago, the shimmering lights and dark alleys of the city – he didn't like this extravagance. But it was free, María Christina owned it, or really, the Ragman owned it and she managed it along with everything else – and some of the biggest *hijos de puta* came here to gamble and fuck teenage girls and snort thousands of dollars up their heavily excavated noses. But right now no one was using the place, so it was his.

It was a long way from the Mexico City dump, and he was as always aware of this and sad and guilty and proud at the same time. And what if instead he'd grown up in some little hacienda in a Cuernavaca suburb, with a small garden in front and a big one out back, what would he be doing now?

On the house line he ordered *camarones al mojo de ajo* and *steak asada* and a bottle of Jose Cuervo Añejo Extra, and while he was waiting called a number from memory, on his cell phone.

"It's me."

"She said you were coming."

"She tell you what it is, these guys?"

"She said."

"So anyone comes into town looking to sell, anybody new, anybody different, you tell me."

"*De acuerdo, hermano.*"

"I'm not your fucking *hermano* you fuckhead, and if you let them slip through your fingers I will fucking kill you. You understand?"

"No need to get rude, *hermano.* Maybe if you rude I kill you first."

Diego burst into a warm deep laugh. "You never change, motherfucker. I like that."

"She said you will make a withdrawal, two hundred grand, to offer them, *sí?*"

"It is only for show. Not to do."

"I think is crazy. You could lose it…"

"She says do it. You want to argue?"

"Not with her, no."

"Good."

"So these guys, tell me about them."

After Diego told him what he knew about the two gringos the man went quiet for a few moments. "This should not be hard."

"Remember, they are stupid. They know nothing. The football one, he thinks he is tough. The New York one, he thinks he is smart."

"So they are easy."

"The moment they show up, I want to know."

"Anything else?"

"A girl. You got a young one?"

"I got a new one, Guatemalan. Nobody's had her."

"And I'm the Pope."

"She's fourteen, amigo. It's your luck."

"Fourteen is nothing. I can get plenty of that."

"I'll send her up. You wait, you see."

"She isn't perfect, I send her back."

"You won't, I promise."

THE CAVALCADE PRIVATE TABLE was down to seven players, as one of the hedge fund guys had just walked away with an angry glance. The Mexican parochial publisher was still there with his coke, oxygen and cognac, the hooker's panties aslant his bald pate. One of the Hollywood stars had his hand on the other's arm as the pile of chips diminished in front of them, and Zack wondered were they gay?

The old crone in a black evening gown with tons of diamonds dangling like an albatross from her wrinkled neck – could they be false? The two Chinese guys had taken off their coats and rolled up their sleeves; one had a black girl with short frizzy orange hair standing behind him with her arms round his chest and one hand in his crotch.

Money here, Zack told himself as he slid into the eighth chair. *Money to be made.*

All was well. He had the overwhelming cocaine sense of power, righteousness and his good path across it, in harmony with events. Lovely and lustful and lots of money to be made.

The comforting room, wide and vast, with Michelangelo paintings across the ceiling, white cumulus in a blue sky, God reaching out his divine fingers to a naked nymph, sly and erotic, her hand between God's thighs.

How wonderful it was.

How real.

The warm damask curtains down the cultured stone walls, the floor tiles like the ones he'd seen years ago in Pompeii, the divans and ottomans in scarlet silk – sure, it was all fake, but wasn't it *real* too? Isn't the fake, when you look at it, real? Isn't that the secret to Vegas?

He'd already lost a few thousand of Haney's twenty grand at Texas Hold-em, and was down to sixteen, maybe...No, fourteen-five. Fourteen thousand three hundred and sixty-nine, to be exact. *You motherfucker, be honest.*

Seven card stud: his baby. Back at Notre Dame it had made him good money in dorm rooms full of weed smoke, laughter and Nirvana.

Cruikshank dealing; Zack remembered him presiding over great wins and losses, but always on the downside, in the end. Not now, though, Zack decided. Had my down time on Texas Hold-em. I'm due.

He slid his chair up to the table. He had the dealer button – how symbolic – so he'd be the last dealt and would know what everyone'd done before him. The groove.

The nap of the table beneath his arms was worn and the tan underfabric showed through. And thin spots on the table where chips had been shoved, rings on rings of glasses set into the soft nape like overlapping Olympics logos.

The rich and the wannabee rich, coming to Mecca to be fleeced.

Like the bond market. Like the ocean. The medium guys feed on the millions of little ones, and the big guys feed on them. "How do you get to be a billionaire?" a famous businessman had once told him. "You eat millionaires."

Jack of Hearts down on the first hand. A lovely card. Totem of good cards to come.

His second downcard a ten of Spades. Could mean anything. Not to worry.

Across the table the parochial publisher took a quick look at his down cards and snickered into his oxygen. *Fuck you*, Zack told him. *Don't pull that shit.*

King of Hearts his first upcard. The only other face card on the table a Jack of clubs. So his having all four Jacks now out of the question, odds lowered on a three.

He felt a surge of power. Might as well go in hot. He dropped a white five hundred-dollar chip.

It pissed people off when you started this hard. An early bluff or an amateur misjudging the next hands. We'll get him for that, he felt them thinking. Tough, he was going to stick it to *them*, make *them* pay. His skin felt electric, his muscles: he was *on*.

Holy shit. His next upcard the Ace of Hearts. He tried to keep his face calm, disinterested. "Ace high bets," the dealer said.

Another white five hundred on the table.

"Meet and double," said the parochial publisher in his rude English.

Holy shit, two more chips on the table.

His next upcard the ten of diamonds.

"Ace high bets," the dealer repeated, as if Zack were a slow student in need of encouragement.

"Check."

"Check," the others repeated till it reached the parochial publisher who was showing two sevens. He dropped a white five hundred on the table. This was getting hot; Zack decided to call and take one more card then bail if it wasn't good.

"Meet and raise," a squawky voice, rough with cigarettes and brandy. The old crone in the diamonds, showing a nine and queen of clubs. Nothing, or maybe a club flush? Zack had the seven so she wasn't going lower.

Fuck the odds. "Raise you five hundred," he said. *You crazy fucker. You can't win this.*

"Hit and double you," the parochial publisher said.

Oh fuck. You are not going to fight this.

His next upcard the Queen of Hearts, lying out there next to the king and ace. And with the Jack of Hearts in his hand.

"Hit and double you." The diamond crone's squeaky voice, her jaw thrust forward, the chandeliers scintillating in her black eyes, now with two queens and the nine. She scowled at the parochial publisher. "You heard what I said."

Oh Jesus this was getting out of hand.

The movie actors and one Chinese guy dropped out.

"I match and double you," said the parochial publisher, his upcards a two, three and five.

"Fuck it," Zack raised a finger for the last, a downcard.

The dealer dropped it before him like an offering. Like something sacred. Or deadly. He wasn't going to look at it first, pretend he didn't need it.

He tipped an edge. They all watched him, fearful, exultant, curious.

Ten of clubs. His heart sank; he tried to keep a nonchalant face.

The diamond crone had two pair, sevens and nines. Zack had her beat.

He had the hottest cards showing on the table. Could he bluff this out? He laid a five hundred chip down on the table. His remaining pile was getting small – how did it go this fast?

"Meet and raise you," diamonds said.

"On you," the publisher said.

Jack called, laid them down. Two tens and two Jacks.

"Sorry, my friend," the parochial publisher laid out his hand. Three sevens.

Hey, Jack told himself, he still had plenty of cash on the Swiss Bank card. What if he took a couple more thousand, see how much he could get back with it? He wasn't a gambler, not really, but when he was on he was good.

Half an hour later it was gone. Nothing left on the Swiss Bank card. Nothing left of the twenty grand Haney'd fronted him.

Zack walked out with his head spinning, as if he'd committed a crime for which there was no sanction, no absolution. He had damned himself.

MONICA had just come home from the ER when Steve reached her. "You may not remember me," he said. "I'm Zack's broker, have some good news for him."

Her voice on the far end of the phone sounded exhausted, dispirited. "I haven't talked to him in days. I thought he was with you."

"Too much snow, we had to give up hunting. He's in Vegas but his cellphone doesn't work. I think it got broken on the trip."

"Maybe that's why," she brightened, "he hasn't answered my calls."

"I know he's been thinking about you. I'd like to meet you sometime."

"Me too," she said, but it didn't sound real, an afterthought.

"When he goes to Vegas, you remember where he stays?"

"I've only been there once. We stayed at The Cavalcade."

He could hear the distaste in her voice. "You didn't like it?"

"It's disgusting, Las Vegas. Not for human beings."

"Thanks, I'm sorry to bother you."

"It isn't good for him there," her voice heavy with weariness. "Tell him to call me."

CURT WANDERED THE CASINO, stunned and lasciviously disgusted, a kid at a salacious carnival. He'd heard it was like this but had never paid attention. It was another planet, more than that – another universe, dimension – the falseness, fake excitement, the lie of every single thing. *We welcome you.* Of course, *we're going to take your money.*

And what happens in Vegas doesn't stay in Vegas. After we take your money, or you spend an inebriated hour with a hooker reeking of perfume, old sperm and tobacco, your life will be ruined forever. The life you thought you had.

Like a hooker, Vegas pretends you turn it on, that it's there for you, wants you. But it's not there for you; you're there for it. Like this cocaine Steve and Zack had gone crazy for.

The blazing lights seemed to him nothing but terror of death – didn't they understand, these people who chased each other over the cliff to get here? That it was their fear of the dark eternal night where we're all headed, that they were trying to blot out? With this mirage of light and excitement, the faked orgasm of a twenty-year-old hooker. It made him shiver, nauseated, nearly enchanted.

"You should come home," Diana had said when he called. "I miss you."

The signal was poor; he strode back and forth in the parking lot. "I've miss you too, dammit, down here in all this weird foolishness."

"A fox got through the hog wire at the far end of the coop and took two good hens. You know them, the Rhode Island Reds who always nest by the wall?"

He tried to imagine it, home. The cold wind down the frigid snowclad slopes. The icy intensity of the air, the ammoniac reek of the henhouse. "Them? I love them."

"So when you get home you fix that hog wire."

He felt a moment's aching loss for those two hens, he *had* loved them. Two out of sixty maybe, sixty-five. But he'd known them, cared for them, wondered were they sisters, how they always hung out together, protected each other. "I'm coming home. I'll deal with it."

"And Belle pushed over the jack fence by the creek. She didn't need water, she was just getting out. So the others had to follow, follow that bitch."

"Tell her when I get home I'm going to shoot her. No, even worse, I'm going to take away her oats."

"So Andy Martin had to chase all over two sections on his four-wheeler, finally drove them back…"

"Tell Andy I owe him."

"Just you get home."

She was gone. He paced the wide dirty parking lot that stank of asphalt and gasoline, looked up at the brilliant lights reflected on the oily clouds. In Montana at night you can see thousands of stars. Here not one.

Stars put us in our place, guide us; we're lost without them. Lost like my two stupid dudes.

His anger at them, he'd realized, was easing. They were fuckups but he didn't want them hurt. Wanted to talk them out of this. For four years they'd been good guys. He needed to ask them *why*. Why they'd done what they'd done.

Just walking around the casinos he wasn't going to find them. And if he did? He imagined halting before them, making them look him in the eye. "How many years," he'd ask them, "have I guided for you?"

"Just you get home," Diana had said.

He thought of her the first time, fiery naked in the Cheyenne Caves hot spring way back in the tall pines, her body lithe and star-silvery, her thighs gripping him, her eyes flashing in the darkness. The ardor of sudden unexpected love, of complete communion, and above them the black cliffs alive with stars, the heated waters of Cheyenne Caves enveloping them like a womb. And the spirits of a hundred thousand murdered Cheyenne and Sioux watching over them like parents over a newborn child.

A HESITANT KNOCK at the door of his suite. Diego let her in, five feet two maybe, skinny girl with proud little tits, long gleaming sable hair a waterfall over one shoulder. When he held the door wide she didn't want to come in.

"It's okay, *florita*, I won't bite."

She darted in, looked up fearfully, circled the room glancing out the windows, the streets so far below glistening and headlight-bright.

"*Qué pasa?*" he smiled, "you never been this high before?"

She faced him, fingers locked, palms down, face tense. "*Qué quieres de mí?* What do you want from me?"

"Hey, relax." He went to the fridge, popped a bottle of champagne, sat on the wide leather couch and poured two flutes. "Come," he patted the couch beside him. "Sit and tell me your story."

Her eyes danced left and right, wouldn't meet his. "Come," he said, a little harsher. "Sit."

She did as she was told. He could smell her nearness, her oily black hair, her musky skin. Heard her breathe. "I ask you again," he said roughly, "tell me where you come from. How you get here."

As he would have said to María Christina, it was a story of our people. How we were before Columbus "discovered" a world already full of humanity. Sure, he, Diego, had not gone to university like María Christina, but he had read things, had learned about it. The priest who lived in the Mexico City dump had taught the children to read and write, the history of their people, till *el Vaticano* found out and accused him of what they called *liberation theology* and called him back to Rome, a castle on the other side of the world where the Pope lives.

Where the Pope decides what should be right and what wrong. What is right for the church, or might harm its steely grasp over the world's poor...as the Ragman's cocaine and heroin spider webs trap the poor – how the image of an imaginary good pulls them in...or, if you wish, give them a little of it, then a little more.

Doesn't take long to hook them, and first thing you know they're going to Mass every Sunday.

And they are hooked. Nearly always till they die. But it doesn't matter they die, for they die loving the delicious beautiful religious heroin in their veins. In the love of their Lord. And all their sisters and brothers following along like sheep behind them.

What he would have told María Christina of the girl's story was nothing new, how the girl's parents like a million other Guatemalans had been chased from their homes by the Generals' dictatorship created by these United States, and which murdered a half million people in a country of five million, "disappeared" another forty thousand, and tortured twenty thousand more to death in Guatemala City prisons...all because the farm workers, these "enemies of the state", weren't satisfied with a dollar a day laboring in the concentration camps of United Fruit (now known as Chiquita bananas) – originally owned by the Bush family, the family that made two Presidents, and which told the American government to attack these peasants for the crime of wanting more than a dollar a day, accused them of "Communism" and finally instructed the CIA to "go down there and solve this." From which came the murdered presidents, the military dictatorships, death squads, the torture prisons and the Latin American tragedy that the United States had instigated for more than six decades...

But, as María Christina had told him, everybody already knows this. So get over it. We must all get over what the *norteamericanos* did, and destroy them in a different way. With cocaine. With heroin. With immigration and taking over their government with political contributions. With taking everything they own.

Revolution failed. Freedom failed. We will get them another way.

He could hear María Christina now, her soft and modulated multi-tonal voice with the rumbling "r" so true and sensual. As if I could ever forsake you, María Christina. Nor your father the Ragman who raised me up from the Mexico City dump to this suite in America's shining Heaven, the place that thinks it is what it wants to be. Where everyone is alone and everyone's a victim. Especially the winners.

He rustled his shoulders. It gave him an exciting shiver up his spine to think like this.

"And now I am here," she said.

"I don't know your name."

"Aemilia."

"Aemilia." It was an exhalation, something breathed out, like a truth.

"And what is yours?" This was very forward and she knew it: he saw the fear in her eyes. The dark-shadowed black eyes with dark lashes. *O Cristo*, he thought.

The padre who came to the Mexico City dump was tall and spare with a long chin and dark sad eyes. One time, after he'd taught Diego to read and write and began to speak with him of deep things, he told him what had happened to him and asked *what should I do?* He had been robbed and beaten by one of the dump gangs, and he wanted to know from Diego was it okay to have them punished, or should he turn the other cheek?

"Punish them," Diego said right away. "It is the kindest thing for them."

"How so?"

"To make them whole again you must show them the connection between what they do and what happens to them. That life truly does have a purpose and there is such a thing as good. And also, if they get away with beating and robbing you, a priest, what will they do to someone else? To a mother with child? To a bearded old man?"

So the priest had gone to the gang who ran the dump and explained these things. And the thieves had been punished. And for many months the people of the dump lived in peace.

"So, Aemilia," he said when she had sat there silently for a while, moving her fingers to and fro in her lap as if weaving something. "What was it like, your village?"

"It was on the edge between the jungle and the river. The river was big and was full of fish that we dried on wooden frames. We had nice houses of clay and straw. We were happy."

"*Y entonces?*"

"*Entonces* came the soldiers. You know all that."

"I had two sisters." Why was he telling her this? "They were killed when I was fourteen. One after the other."

"Good Lord." She looked up at him. "I am sorry."

He listened for two hours to her story, the flight north, how her mother sold herself at the border so they could get across, her mother and father dying when a truck of farm workers went off the road and rolled over near Salinas.

"And now I am here," she said again.

"What do you think," he turned the question over in his head, "will happen afterward?"

"After tonight?" she hunched a bit. "I am supposed to go in bed here with you."

He smiled. "Do you know what that means?"

"You put your peepee in my peepee. Like dogs and pigs do."

"I meant what will you do, in these years that will come? Who will you be?"

She squeezed her arms against her body, rigid. "I am in God's hands. How can He go wrong?"

"What about the army and death squads? Was that in God's hands?"

She retreated into herself, looking down at her folded fingers. He watched her slim lovely thighs in the short skirt they'd dressed her in. Oh Jesus she is beautiful. What was the Lord's mother like, Mother Mary, when she was fourteen? Was she this hot?

I bet she was. And I bet she was doing it, too.

He could taste the place between her thighs. Someone had to be first.

He imagined adopting her, putting her in a gringo school, finding her family, what was left of it, giving them money. Like she was his little sister.

You're getting soft, *hombre*, he told himself.

That's dangerous.

IN GOD'S HANDS

STEVE STROLLED INTO THE CAVALCADE and headed for the young woman at the main desk. Curly black hair, wide pretty face, Hispanic, twenty-five maybe, a little overweight and tired-looking. Wedding ring, circles under the eyes. You're doing a day job and this one too, he decided. Kids at home, husband maybe out of work?

"Hey," he gave her his best smile. "I need your help."

She checked him out, the good clothes, expensive haircut, the suave gringo manner of a guy who made money here, didn't lose it. "What kind of help?"

"My friend Zack Wilson told me he was here, I need to knock on his door but I can't remember which one."

She shook her head slowly. "I can't tell you that."

He nodded at her computer. "Just check he's here?"

"I can do that."

He watched her find the name, the room number, slid a hundred-dollar bill across her counter. "Please help me – I need to find him, help him, his Mom's sick…"

She looked at the hundred, at him. "If you bring this back on me…"

He shook his head. "Ain't happening."

The hundred vanished. "Floor 49, the Normandy Suite. Last elevators on the left."

He knocked softly at the door. No answer. Knocked again. Again.

A fuzzy voice.

"Zack!" he whispered. "It's Steve. I've got a buyer for our stuff."

THE GIRL HUDDLED AGAINST DIEGO as if to keep warm. Like in winter when his family clumped together in the back of their trash den in the Mexico City dump, under newspapers. Like maybe in this girl's jungle village, and everyone sleeps in a pile.

She felt slim and gracile against his muscular frame, his arm easily around her. After a while she stopped shivering and he massaged up and down her slender spine to warm her. Listened to her soft breathing. *Como el viento en las hojas.* Like wind in the leaves.

Her breath like jasmine.

"I am in God's hands," she'd said. God who would make her a young hooker in Vegas till she wasn't young any more, then a hooker, then an old hooker. But always she'd be sending dollars back to the family in Guatemala – *was it God who arranged this?* So that someday maybe a little nephew or niece becomes a doctor, a banker in this silver and gold Heaven and Hell known as America? *Que mala, la vida.*

Fuck you, God, if that's the best you can do.

His cellphone rang *Necio*, the Mexican hit he loved because of Carlos Santana. He carefully slid his arm from beneath the girl's head and answered. "*Sí?*"

"There *is* a guy, over at The Cavalcade. He is not in the business. Nobody knows him. But he's selling."

"How much?"

"How much you want? That is what he is saying."

"Just one guy? Not two?"

"Just one. With a woman."

"How do I find him, *amigo?*"

"In the Normandy Suite, 49th floor. He and the woman. They are there now."

"*Gracias, hermano.*" Diego slipped from the bed. "I owe you."

Quietly so as not to wake the girl, he got dressed, took a Glock 19 and an Advanced Armament suppressor from his backpack, screwed in the suppressor, slid in a magazine, put a thousand dollars on the bedside table and slipped out the door.

"SO I KNEW you'd come to Vegas." Steve stood in the center of the room, angry and tense. Zack pale-faced and unshaven, his muscular torso in the dingy-shirt and sweats he'd thrown on before answering the door. Emily under the covers naked.

"You *do* realize I had to move our stash?" Zack said. "Once DEA nailed you at Newark, you idiot, we couldn't chance leaving it there. What was I supposed to do?"

"You should've told me. Should've answered my calls."

"Right, when you're being listened to by DEA and probably Colorado cops and maybe the folks who own that stash, you want me to *answer* you?" Zack glanced sideways toward the bedside table, not meeting Steve's eye.

Or maybe, Steve thought, Zack was looking for Curt's Ruger if it was hidden there, in the bedside table. Steve almost pulled his Beretta: *No, not now.* "I had to come *searching* for you!" he said. "You weren't *ever* going to tell me where you were, where you had our stuff…"

"That's not true." Zack paced, turned back to him. "Don't you realize you could be toxic? You could fuck our *whole* program! If DEA found you at Newark they're probably following you now. And everything you say or do only makes things worse."

"Both you guys," Emily sat up holding the sheets and blanket to cover her breasts as in some old Hollywood film, "you shut the fuck up. Steve, Zack is right. You probably *are* toxic. If you want this done, leave it to us." She turned to Zack, "and Zack, you should've found a way to let Steve know…"

"I knew where you were," Zack said to him.

"You didn't know shit. You were thieving it."

"I put a sample out to some folks," Zack said. "They may be interested."

"How much?"

"Two hundred bricks. Maybe more."

"I got a guy back east. Offering three million bucks but he's stuck at twenty-five a brick."

"Let's sell all we can here first," Zack said. "It's a shorter drive from Denver to here than Denver to New York. Then whatever we have left we drive back east, for your guys."

"No more arguing," Emily said. "Just get this done."

RAIN splashed across the Range Rover's windshield, gleamed on the asphalt and hissed under the fat tires. Diego drove carefully – now was not the time to get noticed by some *hijo de puta policía* so that later if bodies showed up the cop might remember him out in the middle of the night when most people are in bed screwing or sleeping, or had lost their money and are sitting in their rooms trying to figure out how to get through the night. How to find their way home.

He parked a quarter mile down the Strip from The Cavalcade, pulled a rain poncho over his shoulders, tugged the Glock closer under his arm, keeping it dry, feeling affection for it like for the girl Aemilia – how strange to know her name, *en verdad* a little sister.

But his little sisters had been killed, hadn't they? So you don't have a little sister, *hijo de puta*, so don't talk like that. The gun so warm against his ribs. Better than a little sister. Almost.

The doorman blocked him. For a moment the old fear, the old insecurity, *who are you, dirty little Mexican, dare come in here?* Then he made himself remember, *María Christina cares for you. You can go anywhere, do anything.* "I've just come from Caesar's Palace," he said. "They closed the tables, said yours are still open."

The guard tugged out a phone, punched a number. "What's going on up there?" He listened, nodded, turned to Diego. "You're on. Ace of Hearts room, second floor."

Diego took the chrome-walled elevator up to the second floor and then the stairs down to the main elevator stack and the staff lockers below.

"SO THIS GUY you know," Steve said, "he'll take some?"

"I think –"

"You *think?*"

"Fuck you. You don't have proof either. This Wall Street guy –"

"Guys!" Emily snapped. "Stop arguing. Let's get this done."

"He's got a sample. He'll be back to me tomorrow. He'll want a lot."

The doorbell buzzed. Steve looked at Zack. Zack shook his head. The buzzer buzzed again, longer, strident. Steve stepped into the bedroom, Zack went to the door. "Who is it?"

"Room Service, sir. A gift from management."

"Tell him come back tomorrow!" Steve hissed, from behind the bedroom door.

"If it's from Haney I gotta take it…" Through the peephole Zack could see a small man in a bellboy uniform almost too big for him. A stainless steel trolley with a white cloth and on it a silver tray, ice bucket and two bottles of champagne.

Zack opened the door.

The bellboy came in pushing the cart ahead of him. "Would you like me open one, sir?"

"Sure," Zack said. "Why not?"

The bellboy pulled a long-barreled gun from under the white cloth. "You and the woman, you both stand in the corner there, hands on heads. Quick quick. *Go!*"

"What the fuck are you doing coming in here like this?" Zack yelled. "Who the fuck are you?"

"You stole everything was in our plane. We want it back."

"I didn't steal anything!" Zack said.

"You want to live, you tell me where you put our stuff. I make a call, it gets checked out, if it's good I let you go."

"Soon as you find it you'll kill us," Emily said, managing to cover her crotch with her hands and her nipples with her upper arms.

"So you do admit you got it?" He pointed the gun at her.

"Fuck you, jerk." She huddled tighter against herself.

"Leave her alone." Zack stepped in front of her. "And mister, we didn't steal anything of yours. So please go find the people who *did* steal it, whatever it is. And leave us alone."

"Thirty seconds," the Mexican said, "Till I shoot her. If you don't say."

"Tell him," she hissed at Zack. "*Tell* him, for *Chrissake!*"

Out of the corner of his eye Zack tried not to watch Steve as he stepped from behind the bedroom door with the Beretta in his hand and came up behind Diego.

Outside the rain was splashing down the floor-to-ceiling window shimmering the city lights. The glass rattled when gusts hit it, wind howled past the glass.

"You, behind me," Diego said, "you come any closer and this woman dies. If I let go this trigger she dies. So you can't risk shooting me. I need you to come round in front of me and put your gun on the floor. Or I kill her."

"Put the gun down," Steve said. "Or *you* die."

"Don't play with my life!" Emily begged.

"Put the gun down," Steve said, "then walk quietly out of this room and we never see each other again. Because we don't have whatever crazy thing you're looking for –"

"You know what I am looking for," the Mexican said. "What you steal from our plane and take down the mountain and drive away in that guy Curt's pickup truck. Ever since then we've been hunting you. And now we have you."

"You're the guy with the gun at your back," Steve said.

"So even if you kill me, *hombre*, this gun fires, the woman dies. And don't think there won't be ten guys coming after you then, ten guys all better than me? Because then we'll be really angry at you. So give us back our stuff and all this goes away."

"Do what he *says*," Emily said. "*Please…*"

"Nobody's dying here," Steve said. "Our bellboy's going to put away his gun –"

"Give us back our stuff," the Mexican said. "Sooner or later you will have to give it back. So do it now, get it over with. Then you can go back to your lives. You will be much more happier."

"How do we know you won't kill us?" Zack said.

"What's the advantage to that? Then we have a murder rap over our heads, all kinds of shit comes down, it's ugly, man." The Mexican shook his head wearily. "Just give us our stuff."

"He's right, Steve," Zack said. "Let's just end this, before anyone gets hurt."

"I have no wish to hurt you," the Mexican said.

"So you want us to stay here," Steve said, "till you guys check out what we tell you?"

"I have five other guys here," the Mexican said. "We cover everything you do. Even if I'm not here, you are still covered. So, please."

"There's some missing," Zack said. "Got stolen from Steve, here."

"I was given a name," Steve said. "In Fountain, a place south of Colorado Springs. But they knocked me out and stole twenty kilos."

"You tell me all about them," the Mexican said. "We will find them."

"Yes," Steve nodded. "I would like that." He thought of the girl Emerald, what it would have been like. "Your stuff is at Maxi Self-Rent in Denver," he said, the address of the old self-storage they'd had before Zack had stolen their stuff and taken it elsewhere.

Zack looked at him in disbelief. "What's *that* going to do?"

"It's all right," Steve cut him off, "to tell them." He raised his hands in defeat. "It's over with. Time for us to go home."

"You motherfuckers better agree," the Mexican said, "or I kill you both." He glanced at Emily. "I shoot you *all.*" He turned to Steve, "Listen, you, it's so much easier – you give me our stuff and I give you two hundred thousand dollars, okay?"

"Why would you do that?" Zack said.

"Because it is so much more easier, *hombre*. It is cheaper than we buy it again, put it on a plane and fly it up here again, okay?"

Emily walked naked to the dresser. The Mexican stumbled back, laughed. "Get over there or I blow your head off."

She ignored him, pulling into her panties, tights and bra and the sinuous black dress she'd dropped over the TV. "I'm out of here."

"Go there," he rasped. "With *him*, in the corner."

"You'd kill me?" she came closer, "I've done you no harm."

"Get back, lady!"

She shoved away his gun. "Just let me out –"

He shot her in the right eye and she toppled backwards on the floor. Zack ran to her screaming, cradled her head, dropped her and rushed the Mexican. Steve fired at the Mexican and missed, hitting his gun that spun from his hand and smashed against the wall. The Mexican hunched over his shattered hand and ran out. Steve sprinted after him down the carpeted hallway not daring to shoot because of the noise. The Mexican spun round and with a swish of his other hand flung something that stabbed into Steve's ribs, a piercing pain that brought him to his knees, the Mexican's footsteps fading down the stairs.

Don't bleed on the carpet Steve told himself, staggered back to the room, arms clenched over the chunk of steel in his chest, the hot blood spilling between his fingers down his stomach and legs.

"She's *dead*!" Zack screamed at him.

"Oh Christ." Steve knelt beside her.

"You *killed* her!"

"Oh God now what are we going to do?" Steve lifted her head, blood spattering out the back of her brain and mixing with the blood that was running down his chest. "We can't call 911."

"Now, fuckhead," Zack screamed at him. "*Now* what are we going to *do*?"

Steve looked down at his shirt. One blade of a four-bladed throwing star was buried in his chest, between the ribs. The pain was like fire.

He got to his feet, stumbled into the bathroom, pulled the throwing star from his chest, took off his shirt and held a folded washcloth tight over the wound. How could anything hurt so bad? How could this have happened, so fast?

WHAT HAPPENS IN VEGAS

CRAZY. INSANE. Emily's blood spurting down Zack's arms and spattering on the carpet was like the death of goodness. *Her vacant eyes and slack mouth.* Just seconds ago she was *here*. He was going mad. Oh Emily I loved you. I *love* you. Emily *Emily Emily…*

I never told you.

Steve lifted Emily from Zack's arms and carried her into the bathroom. "What the fuck you insane motherfucker you doing?" Zack screamed.

"I'm putting her in the tub. All this blood…"

Not possible. It went round and round howling through Zack's head but there was no way it had happened. That Emily was *dead*. Strangely, he wanted Monica to be there, tell him what to do. *Monica please help me Monica.* He imagined her in the Emergency Room, saving lives. *Save Emily, Monica. Please save Emily…*

How could Emily be right here, alive, then be not? How had the Mexican done it? Was it just a piece of metal out of a metal tube and then you're dead? Then her thirty-three years of brilliant happy and unhappy flirtatious affectionate beauty annihilated?

In the bathroom he washed her blood from his wrists and hands with a bottle of antibacterial soap. What are you worried about, he wanted to ask the makers of this soap, this antibacterial foolishness? Don't you know all life is dangerous, every instant? Look what it did to her.

I did this. I'm the one who brought her here. Used her to sell the coke. Used her to death.

He collapsed over the sink. If only I could go back, Lord. *Please,* if only we could just go back.

DIEGO RAN down the stairs with his shattered blood-pulsing hand gripped against his stomach hoping no one would see him, that he wasn't leaving blood tracks and Oh God he'd fucked up. María Christina would be looking to kill. He'd failed her.

He searched for the Range Rover, pain thudding through his hand up his arm making it impossible to know where he was. But he found the car, found the key in his pocket and somehow put it in the machine and drove away, driving nowhere, his heart a knot, ideas screaming through his head. Should've killed them all. But then, how to find the coke?

How to find it now?

He had to make them talk. Then kill them.

Scum from the Mexico City dump. You worthless thing.

He U-turned on Fremont and sped back to The Cavalcade. Kill them all. All except the one who would tell the truth.

At The Cavalcade he pulled over, the engine idling hard, and pulled out his phone. "I screwed up," he said when María Christina answered.

"*Qué dices?*" He could hear she was in some big room, lots of voices.

"A mistake," he said. "Please forgive me ..."

"I don't understand you," she said softly. "Call me in business hours, we can discuss this."

"Where are you?" he said, shocked by his forwardness.

"This is the Democratic State Convention," she whispered. "A late night meeting. Who *are* you? Why are you calling *me?*"

He shut off. Whatever he did now, she had told him, he did on his own.

He would prove himself. Whatever she needed, he would do.

"WE *HAVE* to get her out of here!" Steve gasped, clutching a bloody washcloth to his chest.

"She's dead," Zack stuttered, staring, not seeing, voice hoarse with tears, with sorrow, with refusing to understand. "Emily is *dead!* What are you going to do about *that?*"

Steve glanced blindly round the room. "We have to *solve* this!"

"Let's call the cops – *please*, let's do it?"

"Really? And tell them we were selling three hundred kilos of cocaine to Vegas dealers? Three hundred kilos that we stole from a Mexican drug ring, that we should have turned in to the cops but didn't, that we *hid* from them – add that to our list of crimes. And we stole Curt's truck, lied to that Montana Sheriff's Department, Colorado State Patrol and DEA. We used rental premises illegally to store a Schedule II Controlled Substance, and transported it across state lines. And because we stole three hundred kilos of cocaine from the Mexican who killed Emily, we can be ruled as accessories to her death. You want to explain all this to the cops?" He shook Zack's good shoulder. "You *want* that?"

The impossibility of it all was staggering. Zack's stomach turned. He swallowed bile, realized he was going to die and hoped it was true. How did he fall this fast, this far? Poor Emily. God, *poor Emily.* Why had he asked her to come?

Her body crumpled in the tub. Blood oozing from her nose, from her sagging mouth. Out the back of her brain.

What happens when a bullet blows out your brain? Where do your memories go, your mind? Your intense self?

Why did she walk toward her killer? Did she think he wouldn't fire? That he'd be kind?

What could he tell Wally?

Oh God what have I become?

THE WORLD WAS RUINED. Steve would save what he could, for Marcie and the kids. Didn't matter if he died, except for them.

Didn't matter if he lived. Because Emily died. Because he should've shot first and didn't.

He stuffed paper towels into the hole in the back of her head, tore the sheets off the bed and wrapped her in them, undid the plastic mattress cover and zipped her into it. She was heavy; he imagined Zack and her making love just an hour ago, she riding his hips.

How did this happen, so fast?

The Mexican shot her. It's not my fault, Steve told himself. *Dear Lord not my fault.*

He fought the hunger to call Marcie. Two a.m. her time. Anyway, what could *she* say? What would happen to her if he told her?

"When's the last time Emily can be traced?" he asked Zack standing there like a broken tree. "The last time you called her, where was she?"

"She was…" Zack broke down, couldn't speak.

Steve whacked him across the face with the back of his hand. It felt good, made a good sound. Now maybe Zack would listen.

"I called her," Zack said slowly. "I called her cell phone."

"When?"

"When I was coming to see her. Called her in Aspen and she came down to Glenwood." Zack tried to remember but it was too hard.

"You brought her into this," Steve said. "Not me."

The punch came out of nowhere smashing Steve's jaw, the shock electric up his face into his head and down his neck and chest. He found himself on the floor, for a moment unsure who and where he was. He sat up. "You sucker punched me."

Zack stood over him. "Stand up and I'll hit you again."

"I have a knife wound in my chest and you hit me." Steve lurched to his feet, wanting to hit Zack but that was foolish, Zack the NFL linebacker would demolish him. "We have to drive into the desert," Steve said. "And let her go."

Steve looked for the hole in the wall where the bullet that had gone through Emily's brain had lodged, couldn't find it. Walked back and forth saying "It has to be somewhere," then saw it had hit a fabric print on the wall and buried in the concrete block behind it. He pinched the fabric together over the hole. And his bullet that had smashed the Mexican's gun lay on the carpet, spent.

They washed the blood stains from the carpet with the anti-bacterial soap and dried them with the hair drier, opened a window and turned the heat on high, wiped the blood off the bathroom tile floor, scrubbed the tub, took the Mexican's shattered gun, and packed up.

Steve checked out the elevators but they were too crowded, party people coming up and down, hookers hugging drunken clients, *Honey I'm going to give you such a good night...*

Back in the room he threw Emily over his shoulder, his injured chest ripping open, waited in the hallway for silent Zack to lock the room. He carried her down the service stairwell forty-nine stories to the main floor then two more to the parking garage and no one stopped them except on the seventh floor some party girls came out giggling and looked at him like he was a murderer. "What you got there?" one girl said, eying the bundle of dead Emily under the sheets and mattress cover on his shoulder.

"Potted palm," Steve said, pretending inebriation, hoping the blood down his chest didn't show. "My buddies stole it from my room. College football stunt." He nodded at Zack. "We're taking it back."

"You *go*, Darlin," she laughed.

Drunk as a skunk, Steve thought. But what's she going to remember when she wakes?

FROM VEGAS they drove northeast into Utah, Steve first in the Eddie Bauer with Emily in the back, Zack following in the Pathfinder, down the wide concrete strip across the dark ragged desert under the aching stars, the cold blue universe free of any care for humankind, where rats, rattlers, ravens and people stole whatever solace they could find.

Highway lines and dead jackrabbits flitted past; the air was cold and sharp. Steve stared at the road ahead with the exhausted vision of a murderer – *that's what he was if you got right down to it* – tried not to think how horrible, how insane this was. Tried to imagine a way out.

For moments it seemed unreal. Then when he realized it *was* real the pain was even worse. This horror and sorrow like a chainsaw in the gut.

One he had no right to complain about because he was the one who started it.

It was *he* who lured Zack into this, stole the coke from the plane, took the horses then Curt's truck, broke all these other laws since. And now because of what he'd done, Emily was dead.

Zack's headlights in the mirror were a steady reminder. Zack must hate him. With a murderous hate. Now on top of everything else he had to watch out for Zack.

As the highway flitted under his tires he kept looking for a way out.

If the hotel checked the room might they see something? Blood? The bullet hole in the wall behind the fabric print? The theft of the sheets and mattress cover would piss them off.

But there was no way to connect with Emily. She hadn't made any calls and hadn't used a credit card, according to Zack. No one knew she was even there. Or that she was dead.

No victim, no crime.

An hour north of Vegas he turned east toward Overton then northeast on a gravel road five miles to the Virgin River canyon, halted at a gritty windblown rest stop overlooking black cliffs and far below a thin cleft of star-bright water.

ZACK got out and walked to the edge. The black emptiness below was taunting and nauseating; he backed away so as not throw himself over.

He opened the Eddie Bauer's back. Emily's hip under the plastic mattress cover felt cold and rigid as soft marble. Emily in her tattered happy life, this living being, this lover of sun and fun and champagne and the exciting mystery of life, her vast joy in pleasure itself – wasn't she right and the rest of us wrong?

Look where it got her.

Why had he called her? Because he'd wanted to sell coke to Wally. But once he started talking with her it made him want to see her, his cock hard just hearing her voice. *Had* to fuck her, like the old days when they got so hot they had to shower afterwards, wash off the sweat.

Now the bullet in her eye, out the back of her brain. Taking Emily with it.

Steve who'd led the Mexican to her. To *us*. The bullet smashing through her brain. *Steve*.

He slid Emily from the Eddie Bauer and carried her toward the cliff. From the ground came sinister crackling noises. "Oh fuck," Steve said. "Rattlers."

"Why don't you step on them?" Zack said, aching to push him into the snakes, off the cliff.

"Hey, man, not to worry." Steve stomped to chase away the snakes.

"How you know this place?"

"Came here with Marcie, our honeymoon. Raft trip."

Zack knelt with Emily at the cliff edge and unwrapped the mattress cover and sheets from her body.

Steve dropped to his knees beside her. "I just never *knew*."

"Knew what?"

"How we could go so *wrong*."

"We didn't go wrong. We just followed who we are."

Steve looked away. "Have to undress her. Can't leave anything could be ID'd."

Zack said nothing, breathing loud.

"I'll move back," Steve said. "You do it."

Zack turned her on her side to unzip the silky black dress but she was already so stiff he couldn't pull it down and had to rip it off.

To unhook the bra from her marvelous breasts and her panties from her luxurious golden crotch seemed like a crime, like rape.

Her skin was pallid under the white stars and black night. She was rigid, arms down her sides, head turned as if not wanting to look at the black chasm beyond her elbow.

Steve crumpled her clothes with the mattress cover and sheets, stuck them between some stones and lit them on fire. It stank of burning rubber, the sparks twirling away on the desert wind.

"I won't do this," Zack said. He would take her somewhere better, a place testament to her beauty and love. He pulled her closer, one last time looked down at her naked beauty, her lovely half-parted lips. Was all love fated like this?

Oh Emily I miss you so.

Dear Monica, I'm so helpless in all this.

Please, show me a way.

Like a parent with a dead child he took a breath, bit back sorrow and pushed her over the edge.

After a long time a rolling clatter came up from below. "Be years," Steve said. "Till anybody finds her." He cleared his throat, spit over the edge. "If ever."

Zack leaped at him trying to push him off the cliff but Steve twisted back, tripped on a rock and fell with Zack on top strangling him one-handed, dragging him to the edge. Steve dug his heels into the rocks but they were too slippery, terrified of the eerie wind moaning up the canyon walls, punching at Zack who kept screaming through bloodied lips, "You're going to die motherfucker. You're going to die."

Zack shoved Steve's face over the edge, the cliff vertical, black, sheer and horribly far down. "I told the cops," Steve gasped. "DEA."

Zack's fingers round Steve's neck relaxed. "Told what?"

Snakes were rattling all around them. Steve tried to slither back from the edge but Zack held him. "Told them what?" he repeated.

"Let me up, and I'll tell you."

Zack let him go and Steve scrambled away from the cliff, ran, stumbled, fell, choking from the grip Zack had had on this throat, could barely breathe, his palms bristling with cactus thorns where he had fallen, his clothes torn by rocks, blood running down his belly from the wound in his chest.

Zack stood over him. "Told them what?"

Beyond the Maze

"I TOLD THEM NOTHING." Steve sat on a rock massaging his bruised jaw and half-crushed throat, blood from his chest ticking on the ground. "You had no reason to kill me."

"You killed Emily. That's why."

"The Mexican killed her."

Zack smacked him. The hurt was enormous.

"By following me," Zack whispered, "you brought the Mexican down on me. On Emily. We were doing fine, she and me, selling the coke, making money. Money for you too. Because once the deal was done I was sending you your half, minus of course the twenty bricks you lost."

Steve stood, trying to get away from the snakes rattling all around them. "So now, you're trying to kill me? Push me over the edge?"

"I should have."

"*I'm* not the reason the Mexican found you. You were talking up a deal all over Vegas, handing out samples, hustling people who are in the business full-time, not amateurs like you. So the Mexican's people, of course they hear. They check you out, find you're the guy who stole the stuff from their plane. Then I come into town, get caught up in your crap. And you blame *me* for all this?" Steve walked toward the car, still massaging his neck. "You still don't understand? You never will."

Zack followed him, his fist clenched, couldn't decide. Maybe throw him over the edge. Let him fall down the cliff, let his guts keep company with Emily's, let the ravens eat them. But if two bodies were found wouldn't he be even more at risk? Wouldn't they show a link between Emily and Steve, that someone had pushed them both over? How many years in jail, he wondered, will I already get, if this goes south? And if I kill him how many more?

There had to be a traceless way to do it.

DIEGO DIDN'T DARE go to the hospital. Twice he'd called María Christina but she didn't answer. Did she no longer care for him? Did she not recognize his number? Had he done something to offend her?

Or didn't the scrambler tell her who it was, and where? How could that be?

Maybe was she just pretending to care for him?

Finally he called a good friend whose name he could not remember.

"Ah, my good friend," his good friend said. "How are you?"

"I need a doctor, a nurse. Anybody. Any *fucking* body."

"You hurt?"

"You could say so."

Five minutes later his good friend called back with an address on Windmill Parkway. "Go in this door, code is 1769, second floor and down the corridor to the end, knock on that door."

"When?"

"Now. And now get out of my life."

STEVE drove north on I-15 in the Eddie Bauer, Zack behind in the Pathfinder. They'd talked about dumping one car and going together but neither was willing to give his up. Because the other guy was getting crazy, you couldn't risk riding with him. No telling what he might do.

He might kill you. You know he wanted to. Just like you wanted to kill him.

So you kept a gun close. And hoped he was stupid or lazy or maybe didn't really intend to kill you.

It was raining when they reached Cedar City at 3 a.m., as far as they could from Vegas without falling asleep. Steve got a room at the Quality Inn and Zack across the street in the Abbey.

3: 42 a.m. Hands behind his head Steve stared at the ceiling. At the red spot of the fire alarm. At the flicker of the clock radio's flashing red strobe on the papered walls. The green light at the foot of the little refrigerator. The streetlights outside wavering against the rain-streaked glass.

Why was he here? Good God *why* was he here?

He tossed in the wide empty bed. Nearly seven in the morning now in New York. Marcie'd be making tea then oatmeal and hot chocolate for the kids then getting them up and dressed and smoothing their hair and making them happy despite another day of educational indenture, a concentration camp for children to keep them out of their parents' lives, then Marcie racing downtown to the office to spend the day "reaching out" to anyone who might want to buy a hole in one of the thousands of cliff dwellings in Manhattan. No matter the cost.

Like rats in a maze we think we know the way.

We may, but we have no idea what lies beyond the maze.

THE DOCTOR was a sleepy young woman with pale hair that kept tumbling over her brow. "This is a bad wound," she told Diego. "You must go to a hand clinic, doctors who really understand how the hand works…"

"You're what I've got," he said, exhausted from the pain. "Do it."

"I can't sew these torn tendons…Are you *out* of your *mind?*"

He leaned up at her from the table. "How much your medical school bills?"

She appraised him. "Screw you."

This surprised him. "I give you ten grand extra. Sew me up best you can. Or I will just wrap it up and live with it."

"Not possible."

He tried to shrug. "So let's do it. Who knows, someday you might become a great surgeon." He tried to smile. "I believe in you."

ZACK STILL WANTED TO KILL STEVE. But how to get away with it? Afterwards, he'd send Steve's wife some money. He'd agree to thirty cents on the dollar for the auction rate securities, send her half that. That should shut her up. Maybe she's already screwing other guys, won't care Steve's gone?

Who would know?

Who cared?

DAWN spread across the desert of another planet, barren ochre, pale and dusty. Trucks howled back and forth on I-15 as if they and not humans ruled the earth. Diesel stink undulating snake-like on the bitter wind, genuflecting sagebrush gripping eroded bedrock, coyote starvation on the ragged stony slopes, the sorrowed resignation of a cattle-ravaged land. *Oooooh*, the wind sighed. *Dooomed.*

They drove northeast on I-15 then across Utah and western Colorado through a new snowstorm on I-70, to Glenwood Springs. Feeling like a murderer Zack put on his gloves and drove Emily's 500 SL from the Hotel Colorado parking lot back to Aspen, Steve following close behind. Half way up the mountain Steve threw the Mexican's shattered Glock into a ravine, and at another turnout tossed Emily's smashed phone over the edge. At Aspen Airport Zack left the 500 SL in long-term parking and halfway down the mountain threw the keys far into the trees.

Steve drove them back to Glenwood where Zack picked up the Pathfinder and they took I-70 down the Front Range to 470 to Lucent Boulevard then Highlands Ranch and Good News Self Storage.

"I never wanted to hide this from you," Zack said, flashing his headlamp into the unit so Steve could see the kilos stacked in even order, white in the glaring light, each one with its black scorpion logo. "There was no choice. I had to move it when you got busted in Newark."

"I don't care," Steve said exhaustedly. *If I'm going to take him down,* he told himself, *it has to be soon.*

They paid cash for two rooms at the Everglade Motel, one at each end. It was a dark place hunched over a broken parking lot alongside Santa Fe, a relic of when Denver was still a cow town, this motel waiting to be torn down to build a Costco, Sam's Club, Whole Foods or Home Depot to fill the needs of the fifty thousand new homes that hopscotched across the prairie every year. The all-night trucks rumbled past on one side, Warren Buffett's 200-car coal trains from the Wyoming strip mines on the other side, every twenty minutes, all night, all day long.

Neither slept, with the noise, the fear, the worry, and knowing the other guy could come through the door any moment, shooting to kill.

Each, in his own room, tried to imagine what it's like, being hit by a bullet.

FAIRPLAY

"THEY'RE BACK IN DENVER," Whitney said. "Still can't trace their phones but the last credit card hit was at Beau Jo's Pizza in Idaho Springs, and before that was the Conoco on Main Street in Green River, so they're headed east, and that's Denver."

"What are you going to do about it?" Curt said.

"We still can't trace the cars, so we wait for more credit card data."

"You could've got them in Vegas."

"We want them with the goods. *All* the goods."

"And now, you guys can't set up roadblocks?"

"I've asked Colorado State Patrol … but they see so many deals every week, no way they can cover them all. They said maybe they'll set up one or two roadblocks …"

"I know these guys. That's not going to catch them −"

"One bit of good news …" she half-smiled. "I just learned that Steve got caught at Newark Airport three days ago with traces of coke in his pocket…"

"They didn't arrest him?"

"Not enough evidence. Some fancy lawyer got him released right away."

He shook his head, numbed by it all. "If that plane hadn't crashed, nobody'd even *know* about this deal."

"YOU CAN KILL me any time." Steve leaned toward Zack across the table at Barnaby's Steak City in the Aspen Glen Shopping Center. "So I don't understand why you haven't tried."

Zack waved his good hand at him, a dismissal. "From day one, we've been in this together."

"You don't believe that. Not for an instant."

"True. I didn't want any of this. You dragged me into it, with no way out."

Steve snickered. "You always had a way out. You just didn't take it."

"And now what?"

Steve held his wine glass against his cheek as if drawing the coolness from it. "Your Vegas friends say they'll take two hundred kilos, maybe they'll take more, so we take all the kilos to Vegas and see what happens."

"And the Mexican? He's just going to be nice and forget us? He knows who we are, or how else did he find your room? How we going to get away from *them*?"

"They're not sure we have their stuff. They just suspect it. And now he's wounded and maybe we've gone to the cops, told them he killed Emily. So he doesn't dare surface again."

"And the cops?"

"What have they really got on us? That we stole Curt's truck? Your arm was broken, we had to get to a hospital. Nobody's going to nail us for that. And that I had a trace of powder in my pocket? No big deal. And we can't be jailed just because we'd shut off our phones for a few days and didn't know they were trying to reach us. We'd come down to Denver, you went home to New York for a weekend, we drove to Vegas then back here to Denver. Just two old buddies having fun."

"So why would we drive back to Vegas again? It doesn't make sense."

"Who's to say we can't? And we're taking a back way. I've been looking at the map ..."

"So that's what you've been doing."

"If the Mexican or the cops or DEA are looking for us, they'll assume we'll go back to Vegas the same way, I-70 to I-15. So instead we head southwest on smaller roads, where nobody'll be looking. We can make Durango tonight."

Zack glanced out the window. "Not with this snow coming down."

"Once we get to Vegas, unload the stuff, we're free."

THEY LOADED THE KILOS under a tarp in the back of the Eddie Bauer and left Highlands Ranch on 285 southwest in a deepening snowstorm, Steve first in the Eddie Bauer, Zack behind in the Pathfinder, Denver's suburbs climbing into rocky conifered mountains coated in houses, broad valleys filled with gas stations, shopping centers, box stores and fast food, all half-veiled in driving snow.

Three hours on 285 to Poncha Springs, the road slippery, oncoming cars difficult to see even with their headlights on. They got low-price gas at Western Convenience then turned west on 50 through Gunnison toward Montrose.

We can still get to Durango tonight," Steve said.

"Not with this snow."

It thickened, a sleeting blizzard, the road icy as they crossed over the Gunnison dam.

They grabbed a late lunch in Montrose and took 550 south. The road climbed toward Red Mountain Pass, 11,000 feet the map said. It narrowed, no guardrails, the cliffs vertical, the canyon vast beneath them. Trucks came the other way, on the edge of the road, throwing up ice and billowing snow.

Zack called Steve. "I can't make this, my car's sliding all over the place, almost skidded off the cliff…"

For an instant Steve thought wouldn't it be great if that happened, remembered that Zack was the only one who knew who to sell their stuff to in Vegas.

Ahead, suddenly, the traffic began to back up. "Road Work 2 MI," a yellow sign said, half-covered in snow. Steve hit the flashers and pulled off at a turnaround.

"What the fuck?" Zack said, rolling down his window.

"It's not road work according to the Google app. It goes down to one lane, cops watching every vehicle as it passes."

"What the fuck? It can't be us…"

"I got a bad feeling."

"So now what?"

"On Google there's a back road, goes south up into the Uncompahgre Mountains then back down to 550 to Durango."

"There's too much snow up there, we can't get through."

"We both got all-wheel drive. If they plow those roads it'll get us through. At least we're avoiding the roadblock."

"No way."

"You want to get to Vegas and sell this shit? Or you want to be arrested on the way? I'm the one sitting in the car with all these kilos. The one facing life if I'm pulled over."

Zack looked past him up the mountain settling into darkness. It was severe and steep in last light, gleaming black cliffs, the road tracing a slim line up through tall conifers with deep snow between them. "What if those back roads are closed?"

"Map says the county plows them. On the satellite they're open."

"And you really think that traffic jam down there was for us?"

"I said it could be. And I can't take that chance."

"Relax." Zack felt a swelling optimism, a remembrance of friendship. "We're not getting arrested. We're going to sell this stuff in Vegas and be rich." *Like I already was,* he started to add. But didn't.

"THEY HAVE LEFT DENVER," María Christina told Diego. "Going back west."

"How you know this?" he said, as always stunned by what she could find out.

"DEA, they think it."

He tried to hold his bandaged hand in a less painful position. "How they know?"

"They picked up one rental car on a traffic light camera, a white Pathfinder with Colorado plates, I will give you the license. In a place called Fairplay."

"I know this Fairplay." The pain killers made his voice sound sleepy. "It is beyond the first mountains on a big valley that goes many miles south. Sometimes we have flown up that valley, below the ridges."

"You must always be careful, Diego. Not foolish."

This warmed his heart, what she said. "These guys, DEA is following them?"

"Of course. And we are following DEA."

"So I must be careful of them too?"

"You know that." She said nothing, then, "Whatever you do, get these guys and find our property before DEA does."

"These guys maybe are going back to Vegas."

"I think so too. Our friends say perhaps they have done a deal, that these two guys are going to sell our property."

He thought a moment. "Perhaps I should go straight to Vegas, wait for them?"

"We can't be sure they're going there. Why not go as far as Fairplay? What do you think?"

He felt a rush of pleasure she should ask. "I will drive to Fairplay. Looking everywhere for this white Pathfinder ... I will find them."

"Check motel parking lots at night. That's the best place."

"How beautiful that would be. To do it there."

"Not before you get back what is ours."

"After that," he said softly, cradling his hand. "After that."

She shut off. He called Curt. "Where you are, my friend?"

"I'm not your friend," Curt said. "And I wouldn't ever tell you where I am."

"Fine, fine, be like that. I am just letting you know, your two thieves, they are driving southwest on 285. Maybe you like me to help you find them?"

"Where are you?"

"*Why should I tell you where I am* – is not that what you just say to me?" He chuckled. "Don't worry, my friend. I am more honorable than you."

"Honor has nothing to do with it."

"Just joking, my friend. I am going southwest, Fairplay, maybe farther. You want to meet somewhere? Maybe together we find them."

"I'll think about it."

"Don't think too long. You could miss the fun."

How the World Works

"IF WE CAN'T get through this blizzard," Zack yelled into the wind, "we'll be up here all winter." He stared ahead of them up the steep narrow track sinuously ascending the near-vertical slope. The dusk had turned icy, their vehicles slithering, and finally Steve had pulled over.

"Like I said," Steve answered, "what if they're watching the main roads?"

"I think you're imagining things."

"You want to go back down? Okay, you drive the car with the cocaine. I hope you get caught."

Zack nodded at the cast on his arm, at the Eddie Bauer. "I'm not driving that piece of shit with a broken arm."

Steve nodded as if this were expected, that Zack would complain but not step up to the plate. "Okay then, I'll continue to drive the cocaine, though I'm injured too."

Zack gave a rasping laugh. "Poor baby."

Steve turned and trudged toward the Eddie Bauer. *Once I learn your contact in Vegas, I'm going to kill you*, he started to tell Zack but didn't. No use letting him know. Though, he thought ironically, he probably already does.

The blizzard had grown so thick that unless Zack drove right behind Steve he couldn't see him, just this wall of snow twisting and tumbling across his windshield, piling on the hood of the Pathfinder, obliterating his headlights.

He could not think, couldn't take his eyes one instant from the white tempest whirling across the road, tried to remember how they'd reached this point, couldn't concentrate on anything but how to stay on this treacherous path through cliffs of flailing white, trying to follow the tracks made by Steve's tires. But Steve's tire tracks were obliterated instantly by the wind.

COWBOY BOOTS UP on his DEA Denver desk, Duane McCord put himself in Zack's place. A football hero, smart enough to quit before your body's totally ruined, and now you're a TV star who fans trust because you not only talk the talk but you'd damned well walked the walk. Had survived thousands of high-speed collisions with other guys as hard and ruthless as you.

Duane's nephew Jason had played three years at Boise State as a second team wide receiver and kick returner, an incredibly tough, smart kid who could now barely walk and couldn't raise either hand above his shoulder. So for Zack to have been a linebacker through seven seasons in the gladiator arena of the NFL, in one of the most destructive positions in the game, he must have a physical and mental hardiness beyond belief. Like a guy who made a career of running into fast-moving locomotives and knocking them off the rails.

So how did this same guy end up on the wrong end of a ten-million coke deal? And why? Despite being a cop for many years Duane had an innate sense that most folks were good, we just had to weed out the bad. And Zack wasn't that bad.

Something felt out of place.

DEA had gone through everything: Zack's bank statements, his investment accounts with Steve Montclair – twelve million in bonds of some kind – all his emails, his phone, which was now curiously silent. And Whitney Castro had made fourteen calls to Zack's agent Rob O'Brien and his producer Benny Silva.

"Where the *fuck* is he?" Silva had fumed.

"Gee whiz, I'd like to know too," Whitney had murmured, voice low and dulcet. "I really *need* to interview him, for *Rolling Stone.*"

"*Rolling Stone?*" Duane had said when Whitney told him. "What the heck does Zack Wilson have to do with rock'n roll?"

"Oh it isn't *that*. He's dated some of the hottest vocalists in the industry. That was how *I* was going to get in. He's apparently rather special in bed..."

"Get in *where?*"

"Well, you know, find out if that's true."

"Just focus on finding this guy," he'd growled.

"What the Hell do you think I'm doing?"

It hurt, that she'd snapped at him. But she was the absolute and very best, and he loved her. "I believe in you," he said. "Like you're my own daughter. But sometimes you worry me, the risk." He cleared his throat.

What he meant, he realized, was that if Zack was going to be tracked down, Whitney would be the one to do it. Despite the risk.

And the worry was she didn't give a damn about risk.

He caught himself. His calves were numb from having his feet upon the desk. The air in the sealed office felt thin and dry, as in a prison. *Whatever you're doing,* the words came to him, *you're doing to yourself.*

He was getting a little old, that was true. Couldn't even keep up with his granddaughters at soccer, they dribbled the ball all around him, flicking it back and forth between their fast-moving feet quicker than he could see.

It reminded him of Cicero in his marble-palaced retirement on Capri: "Be sure that it is not you that is mortal, but only your body." Cicero had actually said that, the old fart. And it was the "Be sure" that counted. Telling us to mind our souls, lest they also rot.

Maybe, Duane McCord decided, Cicero had trouble keeping up with *his* granddaughters.

Just find Zack, he told himself. *The rest is horse hockey.*

"Check out all the Vegas hotels, he reminded Whitney, "see if he's reserved anywhere. Tell the local team be ready. We're going to take these guys down."

"THEY'RE GOING BACK to Vegas," María Christina said.

"You think this?" Diego said, astonished at his forwardness, "or you know?"

"I know what DEA *thinks.*"

"You trust them, *estas putas?*"

She brushed past this. "Don't worry, they're not on the good road."

"*La buena camina?*"

"They don't even know these guys are going to Vegas. And that they have what they stole from us … All DEA has is their *cartas de credito* and one license plate."

"Stupid fucks, anybody can get that. That is *all?*"

"I promise you."

"*Diablo* … Our friends in Las Vegas, they don't hear anything?"

"Not yet. They are asking. Soon or later, they'll know."

"So I go, straight, to Las Vegas?" Diego tried to imagine driving all that way with his damaged hand.

"Maybe not yet. Somehow I feel maybe you should stay *there*, where you are now. I don't understand this feeling but I have it. That you should stay *en la montaña.* If we can take them in these mountains, somewhere where nobody knows …"

"Before DEA gets there."

"So there is no trace."

He thought about this, if it would be difficult. "Yes."

"This Montana cowboy –"

"I am working him."

"Get him out of the way."

"No, María Christina –" Again astonished at his forwardness Diego pressed on, "he's the only one can identify these guys. Everybody else is working from pictures. Let's keep him *in* the loop. Let's *play* him."

"Use him." Her voice turned sharp. "Then kill him."

STEVE HARDENED his heart and added up the facts:

First, Zack had stolen their coke, was going to sell it to his pals in Vegas and keep all the money. So he'd want to kill Steve to avoid sharing it, to cover his theft.

Second, Zack thought that he, Steve, had caused the Mexican to kill Emily. Zack had even said he would kill him just for that. Zack didn't understand that he himself had led the Mexican to them by hustling their coke all over Vegas. That he had brought her to Vegas. That *he* had killed Emily.

Third, Zack also blamed Steve for losing the auction rate securities. *I did my best*, Steve told himself. It was Citigroup who stole them. It was Wall Street, who owns us all. I was trying to do good by him. But now he wants to kill me for that too.

So three good reasons he wants to kill me.

The question is when. He could kill me now, sell the coke and get away with it all. So why hasn't he killed me yet? He tried to push me over the cliff, choked me. Why not do it now? No reason for him to keep me alive, so many reasons not to.

Steve thought of the night he'd gone down to Fountain, the woman Emerald. He'd got knocked out by that drink, found himself naked and freezing in a field, was lucky to find the car keys, get home alive. And when he'd tried to find them the trail went nowhere.

And he'd lost twenty kilos. For that too Zack might kill him.

This life he was living, Steve had long ago understood, was a desert without end. But there hadn't been an escape, a way out. Now if he had all the coke money he'd buy a sailboat or a farm somewhere, get the kids out of that PC Manhattan school, bail out of that social-climbing apartment on the upper East Side, rescue Marcie from denigrating herself with the pretenders wanting to buy a hole in a cliff in Manhattan and thinking *that* made them special. Break himself free of the endless indenture of Wall Street, the treadmill, sucking the never-satisfying tit of money.

What about Montana – moving there? What would he do?

It would be good for the kids. The real world.

What if he went on real runs, in the countryside, instead of on a treadmill?

"SO WHAT YOU GOT?" Kenny Stauffenberg said.

"I wish I knew," Duane McCord said.

"That's a pretty sad statement for someone in your position."

"For amateurs these guys are good. We can't find them past Poncha Springs, where they got gas at a place called Western Convenience. The sale was for a hundred and ten bucks, so they ran one card for both tanks. And they bought a shovel."

"A shovel?"

"And a tow chain...Like maybe they planned to be driving in snow..."

"That could be anywhere."

"We found where they had the coke stashed."

"Where's that?"

"But we can't find traces."

"I said, where's that?"

"Highlands Ranch."

"Weird." The one time Kenny had seen it, it had seemed an endless convolution of cookie cutter houses, malls and roadways. *Someday these things*, he'd thought, *are going to cover the world.*

"You been talking to your cousin?"

"Curt? That's my wife's cousin."

"You Montanans are thick as damn thieves."

"That's how we've survived. And why Montana doesn't look like Colorado." Kenny cleared his throat, an announcement of serious things to come. "We need you guys to be open with us. We want these two dudes, make it a Montana thing. They broke the law in Montana, damn it. We want to prosecute them here."

"You find them," Duane said after a moment, "and they're yours. We find them, they're ours."

"And on that basis you actually want me to *share* information with you?"

"We already know what you know."

"What's our final goal here, you and me? For our nation? For America?"

"To catch these scumbags?"

"So let's work together. All the way. And if it turns out we've both helped, we do a joint announcement?"

"Yeah, right."

"What if democracy actually does work? Wouldn't that be great?"

"You guys've been living too long up there in the woods," Duane McCord said. "You don't have the faintest idea how the world works."

BULLETPROOF

"**Y**OU SURE can pick a road." Zack stared up at the trees like thousands of black spears high above the narrow snow-deep canyon. He paced the road a few feet, shaking snow off his boots and trying to see over the head-high wall of plowed drifts on both sides.

"So we spend the night up here? So what?" Steve brushed snow off his shoulders. "How many nights we've slept in a tent at thirty below?"

"You think I'm a pussy?"

Steve snickered. "Keep your eyes on the ball, Zack. We're going to make nine million dollars –"

"Not really. Not with the twenty kilos you lost and all the kilos we left behind when the Mexican chased us in the snowmobile."

"We still don't know if it's the same guy... why would it be? And maybe your auction rate securities could come back. I asked the New York Attorney General to join my civil suit against the banks, Merrill Lynch, Citigroup, Swiss Bank, all those thieves who promised these damn instruments were cash-equivalent when they sold them to us."

"When they sold them to you."

"And now they're trying to cover their balance sheet by telling us *fuck off, you gave us your money you stupid shits, so it's our good luck and your bad. Take your vanished life savings and your empty retirement fund and shove them up your middle class ass.*" Steve looked away, surprised, after this, to see it so clearly.

Zack felt sudden comprehension, near compassion. That Steve had gotten screwed too. They'd both been screwed by Wall Street, by the same crooks. Steve was in pain, you could see it. And he, Zack, had been so tied up in his own pain he hadn't noticed.

Hadn't cared. Angry, sarcastic, trying to hurt Steve for losing the money. For his broken arm. When Steve was already hurting. And had a wife and kids to protect.

"You're right," he said, "that we've been going down the wrong road here." He saw Emily bleeding in the bathtub, heard her body clatter down the cliff. "This is a horror show, let's get ourselves out."

Emily's voice came back to him: *Just get this done.*

"We have to take care of each other," Steve said. "No more war."

"GO TO DURANGO," María Christina said. "They are coming there."

"I am almost there … it is hard, with this snow."

"The snow is bad for them too."

"There was a roadblock, on the road south from Montrose."

"They didn't say this, DEA."

"They don't tell you everything?" Diego was again shocked by his forwardness. But then again, this woman, some day she could be his.

She laughed. A subtle laugh, but he caught it. "When you get to Durango," she said in her throaty voice, "let me know. If necessary you must be ready to drive back north, meet them somewhere."

"A side road. Somewhere quiet."

"As you wish."

WIND HOWLED through the black conifers on the cliffs above. Snowdrifts scurried up the road at them, biting their faces. "The really sad thing," Steve added, "is you don't need me but I need you."

"After what we've just said," Zack stared at him, blinking at the snow, "you still think I'd cheat you?"

"We've been through the wars together, you and me, how many years?"

Zack felt a flush of warmth. "Since I hit the NFL."

Steve gave him a sudden sharp hug. "You sure hit it."

The thought gave Zack a feeling of onrushing gratitude. For what Steve had done for him. "We're back in the old days. I will look after you and protect you. Whatever it takes." He clenched Steve's hand, hard. "Back to brothers." Unexpected emotion warmed him. "Brother to brother."

"Brother to brother. We're going to make this work. In the morning we're getting the fuck out of here, down to the main roads if we have to. To Vegas to sell this shit."

"We should sleep in the same vehicle," Zack said. "Conserve the heat."

"You think I want to smell your farts all night?" Steve slapped Zack's good shoulder. "Good night, brother," and turned to the Eddie Bauer, its unlock lights flashing across the frozen landscape like in a technicolor movie.

Entombed in the Pathfinder Zack worried that Steve could come up in the darkness and shoot him. So he kept Curt's Ruger right by his side, good hand over the action. But that wasn't enough, if he fell asleep. He couldn't figure what to do about it except stay awake all night watching for Steve's shadow to creep toward him across the moonlit snow, gun in hand.

Despite all they'd said.

He rolled around in the sleeping bag to face toward the Eddie Bauer, keeping the Ruger in his good hand. He'd be shooting through glass, and Steve too. But glass was more deflective shooting out than in, at the distance of one foot rather than three. He should keep a window open, to avoid distorting the shot. Perhaps the only shot he'd have.

And with the window open, freeze to death?

When he looked back over the recent past, Zack could see that everything that had gone wrong was due to Steve.

So why was he willing to be friends again? To split the stuff? When he, Zack, had worked hardest for it? When he'd found the buyer? When he was the one paying the dues?

Every time Zack tried to push it out of his mind, the Mexican, the silenced gun, the bullet, Emily. Steve's shot that smashed the gun from the Mexican's hand, Emily bloody in the tub, in the mattress cover, in the back of the Eddie Bauer, the clatter of her naked body down the cliff.

It was worth killing Steve, just for that.

But hadn't they been friends? What if Steve *meant* what he said?

IN THE BITTER blackness of the Eddie Bauer, Steve too was thinking of Emily. Hunched and shivering in his sleeping bag, stocking hat over his ears, the frozen Beretta numbing his fingers, he kept trying to remember exactly where on Virgin River he'd pushed her over, how far she would have fallen, and would anybody ever be likely to wander through the rubble at the bottom of that cliff?

And if they did, what were the chances they might find her?

Could she be ID'd?

Yes.

Could they trace her death back to him?

Soon Wally would be back at their house in Aspen. Zack didn't know what she'd told Wally when she'd left – a message, email? A note, taped to the reefer? With Emily you never knew. But Wally was used to it: according to Zack she was always trolling Travelocity and Orbitz for last-minute deals, would head to St. Kitts or Kauai or Lisbon at the drop of a ticket price, particularly if Wally wasn't there.

But Wally would be calling her, going to voice mail. By now he might have called the police and who knows who else?

What if Emily's last email or note said, "Off to Vegas with Zack Wilson"?

"I FOUND THEIR MOTEL," Whitney said.

Duane pushed himself up in bed. "Where?"

"Denver. We thought they were in the area, so I figured they'd find a motel someplace, wouldn't stay with anyone – from what I can tell on LinkedIn, Facebook, all that stuff, they don't know anybody there."

"Good work."

"What, did I wake you? You asleep already?"

"No, I was reading the paper."

"Heck, Duane, it's not even *midnight!*"

"So which motel?"

"I had our people call all the motels in the Denver area, just point out it was DEA calling, wanted to know if either of these guys had checked in, because even if they pay cash they have to show ID...And the motels who didn't want to come across we told them *Okay we'll get a warrant and turn your place upside down,* and right away they got nice."

"Whitney, you can't *do* things like that."

"Okay I won't. So they were at the Everglade Motel, a trashy place off Santa Fe. They never checked out but were gone when the manager came to clean the unit. And guess what?"

"I don't dare."

"We have a second license plate. Every night the manager goes checks off the plates against what the guests have written on the card, to make sure she's not got any non-paying clients. It's a Ford Expedition, Eddie Bauer model, Colorado plate MOU 269."

"Heck, Whitney, that's great work. And you have the rental car?"

"The Pathfinder Zack rented from Avis, with his 'Pigskin Events' credit card? Yeah it was there too."

"And now they're on their way from Montrose to Durango –"

"And one of them, the manager didn't know who was who, has his right arm in a cast."

"Nice. I hope it hurts."

"I finally got Colorado State Patrol to set up an overlook on 550 today but these guys didn't come through."

"Maybe they went a different way?"

"Maybe. Or maybe they just haven't got there yet."

"Is the overlook still up?"

"Damn right...Though the troopers are a little pissed, out there at ten thousand feet and twenty below."

"But maybe so are your bad guys."

ZACK GRABBED the phone. "Hey you," Monica said.

"Yeah, you," he answered, their old drill. He tried to see his watch, glanced out the Pathfinder's windows at the frigid night. "What time is it?"

"Eleven-thirty your time. I just got off shift."

"I was going to call you..."

"Benny Silva keeps leaving messages, he's real mad, wants to know why you're not back. Can you get him off my neck? I've got so many damn calls about people lingering between life and death –"

In the background he could hear hospital loudspeakers and the hiss of poor reception. "I'm sorry, Monica. I'll call him in the morning."

"And this guy O'Brien...Rob O'Brien – did you give these guys my number?"

"Of course not." He felt himself toughen. "I would never do that. I treasure you –"

"Where the hell are you?"

"I wish I knew."

"No, *really* –"

"You can't tell anybody –"

"Why not? What's going on?"

"I'm in Colorado."

"Why? What the *fuck* why?"

"Look, why'd you call? Just to give me shit?"

"I called because I need to know what you feel about me."

"Christ, how do I know, Monica? I love the Hell out of you – is that enough? There isn't a day, an hour, I don't think of you. I've made love with thousands of women but who I want to make love most with is you –"

She snickered. "Cut that stupid shit."

"It isn't stupid. I'm on the edge, wish I could tell you...I may be lost. With no way out."

"Never that is true. Not you."

"I'm not as bulletproof as you think."

"Nobody's bulletproof. You come to LA General, I'll show you. But you're tough, Zack, nobody ever takes you down."

"Look, I'm all fucked up."

"Let me go outside, I can't hear you." The sound of her breathing into the phone as she walked to an exit, the PA announcements, clatter of feet and voices, the hiss of doors. "I was on call and had to come in because of a three-car accident. Horrible. Even for me it was horrible."

"I'm sorry. I'm sorry for every bad instant that happens to you. I would fight them with my life if I could."

"Thank God you can't."

He laughed softly. "I miss you so much."

"So get back here. That's what I wanted to tell you –"

"I'm coming."

"– that I'm pregnant. Do you want me to kill our child?"

"Jesus, Monica."

"Or do you want to come home and be a Dad?"

"WE CAN'T MAKE THE MORTGAGE," Marcie said.

When Steve had seen it was her number he'd almost not answered, fearing bad news. "We'll get an equity loan."

"We already did, remember? It's maxed."

"Call Malcolm."

"I have. He says nothing more."

"Sell the Benz."

"I did."

"Oh shit." How could he live without it? "How much?"

"Seventy-nine grand."

"*Jesus* Marcie! You got robbed."

"It's what I got. To pay the extra taxes on your last year's income. Before we get fined."

"You don't have any more commissions coming in –"

"You know I don't."

"Fuck, Marcie," he felt like crying, "what are we going to do?"

"This deal," she said, "where you were going to buy a boat?"

"Yeah –"

"How's it going?"

"It might happen."

"Make it work. It's all we have."

BAD DREAM

"I'LL MEET YOU IN RIDGWAY," Curt told Diego. "Just say where."

"The Cimarron Café. Right off the highway, middle of town. What time you be there?"

"I'm just south of Montrose now."

"So you can be here maybe seven-thirty. We have a little breakfast, talk things over?"

"WE'RE GETTING CLOSER," Whitney Castro said.

"Where are you now?" Duane said.

"Montrose."

"Ranch country."

"Man, they don't like black girls out here."

"Tough shit. What you got?"

"Hendersons Country Diner, south end of town, right hand side, the west side ... Place got held up last January seven. Nasty situation, two gunmen, they took a hostage for an hour. Finally surrendered, got thirty to life in Cañon City."

"They'll be out in five."

"So the Diner put in full surveillance, cameras on every angle and on poles in the parking lot, every space covered. And guess what showed up?"

"Enlighten me."

"Steve's Eddie Bauer. And what pulls into the next slot? Zack in his Pathfinder. So we've got them both, in two cars. And I swear they're headed back to Vegas. From Montrose down to Durango and west."

"So the question is where to stop them."

"We wait till they're out of state, most likely into New Mexico headed to Farmington and I-40. Or 160 into Utah. Either way we grab them for interstate transport as well as possession and lots of other stuff plus we get that cocaine. And get two and a half stars on our homework and a pat on the head from the teacher."

"Now Whitney –"

"Or we wait till they get to Vegas and catch who they're selling to and make a big splash that way."

"We could lose them in Vegas. Or before."

"That's the risk."

"No way to put a tag on them ..."

"Not till we have physical contact."

"Which you've been thinking about."

"We know they passed through Montrose yesterday after they left Denver. We have the road overlook plus we can put cameras on 550 just north of Durango. The moment one of those plates shows up we tail them. Sooner or later they'll stop, we tag them and decide where to take them, and when."

"What if they take the back way, Route 145 past Telluride down to Cortez?"

"Same deal. We got them covered coming into Cortez."

"Okay, do it both ways. And any other way you can think of."

"We'll get them," she said, and shut off.

ZACK PACED the squeaky snow, waiting for Steve to be ready. The air stung his lungs like fire and burned his cheeks and coated them in frozen breath. His hands numb even in his parka pockets, his broken arm aching with the subzero chill.

"Do you want to kill our child?" she'd said.

"Or come home and be a Dad?"

The sky had lightened to pale aqua above the spiring firs that grew so thick it felt like being in a trench of darkness, with far above a slit of icy light.

As he paced the Ruger was loose in his jacket pocket, quick to grab. Off safety. That was dangerous, but if shit came down he'd never have time to thumb it off. It felt reassuring against his lower ribs, right side.

Solid and good.

It was better to split nine million and have both of them still alive, than for either to have it all plus another murder waiting to be found.

The problem was Steve might kill him anyway, no matter what he'd said about being brothers and all that. Then Steve would turn around and drive the stuff to New York and sell it, the deal he'd already worked on.

All he had to do was find a place to bury Zack.

And the nine million would be all his.

"Hey!"

Zack spun grabbing for the Ruger then saw it was Steve getting out of the Eddie Bauer and shuffling on his parka. Steve waved and went to the roadside and pissed a yellow hole in the ploughed-back snow, grabbed more snow in both hands and rubbed it over his face and wiped it on the sleeve of his parka.

"So are you ready," Zack called, "to admit coming up here was stupid?"

"It was very stupid." Steve shrugged. "Sorry."

Zack softened, hadn't expected this, it wasn't like Steve. But maybe he was faking? "So where we going instead? You really feel we're being tracked? How do they know fuck-all about us?"

"The credit cards, the car rentals, the other stuff. Eventually they catch up. So we have to sell these kilos fast, before we get caught."

Zack's phone buzzed. "We've got to get out of here," he said, snatching the phone, "before it snows more." He held the phone to his ear. "Hey, Benny, I've been meaning to call you."

"Fuck you have," Benny said. "You've been ducking me for days. So I have just one thing to tell you: You're done."

"What the fuck you mean, *done?*"

"Fired, *kaputt, sayonara, ciao,* you name it. We brought Quinn Stonebraker in last night, he's going to do the Packers game in your place. Young, articulate, responsible. Committed. Does his background work. And that former quarterback status is still a big draw. He's the new you…"

"Fuck you Benny. I'll jump to another network, blow your numbers out of the water."

"No you won't Zack. It's in the non-compete. Two years before you can do a thing. You try and we'll sue your ass off."

"Jesus! Why are you being such a jerk? We've worked well together, you and me."

"We couriered the original docs to Rob an hour ago. He'll no doubt be in touch."

"I'll find a way," Zack said, "to beat you." But Benny had gone.

"HERE IS THE DEAL," Diego said, leaning across the table in the Cimarron Café in Ridgway. "This material –"

"Your cocaine." Curt said. "Or are you still pretending to be Paco, from Denver PD?"

"– it's worth money to us."

"About ten million, apparently."

Diego hunched his shoulders – *maybe.* "Perhaps not that much." He opened his good hand palm up: *who's to know?* As if the money were not significant, and only the justice of the thing mattered. "We want it back."

"I would too, if I were in your shoes. Thank God I'm not."

"Why is that, Mr. Weathers?" Diego looked surprised, mildly offended.

"This cocaine," he said, "I looked it up. It hurts people, makes them addicts, ruins their families, causes robberies and killings in America and hideous wars and widespread murders in Mexico and elsewhere." He looked at Diego, cocked his head. "You're evil, *Mr. Whatever You Say You Are.* You're a worldwide plague."

Diego shook his head: *you don't understand.* "The dangers, the drug wars, is only because *you* make it illegal. Most people, they *want* cocaine. They like it. It does them good. Makes them powerful and happy –"

"And lets them down afterwards. Makes them want more."

Diego opened his palm – *so what?* "What if a low steady use of cocaine makes us smarter? Better able to think new things? This cellphone, these emails, *hombre*, these computers and internet coming through the air at us – is *all* from cocaine. You *know* this. Everybody *knows* this. Is no secret. This technology we are slaves to was *built* on cocaine. Like in television, cinema, sports – is *all* on cocaine."

Curt sat back, chewed his toothpick and stuck it behind his ear. "So what you want from me?"

"I need you help find these guys." Diego looked at him earnestly. "To *talk* to them, tell them they cannot get away with this material. That it belongs someone else. So then no blood, they give back material and go home." He spread his hands. "All forgiven. Bad dream. No more trouble for anybody."

Curt smiled. "And for all this, what do I get?"

The upraised palm: who's to say? "Tell you what, you help me trap these guys, get them to give up my material. Tell them I give them two hundred thousand. *Dollars.*" He raised his hand as if mollifying an objection yet to come. "Some of that you keep."

"That's crazy."

"For us to pay that is cheaper than buying the stuff all over again. And it keeps things quiet – no?"

"I don't believe you."

"I have it already. Cash."

"Where?"

"I know about your problems, the windmills up in Judith Basin. You help me, I help you."

STEVE SHOVELED two tracks for the cars to follow all the way to the top of the saddle where the snow grew thinner because of the wind. From there the universe stretched untouched in all dimensions, white and dark green horizons, the dark blue sky unending.

Going downhill was easier because of the weight of the vehicles pushing forward through the drifts; then the Pathfinder slid off the road and it took a half hour for the Eddie Bauer to tow it out.

"You could've left me, back there," Zack said, wiping his good hand on his jeans.

"What good would that do me?" Steve laughed. "I don't know your Vegas contact."

"You could still turn round, head for New York City. With all this coke."

"We're done with that, remember." Steve held out the coke vial. "We work together."

"I know." Zack took a hit. "Just kidding."

Steve climbed back into the Eddie Bauer. "Don't do that. Not anymore."

"THIS STUPID INDIAN," María Christina said, "what he gets, is dead. In the desert somewhere."

"There's lots of that," Diego said, "out here."

"He's in our way. He is importunate, wants something for nothing. Our property was *never* his but now he wants part of it. It's not our fault these guys stole his truck. He annoys me, this guy."

"He wants to go home, see his wife." Again Diego was astounded how frankly he spoke to María Christina. "Perhaps we just let him?"

"He knows too much. He can ID you."

"He is a stupid cowboy. He will forget me." In his mind Diego saw Curt's canny eyes on his, that Curt forgot nothing. "He doesn't know anything."

"That changes nothing."

"Okay," he sighed, feeling estranged, empty, thought of his injured hand. "So how do I do it?"

"That's your end of the game. Just get it done."

WE CAN FIX THIS

"**F**OUND THEM!" Whitney said. "We got ten seconds of real-time satpix before the clouds closed in again. Their two vehicles on a logging road west of 550, about nine thousand feet, stopped maybe due to snow, can't tell."

Duane scratched the back of his neck where it suddenly itched. "So go get them."

"Can't. Snowing hard again, the choppers can't get near it."

"So?"

"So we block the roads below and when they come down we have them."

"Or if the clouds clear –"

"Of course. But choppers are expensive, and La Plata County only has two."

Duane thought a moment. "No way to get ours out there, in time."

"No way."

"So send some guys up there on snowmobiles."

"Guys? No way, I want this done right. Soon as the Sheriff shows up with the machines, *I'm* going up there."

"Be careful, Whitney," Duane said, suddenly terrified of losing her. "Whatever you do."

"HERE IS THEIR GPS." María Christina read it to him, one digit at a time. "This is where DEA last saw them, from a satellite. It is snowing there now?"

"It's snowing, very hard."

"They are stuck, then. Good."

"So DEA knows this too?"

"They think maybe these guys have moved on ... You should go up and see."

The idea excited him. To risk this for Maria Christina.

"I am sending three friends to help you," she said. "Tranquilo and two others."

"Friends? I don't need friends." How could he explain his devotion? "I do this myself."

She had gone.

He called Curt.

"How you know all this?" Curt said. "How do I know it's true?"

"It is true. You come with me, I get you a snowmobile. Together we go up the mountain. We find these guys, you tell them give back our material, I let them go, and you and they have the two hundred thousand dollars." Diego glanced at Curt's Taurus that DEA had rented him at Hertz. "Anyway, that car not get you up the mountain. So you leave it here, come with me."

They stopped at a hack shop in Telluride where Diego rented two Ski-Doos and a twin trailer and hitched them to the back of his Range Rover. He and Curt drove south on 550 looking for a logging road on the right, 4.2 miles south of Silverton.

As he drove, Diego glanced across at Curt. Not a bad guy, really. We Mexicans, weren't we Indians too, once? But María Christina wanted him dead. A shame. Though up here was certainly the best place to do it.

"WE HAVE TO LEAVE IT." Steve stared down at the Eddie Bauer's wheels buried in frozen slush.

"Keep digging."

Steve checked his torn gloves, blood showing through. "We're going to have to transfer it all. To your car." He glanced over the cliff below, eerie and bewitching. "No room to go around, have to be careful."

"Dig some more."

Steve glanced at him. "Maybe *you* could. Here –" he handed Zack the shovel. "Try it."

One-handed there was no way Zack could shovel. Even to hold the shovel shot pain up his injured arm. "I can't."

"We're standing on the edge of a miracle," Steve said. "Let's get it done." He opened the back of the Eddie Bauer, took an armload of kilos and trudged toward the Pathfinder.

It was snowing harder, fat flakes skidding down on the wind, then smaller hard ones, falling fast. So fast it filled their tracks as they went back and forth between the Eddie Bauer and the Pathfinder, and when the Pathfinder was full the two hundred added kilos made it too heavy to go uphill in the deepening snow. The tires howled and smoked but it would go no further.

Sucking in the thin air, Zack scanned the road ahead, which forked in maybe three hundred yards, one fork turning downhill around the bend of a steep slope, the other heading uphill through tall firs and spruce toward a distant log barn with a cliff behind it. "If we can shovel three hundred yards to the fork," he added, "maybe one of the two roads is passable?"

"If the road goes up to that barn, maybe there's a way through," Steve panted. "I'll check that way. You go the other."

"What's that?" Zack raised his good hand, listening.

A distant snarl, an engine. Vanished then back again.

"Snowmobile," Steve said.

"Coming this way."

"How many?"

"Just one. No, *two* snowmobiles."

"Fuck, he's got help. Could be four guys. With guns."

"Let's get out of here."

"Not without our stuff."

Zack looked at him quizzically. "We run, we live. We stay, we die."

Steve shouldered his Winchester. "Not so sure."

All grew silent. No sound of engines, nothing but the north wind through the trees, moaning softly.

STEVE CLIMBED uphill through the deep drifts and fir trees with boughs bent down by snow. The firs looked black against the white ground. The Winchester felt heavy; its sling bit into his shoulder. The cold ate through his jacket into his arms. His cheeks were numb, coated with frozen breath. If he closed his eyes the lids stuck together; he had to reach up aching fingers to pull them apart.

He was breathing hard and the cold cut into his lungs. He feared the snowmobilers would hear him. Whoever they were. If they were there at all.

Could've been imaginary. Or just somebody going somewhere.

A burst of late sunlight slid across the wind-driven snow and up the treetops swaying in the wind, flamed the undersides of the clouds sliding in a sullen near-black rumble from north to south. Frozen chunks scurried across the crust, the snow-deep slope crunched and the ice below it cracked and the wind howled down it.

Get this done, Steve reminded himself, *and the future is good.* Most people quit when they're ninety-seven percent of the way there. He and Zack just had to get their shipment to Vegas and sell it, and he'd be free...all the fears and miseries of the past months would be over, they'd have life again the way they used to.

Except for Emily.

As long as Zack didn't stiff him. Or kill him.

If he was Zack, would he do it?

No, the answer came right away. We need each other. In the end we'll need each other.

To substantiate, to back up each other's stories.

To show we're not dead, because if one of us is, the other probably did it.

But if we do this right they'll never catch us.

He felt a surge of optimism, took a deep breath.

ZACK TOOK HIS RIFLE and the Ruger and followed the lower road downhill and around the bend. It undulated ahead of him along the side of the mountain, in and out of the trees. Here the snow was less deep; if they could shovel the three hundred yards to the fork they could drive out of here.

His phone buzzed, a Vegas number. "Where the fuck are you?" Haney the Rat said.

"On schedule," Zack whispered. "Don't worry."

"*What?* I can't hear you!"

"I'll be there."

"*When?*"

"Tomorrow night maybe. More likely Friday."

"Where the fuck *are* you?"

"Gotta go. Keep you posted."

Zack shut off the phone, stared at the snow-blanketed trees, the wide valley deep in drifts, the road snakelike across the mountain in late afternoon light. He sniffed the fragrant frozen air. How it bit into your lungs. Like magic.

Despite all, they were going to win.

Despite all.

DIEGO STOPPED his Ski-Doo at the top of a hill and crawled through a grove of pines to the edge. With the scope of his Remington he scanned the road ahead. For several miles it undulated over the western ridges. And maybe four miles away the dots of two vehicles, blurry in the telescopic sight.

He slid through the boughs back to Curt. "Two cars. They are stuck. One guy is walking uphill, toward a barn. The other, he is going downhill, around the curve."

Curt crawled forward, tipping his hat under the boughs, came back. "It's them."

"So call them. Tell them I will give them money. Two hundred thousand dollars, to leave my stuff in one car and drive away in the other."

"What I don't understand is why would you do that?"

"Because they have guns and somebody is going get shot. It might even be me, and I don't like being shot. And what can I do?"

he raised his voice, "one-handed? Most likely it's them who gets shot, but then I got a murder rap on me, maybe two murders. What's the benefit to that?"

"This money, how would you give it to them?"

"It's in my Range Rover, *hombre*. I drive to them, they put my material in the Range Rover, I give them the money. Easy."

Curt shrugged. "I'll try, but they never answer." He dialed Steve, then Zack. "It's like I said…" He glanced at his screen. "Battery's going dead."

"You should go," Diego nodded his jaw at the road, where the guys were. "Talk to them."

"What's to keep you from killing them anyway. And me too?"

Diego looked at him. "I work by principles, amigo. You have helped me so I owe you. I am responsible for your well-being. I like you, I would not hurt you. So I am happy to give you and them the two hundred thousand as soon as they agree."

"Where is it?"

"In my Range Rover, like I say. Under the back seat, in a blue toolbox. There are no tools inside. Just the money."

Curt stepped back, the better to see Diego. "I don't want those men killed. Just take your damn cocaine and get out of here. Then I call my wife's cousin Kenny. He brings in the DEA and these guys go down."

"That road leads back to me –"

"Not at all. I don't know you, they don't know you. Nobody does. No need to kill anybody. And the sooner you go, the safer you are."

"So you'd do this, keep me safe?"

"Like you say to me: *I'm not like you.*"

Diego snickered and drove his Ski-Doo one-handed from the road into the trees and up the side of the mountain. Curt waited till the sound had lessened, then called Whitney.

"Where are you?" he said.

"Bottom of the hill. Waiting for the La Plata County snowmobiles."

"Your two guys are up ahead, stuck. The Mexican is going uphill on a snowmobile. He says he has two hundred grand for them, if they give him the cocaine. I don't believe him, I'm trying to get him not to kill them…"

"Stay out of it, Curt. For your sake."

"How come he always knows what you're up to?"

ZACK'S PHONE BUZZED, an 888 number. He let it go to mail then listened:

"Mr. Wilson this is Sergeant Landes with the Colorado State Patrol –"

He killed the message. Five minutes later it rang again, Monica.

"Zack? Is that you? I've been leaving messages –"

"Christ, everything's gone wrong –"

"Why won't you talk to me?"

"I am talking to you –"

"Please, baby, please come home –"

He saw Emily dead and bleeding in the tub. "Jesus, Monica, I don't even know where anything is. Not anymore."

"Just come home, baby. We can fix this."

DIEGO CUT his Ski-Doo engine, shouldered the Remington and climbed the hill through the trees to where he could see the road ahead and below him. On it were the two vehicles and two sets of footprints going from them toward the fork in the road, one set vanishing downhill around a bend, the other rising into the forest toward a granite ridge with a log barn and a cliff behind it.

He scoped the two cars. One, the Ford Explorer, seemed deeply stuck. The other, a white Pathfinder, sat crosswise in the road, as if unable to go further.

All he had to do was drive his Ski-Doo to the two cars, take the one with his cocaine and leave. But both vehicles were stuck. How could he dig it out one-handed? What if he couldn't hot wire it? What if there was cocaine in both cars? If they had alarms that would go off when he broke in? How far away were the guys? Did they have rifles? Pistols?

Were they waiting for him?

He should go get the Range Rover. But then he might lose them.

He thought of María Christina – what would she want him to do?

On the uphill road a tiny figure appeared, moving slowly, leaning against the slope. "You, *hijo de puta*, you stole our stuff," he whispered, and scoped him.

It was a guy in a black parka with a rifle over one shoulder, following the fork in the road uphill toward the log barn with the cliff behind it. Diego sat and watched the distant figure work its way upslope. The problem was that if he shot this one the other one would know he was here. Better to get close and kill him with the knife, but that involved senseless risk and delay.

Knock off the first one and the odds go from 2:1 to 1:1.

But there was still the problem of Curt. How to kill him too. As María Christina had ordered.

He slid the Remington's sling tight around his left arm, set the scope at eight hundred yards and waited, damaged finger atop the trigger guard.

DIE OF FEAR

WHEN ZACK'S PHONE rang again he hoped it was Monica because things had gone bad so fast and maybe she could help find a way through this.

"Zack," the woman's voice said. "It's Whitney Castro, with DEA. How you doing, honey?"

He should kill the call but didn't, bewitched by this sedulous velvet-voiced young woman with the girlish African-American accent so rough yet seductive. As if she were someone he'd *like*. And to speak straight with her, tell her the truth, would unburden his sins.

"I'm doing fine," he said. "What you want?" Wondering how the fuck she got his number. Of course, from Curt.

A trap was closing. He couldn't stop it.

"We know where you are," she said. "And what you've done. But I think we can find a way out of this –"

"So where am I?"

"– and we know all about the kilos of coke, your busted TV contract –"

"So where *am* I?"

"Listen, honey, we *need* you. We want you *out* of there. For years we've tried to take down María Christina and El Trapero and their whole machine. Your evidence can help bring them to justice. You testify for us, and we'll forget your peccadillos."

"How?"

"Easy in these digital days. We change history."

"And Steve's too?"

"Same deal. He talks, he walks."

"I'm trying to reach him but can't get through."

"Service is terrible up there. We're on our way."

"*Where* are you now? Since you're not here?"

"Stay with us, Zack. We can put this all to rest."

"How come the Mexican knew where we were, before you did?" But she'd shut down; the phone buzzed stupidly. He stood on a rock and tried to call back but it wouldn't go through.

"Fuck you, DEA girl," he said to the cold sky, the dying sun. "You sexy hot horny Mama. To Hell with you."

CURT DUSTED SNOW off the blowdown where he'd been sitting, slapped snow off his butt and sat again. In no time at all he'd help Whitney wrap this up, make sure where the credit and the blame went, and get home.

And his two dudes and this shitty little Mexican would all end up in jail.

And that, he thought, would pretty well prove the existence of God. Or at least of an avenging angel.

He rubbed his whiskery jaw with a cold-hardened hand, shook knee-deep snow from his leg. Snow that gives life. Killing the weak to give space to the new. So that selection of the fittest works even faster.

Selection of the fittest for what?

Oh fuck I can't figure that. Wish I could. That we all could.

He walked back to his Ski-Doo, stopped. Now what could he do? He'd gotten in over his head. Should've let it go in Montana, how many days ago? A previous life.

If he tried to warn Steve and Zack, the Mexican might shoot him. But he had to try.

How strange that even when you don't want to shoot anybody, people still want to shoot you.

"I DON'T EVEN understand why you like me," Zack said.

"I don't *like* you," Monica said. "I love you."

He tucked his injured arm closer to his ribs, but the cold still ate into it. "But *why*?"

"You're a remarkable person. You're kind, you're forgiving. Though you're strong you're gentle to those less strong than you. You're a very fine man."

"Jesus, Monica." He'd never thought of it like that. It had always been about being tougher than anyone else. About never losing. Not about kindness. Maybe that was why he loved her, confused as it made him. Because of what she saw in him? Was he really that good?

And the reason he wouldn't commit to her is because *he* didn't think he was that good? That she was a fool for believing in him?

And she an ER doc. Who makes fast decisions about life and death. When the ambulances arrive with smashed and riddled people she's the one who decides who lives and who dies.

And she wanted him to live.

Wind whispered snow grains across the frozen crust. He imagined the universe like this, endless planets driven across eternities by black holes. Infinite cold, and infinite masses of nuclear fire. Where did it all come from?

Why?

STEVE REACHED the granite crest and stopped to catch his breath and check out the little valley leading to the log barn. If they were to drive carefully up this road they could make it, and perhaps beyond the barn the road would descend and the driving be easier.

But they had to move fast, the sun was setting in a vast orange glow over the white western slopes; soon would be another frigid night.

He dialed home. "Dad!" Jason said. "Mom! Susanna! It's Dad!"

"Hey, handsome."

"You coming home?"

"Soon. Can I talk to your Mom?"

"Where are you?" she said when she came on. "Where *are* you?"

He was going to tell her then feared the DEA was listening. "I'm working on that boat." He smiled, thinking *that will throw them.* "Could be done in a day or so."

"Susanna's already aboard. Says she's going to take seasickness pills."

"Tell her I love her." Why was he saying this, as if he'd never see her again? See any of them? "I love you all..." tried not to choke up. "Be home soon."

As he pocketed the phone a horrible hot steel rod smashed through his thigh knocking him down thrashing in agony. His leg was crushed, spraying blood that he tried to stop by gripping the wrecked femur, bone chips washing through his fingers.

"Oh Jesus I'm going to die," he cried, didn't know what had done this – a bullet?

Yes a bullet. He squirmed to safety in the scrub, yanked off his kerchief and wrapped the wound, found a stick and shoved it through the kerchief and twisted it tighter.

He couldn't find the Winchester; it must have fallen somewhere. He tugged the Beretta from his coat and dragged his smashed leg toward the barn. The bone grated on itself and the blood running down his leg froze.

He tried to walk but when he put his weight on his leg the pain knocked him down. He pushed himself to his feet but couldn't move the leg or the pain would knock him down again. If he only had a stick, for a crutch.

Who had shot him? And from where?

If it was the Mexican, how did he get there? *How did he get behind me when I was looking for him?*

He realized he was dizzy, rolled over and half-sat. A black blood trail led from his leg back along his path from the trees. He took off his backpack and cut the sleeve off his windbreaker and bound it close to his groin above the wound. The bleeding slowed.

He took out his phone again and pushed Zack. It made a distant rattling sound. Then went through. *Holy God*, he whispered, *it's working –*

"*Steve!*" Zack said. "What was that shot?"

"The Mexican. Shot me in the leg."

"Holy shit. Bad?"

"Broke the femur. Lots of blood."

"Where are you?"

"About fifty yards downslope of the log barn. I'm going to hole up there, second floor. Let the Mexican come to me. Or I bleed to death. Whichever comes first."

"Don't say that, Steve, I'm coming."

"No. I'm calling just to say don't wait. I'm not going to make it. Take our stuff and get away. Take it and sell it. Go now, before it's too late."

"I'm coming, Steve."

"Just please give Marcie my share. Do that for me?"

"Of course, of course. Where's the Mexican?"

"Probably following me. He'll be coming up the meadow toward the barn. The way I came."

"It's getting dark, that will slow him down. Hold on, brother, I'll be there fast as I can."

STEVE DRAGGED himself to the barn. It seemed to have two levels. Beside it stood a half-fallen log shed with a bare-timbered roof. And behind them a cliff of dark conifers and granite outcrops.

He tried the barn door. If he could get in, up to the second floor, with the Beretta he could cover whoever came up the stairs. It was a good idea, unless the Mexican burned down the barn.

The snow was deep and though it was very cold it melted against his skin and made him shiver. That's alright, he told himself. When I get in the barn I'll cover myself up in straw, stay warm that way. If there's any straw up there.

Whoever had shot at him – had to be the Mexican – by now had reached the spruce clump where he'd been shot. So they'd have his blood trail to follow as well as his arduous crawl through the snow. The Mexican was maybe close already; because of his pain Steve didn't know how long ago the bullet had smashed into his thigh.

The barn door was huge, heavy, frozen shut. He pulled himself up beside it to stand one-legged, the smashed thigh hanging useless, foot hanging sideways in the snow. The barn door bolt was rusted solid. He hammered at it with the butt of the pistol but it would not move.

He crawled around the side of the barn, then the rear. In the middle was a regular door with a round handle. It was locked. He smashed his shoulder into the door but it did not budge. He whacked at the lock with the Beretta's butt, fearing to damage the gun or make it fire.

Someone was coming up behind him. No sound but he could feel it. He pointed the Beretta at the door handle. If he shot, the Mexican would know where he was. But the Mexican was following his track anyway. Could he get inside fast? *Upstairs*, he told himself, and fired.

The noise crushed his eardrums, rocketed back and forth among the hills and dislodged snow down on him from the roof. He shoved at the door and the lock gave just a little, maybe just the door jamb moving and not the lock. He shouldered hard into it, again and again, the thigh agony making him half-cry. The door wrenched open and he fell through it onto a floor of wide rough planks caked with dirt and dried hay.

He raised the Beretta. Nothing moved. No sound.

In the dim light he made out two rows of empty stalls, one on each side with an aisle between them. Then stairs rising toward the darkness above.

The boards under his hands were smooth with age and dirt, and hissed as he tugged his shattered leg along them. Like a blind man he groped on both sides, touched piles of dusty hay, the plank walls of what seemed to be a stall, then more hay on the other side of the aisle, here and there collapsed doors and stalls with rusty nails that jabbed into his skin.

He had to stop panting or the Mexican would hear him.

He inched up the stairs, Beretta in his right hand, dragging his leg in agony, the pain so atrocious he could think of little else. Upstairs seemed to be a wide high room stacked with hay bales in rows with aisles between them.

Oh God why am I here, he begged, but nobody answered.

Maybe the Mexican wouldn't come. Thinks I'll bleed or freeze to death. Maybe he's just gone down to get the coke and vanish.

He shoved aside bales to make a nest and crawled inside. The aged sere grass smelled good, of ancient summers. He laid the Beretta in the straw and squirmed round to loosen the tourniquet but the blood instantly pulsed out. Must have nicked an artery he decided, the femoral. He twisted the tourniquet tight again. Better lose a leg than bleed to death, he reasoned, almost laughed.

As if you have a choice.

As if you're going to live.

He picked up the Beretta. He'd get the Mexican first.

Before the Mexican killed Zack.

Once the Mexican was dead, Zack would have the coke, could get away. He had the contacts in Vegas, could still sell it. And Zack would split it right down the middle with Marcie.

That's who Zack is.

He pillowed his chin on his left forearm, the Beretta in his right hand. Trying not to weep from the pain, waiting for the Mexican to come.

Doorway to Heaven

IT WAS DARK when Diego reached the spruce clump where Steve had been shot. He pushed through the boughs to the edge of the meadow that led uphill to the barn backed against a cliff of conifers and granite outcrops.

Steve's bloody trail zigzagged from the spruce clump across the meadow toward the barn. The barn looked ancient and dangerous in the early starlight. Windows like skull eyes, a tattered snow-deep roof, a half-collapsed log shed behind it.

Once again Diego tried to decide what kind of weapon Steve had. Maybe it didn't matter, maybe Steve had already bled to death.

Maybe not.

But if Steve had a weapon and was able to shoot, then Diego couldn't cross the meadow and close in on the barn without getting hit. Just the thought of being shot made his hand ache.

He climbed alongside the meadow through dark timber. From the top of the dark timber he could cross the steep slope of granite outcrops. And could come down on the barn from behind, where nobody would expect him.

EACH TIME STEVE CALLED MARCIE it went to voice mail. "Please answer, honey," he begged, but she didn't. The home line didn't answer either, and in his pain he feared perhaps the Mexicans had done something to them.

Oh Jesus no.

Pain pulsed up his thigh like a volcano. Crashed through his pelvis, an electric jolt up his spine. Crushed his brain.

He shook his head side to side, inhaled deeply. Tried to figure what time it was back East. His iPhone said 7:23, did that mean 9:23 back there? Or 5:23? He couldn't decide.

How different what she and he had become, he realized, than what we'd wanted, thought we'd be. We drifted astray, lost course, till money was like cocaine and you had to have it like some people need God.

Instinctive to focus on money and not living. Because it represents a delicious threat. That could make you free, by killing you.

Wall Street, Vegas, the cocaine cartels, the NFL, the money that bought the politicians, the media that bolstered all this with its adoration of money, as if money were, like prayer in the old days, the doorway to Heaven...while we told ourselves, *Let's just make a little more money, then we can live.* Yes, *Let's do what our God tells us to do, not what we want.*

Jesus, Marcie, did we do that too?

He knew he was dying when he realized all that matters is love.

A NOISE. A WHISPER. Somewhere on the snow outside. Wind on a grass stalk, maybe, rubbing against the ice. Nothing more.

Steve slid further back into his corner among the hay bales, the Beretta heavy in his hand.

Hiss of cloth on snow. Not really there. He should move, didn't dare. This corner he'd hid in, he realized, had no way out except in front. Where the noise was coming from.

His heart thundered. He tried to slow it. Couldn't. Like a bass drum it shook the barn. Everything black, his heartbeat hammering off it.

In dark you're supposed to see better on the periphery, but when he tried looking at the darkness from the corners of his eyes it made no difference. Neither way could he see anything. Twice more the sound had moved. Closer.

He raised the Beretta in both hands before him, as if holding a cross against the Devil. Slowly the sound came nearer.

His iPhone, Steve remembered, had a light. He tugged it from his shirt and thumbed it and as its light bathed his face he realized what he'd done and shut it off, held it face down on the straw till its light died.

Whoever made the sound hadn't seemed to notice. Steve tilted to one side, fearing a bullet but nothing came.

Just the silence, then the hiss of motion.

His heart throbbed. How could the killer not hear it? Like bells in a cathedral. He wanted to be in that cathedral. Somewhere where God was praised. And people were at peace. Power of life. Not this terror of death. It sickened his stomach, shrank his skin.

You *can* die of fear.

A clink. Very faint, forward, on his left.

He had to do it. Holding his gun in his right hand he raised the phone in his left hand high and away from his body and snapped it on. Two fierce eyes gleamed at him out of the darkness. A big raccoon, slithering backwards, away from his light.

He flicked off the light, sighed, his chin down on a folded arm.

"You should always," Diego whispered, "look behind you."

Steve twisted the Beretta toward Diego who knocked it away and jabbed a knife into Steve's throat. "So where's my stuff?" he said, almost cheerfully, as if they were solving a riddle together.

"I don't have it –"

The knife went deeper.

"Stop," Steve gasped. "Zack has it. In his car."

"And where is this car?"

"Down there. The road."

"Where is he going with it?"

"Vegas."

"He has the contacts? The buyers?"

"Yes, he –" Steve realized before the knife came that he shouldn't have said this, should have made himself seem essential ... the blade sliced his trachea and windpipe in an instant, clunked into his spine as the nerve died; his vision dim, hazy, gone, the brain still working, the brain can go three minutes, it told him, without oxygen. What shall we think about?

Think about this life, what I had.

I can't hear you.

The joy. Everyone I love.

Speak louder.

Marcie'll have another man, the kids another dad. Will they even remember me?

DIEGO WIPED THE BLOOD from his hands with hay. The damaged one hurt beyond what was possible. It will go away, he told himself. It will go away.

Steve lay there, head lolled back, arms widespread, the blood stain widening on the disheveled bales. "Thief," Diego spat, the worst name he could call him.

He cleaned his knife, dried it against his thigh and sheathed it.

Steve's phone rang.

Diego tugged it from Steve's pocket. 212, a New York number.

It went to voice mail. When it had finished he listened. "Hi Darling, saw you tried to call...we were out getting an ice cream. Where *are* you? I've got *great* news, you won't believe it, the Lefkowitz deal came through after *all*, can you *imagine*? They decided they didn't like Gramercy Park – I could've *told* them... They want a fast closing, Lord be praised. A hundred and eleven grand, that's my cut – isn't that *grand*, honey? If you want to we'll buy that boat, cruise a while...the kids'll just have to put up with us. Call me back Darling, *fast*. Oh, and by the way Citigroup emailed their private clients today, they've accepted the Attorney General's ruling – one hundred percent repayment within six months...You're a hero, you pulled it off!" For a moment nothing, then her voice again, throaty. "Give us a call, Darling... *Love* you!"

It makes you almost sad, Diego thought, the way people are. If Harvard Stevie had just kept his little white fingers out of the strawberry pie none of this would've happened. He'd be home with his loved ones, high and dry.

You don't have any loved ones, Diego reminded himself.

María Christina made up for that. Someday he'd prove himself and she'd take him. He imagined their marriage night, her legs widespread beneath him. I will always keep you safe, María Christina.

He piled hay over Steve's body and slipped from the barn uphill, along the ridge of granite outcrops, and down the far side of the meadow where he'd last seen Zack, the wind scouring his tracks behind him.

No one will know I was here.

But soon Zack would know. It would be the last thing he would know.

WINCHESTER IN HIS HAND, Zack climbed through the dark timber till he could see the barn, sinister and dark on its perch atop the meadow and beneath the near-cliff of spruce and granite. He could barely see Steve's trail across the meadow to the barn. But had the Mexican followed it? Was he in the barn too?

He tried Steve's phone but again it failed. For an instant it stunned him that Steve was two hundred yards away but to call him went to a satellite thousands of miles above the earth then back down. And that this endangered them. Made them easier to track.

Coldness touched the back of his hand. He held out his palm. New snow.

He looked up. The stars were gone, flakes tickled his face. If this snow got thick he could move safer, undetected.

He didn't *have* to find Steve. Steve had tried to screw him several times, had lost his money with the auction rate securities. Steve had shot at him – by accident – the day the grizzly got the elk Zack had killed.

When he counted the days it was only nine since the grizzly and crashed plane. And it was Steve who'd wanted to sell the coke, make money to pay back what he had lost.

Like this DEA girl said, Zack could back out now. Let DEA find Steve. If Steve was dead why should he, Zack, risk getting killed by the Mexican just to find Steve's body?

If Steve was dead Zack should retreat back down the mountain and run away. Not even try to take the Pathfinder with the coke, just run away. Leave this memory of coke and killing and start a new life. Monica.

But if Steve was dead he'd have to tell Marcie – there'd be an investigation anyway. What could Zack say, that he and Steve separated in Denver? That he had no idea where Steve was? No, that wouldn't fly, because the DEA girl knew where they'd been. He'd have to testify.

If he did he wouldn't be charged, the DEA girl had said. He could go back to being what he was. Before all this. Monica.

Was Steve dead?

Zack knelt to tighten his boot laces. They were thick with ice. The evil of winter suddenly grew clear to him. That it actually *wants* to kill you.

If Steve was still alive he must be in the barn. Second floor, he'd said. But if he was already dead and the Mexican was there, how to know?

It would be walking into sure death.

He tried Steve's phone again but it still said *No Service.* He stared furiously at the cloud-black sky, at the satellites up there, spinning, signaling into the void.

It gave him a shivery premonition of death. How death will feel as you sink into it.

If the Mexican was in the barn he'd shoot Zack while he was crossing the open meadow. Or wait to nail him the moment he crept inside. So Zack's only choice was to stay to the left of the meadow and climb up through the dark timber till he could cross to the back of the barn, under the near-cliff of spruce and granite outcrops.

But that was not a good choice.

The Mexican had killed Emily. For no reason.

Get him for that.

IN HIS SCOPE Diego watched Zack's tiny dark shape climb uphill through the trees to the edge of the meadow, scan the barn and the near-cliff behind it, glance up at the snow clouds and hold a hand out for the flakes to land on.

"So what the fuck, *niño*, you don't like the snow?" No, this *niño* didn't like snow, staring at the sky. Why would he not like snow? It might save his wretched life. If he ran away now. So he could go on the magic screen again and pretend he knew everything.

And wouldn't end up dead like Harvard Stevie.

No, Diego, decided. Too much fun to kill him.

PURGATORY

CURT TRACKED DIEGO who had followed Steve uphill to a ridge where Diego had paused, widened a space and lain down.

This was confusing. Why had Diego stopped here? Was he tired?

From there Diego started following Steve again, and Curt followed them both for perhaps a half mile to a place in deep pines where someone had been shot – the spattered blood, the broken ground. The bullet had passed through someone then hit a pine trunk that was oozing sap.

It was Steve who'd been hit, you could tell from the boot prints. Peering through the pine boughs Curt could see Steve's bloody trail climb the snowy meadow to the log barn and then circle behind it, below the cliff. He watched it for fifteen minutes but nothing moved.

Interestingly, Diego's tracks no longer followed Steve's. Instead they turned right, uphill through the pines toward the cliff.

If Steve were hurt and in the barn Curt should go help him. If the Mexican had shot Steve, however, he would be waiting behind the barn, and for Curt to go up there would be suicide.

He had to do it anyway.

How to, without getting killed?

ZACK'S TELEPHONE PURRED. Rob, his agent. He didn't answer.

Thinking about Rob made him remember his life before which now seemed foolish and superficial, but he wanted desperately to go back there.

Rob's histrionics as he tried to make money from every molecule of Zack's presence, his photo, his voice and testimonial. But for every dollar Rob made, Zack made seven. So what was he fussing about?

He wasn't fussing. Just trying to understand. Now that things had gotten down to the bone.

In a moment's clarity he saw if he got this stuff to Vegas and sold it, he'd get back on track. Didn't matter there was a two-year non-compete. A million legal ways around that.

But he had too many enemies. Even one was a danger. When ten days ago he'd had none, just Haney and his goons to deal with.

Ten days ago there was no DEA nor that smooth seductive Whitney somebody, nor the Montana sheriff or Colorado State Police or Curt all hunting him. And worst of all this evil Mexican who seemed to take it personally.

Like anyone standing before a suddenly broken future he begged to go back just nine days. But really, he reassured himself, all that had actually gone wrong was he'd lost his money and job. And there was always a way to get them back, or something better.

But, thinking honestly, could he be charged as an accessory to Emily's death? And Steve's too, if *he* was dead? And he'd stolen Curt's truck and shipped cocaine across state lines and set up coke deals and lied to the law and betrayed Monica, and wasn't it about time it all came down on him?

No.

If Steve was dead there was nothing Zack could do about it. Emily was dead and he'd had no hand in that either. The rest a good lawyer could demolish.

He could still get free. Rich and free.

He raised a hand to the sky as if asking benediction, snow quickly filling his palm.

DIEGO WATCHED ZACK come closer through the dark timber toward the cliff. This *niño* was very brave to be coming this way, facing certain death. Or was there a reason for this move? Was it a distraction while somebody else came up behind?

That was the trouble with these fuckers. Some of them were dangerous.

His hand was hurting more and more. She'd been right, that girl doctor in Vegas. He should have it fixed.

Probably he should shoot Zack next time he could see him through the trees. Not an easy shot, and if he wounded him then had to hunt him down when he was holed up, waiting, with his rifle. Diego could get himself killed.

Like when he'd only wounded Steve, so had all the hassle of climbing through the dark timber and across the granite face to the barn, then up the stairs inside, just to cut Steve's throat.

It was time to finish this. He would meet Zack half way.

But if like he figured, Zack *was* a decoy, a bait, then he, Diego, should stay here at the top of the trees and wait for Zack's buddy, the real killer, to come up behind him. Had to be Curt, siding with his two dudes, they must have agreed on a split. But Harvard Stevie was dead so there were only two enemies left, Zack and Curt.

And Curt he had to worry about.

Diego made himself comfortable in the snow and began to scope his back trail, twenty feet at a time. Every ten seconds he turned the other way to check on Zack's progress through the dark timber.

ZACK HALTED at the top of the trees, below the granite slope. From here to the rear of the barn he'd be in the open and if Diego was in the barn it'd be a perfect time for him to take Zack down.

No guns had been fired except the one from far away, the one that must have hit Steve, Zack decided. That had to be the Mexican who fired. And then a nearer shot, by the barn, a different gun. Had that been Steve? Was he shooting at Diego? Or had Diego shot Steve again, with a different gun?

The snow falling hard. Although it would slow him down when he ran for the barn, it made him harder to see, easier to miss. Though did he really want to be in the barn with the Mexican?

The breech of the Winchester had frozen to his hand. Finger by finger he tugged it free, stuck his hand in his crotch to warm it.

He should leave Steve. Steve had caused all this.

It all fell apart when Steve offered him that hit of coke at the crashed plane. No, it all started with the first hit of coke long ago, no, with the morphine for the first bad injuries, no, it was when he'd hired Steve; no, it started way back, one night on a dark street of trash cans and broken bottles.

He imagined Steve in pain, dying. Tried the phone again. No answer.

THROUGH THE SCOPE Diego caught a flicker of motion behind him in the downhill trees. A black shape shifting between two dark trunks. There an instant, then gone.

He lay down in the snow with his elbows under the Remington and put the scope on the spot, slid it uphill a few yards and waited.

Yes. Another blink of dark motion.

So it was true Zack was tricking him, attracting his attention while the real danger was Curt coming up behind. Diego cursed himself for being stupid. Even if he shot at Zack he'd be lucky to hit him in the darkness, and that would alert Curt to exactly where Diego was.

He cursed himself again for only wounding Steve, so that he'd had to go into the barn to kill him, and thus had exposed himself. He could see María Christina watching him, and in her lustrous eyes he saw her sorrow that he'd failed her. It made him want to kill himself.

Now she'd never want him.

No, he told himself. You got yourself in a spot but you can get out. You just have to keep watching where Zack is and wait till Curt gets closer then kill him and swing round and go after Zack. Make sure they're both dead, then there's nobody to bother you when you go downhill to get the Range Rover and drive the coke away.

It was easy, that part. The Range Rover was made for the mountains. Had the tires with the metal teeth in them, to grip the snow.

As soon as Curt and Zack were dead he'd drive the Range Rover to the stuck cars, take the coke and go. And María Christina would be forever loving.

Another flicker of motion between the trees. He focused the scope on it. A branch was jerking up and down, scattering snow. Someone had put a hand on it maybe. He cranked up the scope till just the branch and a few boughs were visible.

A huge crow, gripping the branch.

But what, in the middle of the night, had startled it? Made it move?

CURT WAS WINDED. All these days with little sleep and bad food and jumping from place to place had him tired and despairing. He should be home with Diana, imagined for an instant the back corral with the log fence angling away from the barn, the hoof-packed frozen soil with its dusting of alfalfa, the whinnying, excited horses, the sun-bright peak of the barn's metal roof, the pure blue sky and biting wind.

He should be there, feeding the cattle, mending winter-broke fences, bringing in the eggs, driving the fourteen miles into town for whatever they couldn't make on the ranch. Like lettuce in winter, coffee beans, a bottle of Jack now and then.

Strange he was winded when he'd been so strong and immune to altitude when he and the dudes were up in Montana, the Buffalo Horns, just days ago. Now so weary. But it was the middle of the night. He sighed. He should go home.

Tomorrow he'd find Diego, tell him he couldn't kill Steve and Zack because DEA was coming and they'd get him for it, that they'd catch him if he didn't leave right away. That he should grab the coke and run.

Or was Steve already dead?

Once DEA showed up and arrested Steve and Zack, hopefully they'd get Diego too. Then Curt could go home.

With the saw on his knife he cut a pine branch four feet long, stripped off the twigs, rounded the top and used it like a hiking stick to push himself uphill.

This damn snow so deep when you're climbing through it. And heavy too, so you had to shake it off with each step. Windblown fine snow in your eyes, prickling your face. Down your neck.

He tried to figure when he'd last slept.

IT ALL COMES DOWN, Zack decided, to how you want to see yourself for the rest of your life. If he walked away from Steve now he'd think about it every hour till he died. He would be the kind of guy who deserts someone in pain, in danger. Walks away from an old friend.

The only way to get to Steve safely was to cross the dark timber to the side of the cliff, then find a way across the cliff. He'd be hidden by the trees growing below the cliff – and there had to be handholds on the rock. He could climb down to the rear of the barn that way.

If he could go silently into the barn and if the Mexican was there maybe he wouldn't hear him, or maybe just Steve was there, maybe he could get him out...if he called for help, if he agreed with the DEA girl to do the deal.

Step at a time in the darkness he raised a snow-thickened foot and moved it forward. Then the other. Then took a breath. Then moved a step forward again, then the other. He knelt in the snow, hidden behind a massive pine trunk, took out the phone and called Steve. Still nothing.

The trees thinned at the top of the meadow, he had to duck from one trunk to the next. For a crazy moment he wondered could he tunnel through the snow, it was so deep. He imagined getting snow down the Winchester's barrel, down his neck. Against his aching arm.

Still, how tough he was to have done all this with a badly broken arm – two bones, actually. It was like the old NFL days, you bring home your wounds and try to live with them. Then thought of Emily, her corpse ripped apart somewhere on the rocks of Virgin Canyon.

He wanted to call Monica.

He cleared the last trees, shouldered the rifle, dashed across the open space to the cliff and began to climb one-handed along it, the Winchester off-balancing him and catching on rock.

EVEN IF that downhill motion wasn't human, Diego worried, what spooked the crow? He cranked the scope down a notch to scan a wider area, still saw nothing but the black firs and pale snow frozen in the grip of night.

Maybe it just wanted to move, the crow. Its feet were cold, a coyote or fox scared it. But what had scared the fox?

He faced back across the meadow to where Zack had been, saw Zack's new, hurried tracks across the open space to the cliff.

Couldn't be. He scoped it. Yes, tracks, someone running uphill.

Diego lowered the gun, took a breath. This was not like him, to make such a foolish mistake. To assume Zack wouldn't cross so quickly. In a few instants while Diego was looking downhill to see if Curt was there. *It's what you get,* he told himself. *For being fooled by a crow.*

Furiously he glanced back downhill. Nothing. He stood and scoped it one last time.

There.

In a space between two trees, a man slogging uphill through deep snow, what looked to be a rifle in his right hand. Diego cranked up the scope but the man had vanished in the trees.

Curt. Coming this way.

I tried to help you, Diego told him silently, savagely. *And now you come back to kill me?*

He turned to check the granite headwall. Zack there somewhere. Coming this way.

He could either wait till Curt came closer and he could get a better shot at him, or climb up to the barn and shoot Zack as he was coming down the cliff.

Or better yet, kill Zack with the knife, then Curt wouldn't hear anything, wouldn't know. Would keep on climbing to his death.

Then no one would be left alive who'd seen him. He'd be free.

To take their shipment back, bring it wherever María Christina wanted.

Then, maybe.

"WHERE ARE YOU?" Whitney said, her voice wavering in and out.

Curt tilted the phone, faced south. "Can't hear you."

"Where *are* you?" she yelled. "We're trying to chopper in but can't in this weather… And I don't know where you are –"

"On the side of this dumb mountain. You can't find me?"

"Your GPS isn't showing. Nobody's is."

"It's the dirt road over the mountains to Purgatory. That comes off 550. I'm about ten miles in."

"I can't *hear you!*"

"My battery's beeping. It's running out –"

"Where on Purgatory? The snow's falling too fast, no satpix, no choppers."

"Losing you –"

"Can't you charge it somewhere? I need to know where you are… where your guys are!"

The phone went silent. Curt almost threw it in the snow. Instead he tucked it in his coat, the pocket next to his heart. Maybe if it warmed up he could use it one more time.

And maybe at the top by the granite headwall there'd be service. So he could call her to send in her guys. Before Diego killed someone.

But he had to tell her also that Diego knew what DEA was doing as soon as she did.

Everything Curt told Whitney, Diego soon knew.

Maybe he should mislead her, to lead Diego into a trap. Tell her I'm leaving to testify against him, see if that brings him out of the woods.

Keeping to the dark timber he continued uphill through the pine-scented trunks following Diego's tracks, stopping every three paces to catch his breath.

However fast Diego was moving, Curt had to go faster. Or he'd never catch him.

WHITNEY ALMOST THREW her phone against the motel wall. What was wrong with this phone company, such lousy service? All these damn mountains. Weren't no mountains down home in the hood. Filthy streets calcified with stupidity and sorrows. The drugs turning everyone to walking dead. People who'd never live again.

And now she was losing this chance to take them down. The evil, hated drugs. The evil, hated dealers with their thousands of murders spreading blood across Mexico, the States. Murdering people's souls.

It was because of this lousy phone service she was losing a chance to take them down.

To take this Diego down would be good, but to get María Christina, whore of the universe, whore of Yale and Harvard and whatever else could be used like a high-kill weapon to eliminate people... How many times had Whitney studied her picture, read her files, listened to the intercepts? How many times had she seen her DEA colleagues catch drug lords red-handed, only to see the lawyers get them off?

You keep going, she told herself. You just keep going. In thirty years you're gonna have lots of wins. You're going to be glad you did this.

Yeah, she thought. I already am.

Barefoot she paced the lousy room. It stank of disinfectant and mold. She checked her watch, 04:17. You should get some sleep, girl. When you're too tired is when shit happens.

She set her phone alarm for 05:30, lay down and tugged the bedspread over her. What counted was to seize the shipment before Diego vanished with it. To seize him with it. Perhaps maybe just shoot him. Much as she wanted to, that was not an option. He had too much information to give them. But at such a cost. And to what end?

You get some sleep.

The worst would be if Diego started shooting... And whoever else María Christina has sent in to back him up.

Better that three hundred kilos disappear than a police officer or civilian dies. Better the cokeheads keep killing themselves than we die trying to help them.

When you came right down to it there was no way we could help them.

Just keep trying to dry up the supply.

Like emptying a waterfall with a tin cup.

At 06:00 she called Duane. "I'm stuck in a motel on 550," she said. "Snow's getting worse, total blackout, we got a brief ID on satpix but don't know where they've gone since...We're trying to get snowmobiles up there but they're bogging down. We're getting deputies marooned out there at thirty below."

"No sign of Diego?"

"Not since Montrose, none of them. Except for that one satpic."

"What are you thinking?"

"Soon as the snow stops and we can get a couple planes and choppers up we'll find them. Then we decide when to go in."

"I want them all over the evidence. I want them sleeping with it, eating it..."

"One more thing –"

"What?"

"They seem to always know what we do."

"Who says?"

"Curt."

"Is it your phone?"

"Don't know. Or a leak."

Duane was silent a moment. "We'll find out."

"I'll call you at 08:00. Or sooner if anything happens."

"Something always happens. Just be ready for it."

Too Bad

WITH HIS BROKEN arm Zack couldn't get handholds and had to inch across the cliff one-handed. But it was too steep, he got caught with no way forward, had to back up but there was no way back. Hung there hugging the rock, the depths of the cliff gyrating dizzily below him.

Fingernailing the icy rock, his body glued to its flank, his cheekbone hard against it, he tried to move back the way he'd come but something caught, nearly tipped him off the cliff.

The Winchester's sling, caught on an edge of rock. Twice he tugged at it, but any motion risked hurling him into the void. He'd have to back up to loosen it. But the tiny ledge he'd had one toe on had crumbled, his right foot scrabbled emptily at the space where it had been.

He dug his fingernails tighter into the grain of the rock. The horror of falling, the ache of open space beneath, sucking him out and downwards, telling him *Get it over with, it won't be so bad*... All that made his soles tremble more against the granite seam, and the cold grew harder, his fingers numb, ice-clad stone burning his cheek.

It was only a hundred feet to the bottom. Maybe he'd survive, smashed and gutted on the boulders. He wanted to glance down to see if there were maybe junipers and scrub to break the fall, but couldn't turn his head without falling.

The Winchester was still caught. He tugged it, fearful of pulling himself off the wall into the void. It wouldn't come loose. He took a breath, waited, shaking with fear, tried to decide if the Mexican could see him spread-eagled like this against the cliff. Holding on one-handed, with no way forward and no way back.

His trembling foot made the ledge shake. The quarter-inch wide ledge he'd edged out on, hoping to make it to the path on the other side, was crumbling beneath him and even in the darkness he could see there was nothing to grab at on the way down.

He slid his rear foot back an inch, scraped at nothing, came forward the same inch and dug his toe back into the crease, his gasping loud against the rock.

He would have to drop the rifle. But to move his shoulder to do it would also knock him off the cliff.

He panted, fingers trembling, wanting to let go, tried to shrug the Winchester from his shoulder. It wouldn't budge; he tried again and finally it slid off partway, caught on his coat.

He would have to move his good hand from the cliff. Shaking with fear he gripped harder at the stone with the fingers of his broken arm, forced himself to let go the other hand.

The cliff moved away from him; he caught at it, held. The Winchester bumped down his arm and dropped free. He grasped the cliff again with his good hand. The Winchester clattered as it hit the rocks below.

Slowly, very carefully, he moved back along the cliff to the trees, waited till a cloud covered the moon, and dashed to the barn. At the back door he halted, hearing nothing.

The moon had returned. He scanned the inside of the barn, seeing nothing, then softly climbed the stairs, the Ruger in his good hand before him.

A vast room piled high with bales, no sign of the Mexican. If there were, Zack reminded himself, *I'd be dead now.*

"Steve!" he whispered, loud as he dared. "It's me!"

After a few minutes he crossed to look at the empty window at one end and stepped on something soft. And warm.

Steve's arm.

Zack's heart froze. The Mexican would kill him too. Had heard the Winchester clatter down the cliff. Was perhaps watching from a dark corner, grinning.

He checked Steve's body till he felt the cooling blood, wiped his hand in the straw. How this horror kept spreading. What would he tell Marcie? *Your husband is dead...* The kids, without a father. *Oh Jesus Steve.*

He crouched low toward the stairs, Ruger pointed ahead of him, as if a magic wand that could deter evil, halted briefly at the door and sprinted for the line of trees. Once there he stopped to check his back trail, dark-white in the cloud-shadowed moonlight. No one coming. He ran all the way down to the two parked cars. Still no one chasing him.

The snow had hardened in the night, crackling under his boots. He unlocked the Pathfinder, checked that the black scorpion kilos were still there, turned the key, and tried to drive.

A crunch as the tires broke free of their bed of ice. Carefully, without headlights, he drove forward along the road, going south, toward freedom.

WHEN DIEGO ran down to the road the Pathfinder was too far ahead to waste a shot, particularly in darkness, with its lights off.

He wondered should he go back to the Range Rover but that would take too long. And his Ski-Doo was halfway up the mountain.

He ran after Zack, stepping in the Pathfinder's ruts.

TWO MILES LATER Zack hit a wall. An actual wall, where the road had been cut by a near-vertical ravine.

He got out. If he drove slowly, followed the contour, avoided the clumps of rocks and battered brush he could make it across. *Maybe* could make it.

Freedom. So close now.

The ravine above him was a raw scar half a mile wide that climbed a thousand feet to an overhang where tiny black trees tilted crazily. As the wall descended it widened, with smashed trees and uprooted boulders sticking up through the high-piled snow.

But now when he scanned his back trail he saw someone, a moving spot darker than the early dawn, following his tracks along the road.

The Mexican. Who had a rifle, could shoot from afar.

Zack leaped into the Pathfinder and tried to drive forward, caught on a boulder, backed up and drove around it, tires slithering, back on the road, the Pathfinder tilting, slid to a halt.

DIEGO DIDN'T MIND running. He'd always trained hard, reminding himself that luck rides with the well-prepared, and the surest way to win is to be stronger and smarter than your enemy. So it was easy, this two miles, the rifle swinging loosely in his good hand, the damaged hand clenched against his body, his boots making a steady *chunk chunk* noise in the snow, his breathing steady, the Pathfinder growing larger as he neared it.

Problem was he didn't know what kind of gun Zack had. If he had a rifle, Diego would be an easy target as he came closer.

He halted at a bend in the road, knelt and sighted the scope on the car. Zack was digging at the wheels, didn't seem to have a rifle but maybe had one in the car. Zack glanced back the road toward Diego, jumped in the car and accelerated, got stuck, pulled free, got stuck again.

"Okay, *niño*," Diego said. "You don't have a rifle, do you? I am going to have some fun with you."

He trotted closer, till the Pathfinder was an easy hundred yards ahead. He didn't need to go further; Zack might have a pistol – you never knew. It was getting daylight now, every minute brighter. Once he dealt with Zack he'd turn the Pathfinder around, drive back the way it had come, load the coke in the Range Rover and be gone.

"Hey, Zack!" he called. "Give it up. Leave the vehicle there and walk away. Don't make me shoot you."

BEYOND THE STEEP RAVINE the wall of trees began again. Zack could walk it easily unless he got a bullet in the back. Walk to where? It didn't matter. Not to die was all.

To live was all. He didn't need the money Steve had lost, he didn't need the job he'd lost – there was always another one, he could coach football or be a local sportscaster somewhere. With Monica, it didn't matter if they weren't rich…

If he lived, to expiate the sin of Emily. The loss of Steve, stealing the cocaine and Curt's truck – they were all sins, harm he'd done, but if he lived he could repent, *did* repent.

Lord give me this life, he prayed as he walked toward the wall of trees, waiting for the bullets to smash his back, breath hollow, muscles taut with fear. *Please give me this and I will always work for the good, take care of others, love you.*

A faraway voice was yelling "Diego! Diego! *Stop!*" It seemed like Curt's voice, but why would Curt be here?

When the bullet hit his spine, just below the neck, it cut his brain free, free to do nothing in the last seconds till the oxygen died.

AS CURT RAN toward the chute yelling "Diego!" something yanked at his collar, then came the crack of a rifle and he dove to the ground. Lying face-down in the snow trying to burrow into it as the bullets snapped past.

The first bullet had gone through his collar, the second sang past his ear, the third plowed up snow in his face, a terrifying whack that made him realize what it feels like when it hits you.

In front of him the great steep ravine lurched and groaned.

Crack! – the bullet must have hit the slope behind him. But if Diego came closer there was nothing Curt could do to stop him. Nor could he run; he'd die like Zack just died.

He thought of Diana.

Crack! Diego's rifle fired again. Crack CRACK *CRACK*, more bullets pummeling Curt's nest in the snow.

One tugged at his sleeve, another kicked up snow by his eye.

He had seconds to live. And nowhere to go.

The planet shook, shuddered, the mountain began to slide. A roar, subtle at first, growing, thunderous as the whole steep snow-filled ravine began to slip down, faster and faster crashing on the road and the Pathfinder and Zack's body, tossing the Mexican high in the air then grinding him under, an avalanche of snow twenty feet high, now fifty feet high roaring down the steep ravine and covering all, the Pathfinder momentarily spinning above it, doors flying, then buried again then once briefly surfacing as it and the landslide of snow raced down the mountainside toward the valley far below.

The thunder lessened. Rivers of ice and snow still hissed down, chunks of trees and rock lurched to the surface and were pulled under again. A few crows, startled by the avalanche, ceased their cawing and settled back down in the treetops. It grew suddenly so silent that the tiny roar of a jet plane six miles high was sharp and clear.

Curt stood, shook snow off his coat, took a breath. Turned and slowly trudged back up the road toward his Ski-Doo and drove back to Diego's Range Rover. Under the back seat of the Range Rover, as Diego had said, was a blue tool box. It was heavy. He set it on the hood and opened it. Inside, packed solid, were stacks of hundred-dollar bills wrapped in red elastic bands.

He put the blue tool box in the cargo space of his Ski-Doo and tugged his phone from his pocket to call Whitney, but it was truly dead.

"THEY WEREN'T BAD people," he said to her a half hour later as they looked down at the new avalanche with its boulders and shattered trees sticking up like flotsam on a sea of ice.

"Could happen to anybody, is what you're saying?" Whitney asked.

"To lots of people. Folks down on their luck, lives gone to Hell."

"I know all that."

"It's horrible they were killed. Even Diego. In his tormented way he was a good kid, very respectful, quite honest. And I believe he had a caring heart. How can anyone like me who's had a good life judge him? How can they imagine what it was like? What it made him?

"We want to talk to you about all that. After you get home to Diana."

248

"About Diego?"

"Not just him. We're going after who he worked for, all the way to the top."

"Can you ever touch these people?"

"We have all Diego's phone calls, since Glenwood Springs. With them we might be able to bring down María Christina..."

"Might be?"

She grinned, tugged back her hair. "Too bad about that two hundred grand. Must be down there somewhere, under all that snow."

"I was going to tell you –"

"We'll bring in dogs, try to find the bodies. But with the snow this deep it's unlikely...and in spring when the snow melts the crows and coyotes will get to the bodies first and there'll just be bones." She glanced at the three La Plata deputies who had snowmobiled up with her. "And wherever that money is, it'll be impossible to trace. We won't be looking for it."

He took a quiet breath. "Too bad."

"Yeah," she smiled. "Too bad."

CURT LANDED IN BOZEMAN at seven-forty, rented a car and drove north across the frozen prairies where his ancestors had hunted the buffalo for thousands of years, to the Little Belt Mountains and in the front gate of the ranch at ten-fifteen. A half moon bathed the valley in a succulent light in which the hills of fir trees stood out in their dark ranks of thousands, their black speartops silvery, then down the long valley on the narrow gravel road slippery with frozen snow, the barn light in the distance like a beckoning star.

It was driving him crazy about Steve and Zack but there was nothing he could do. Who wouldn't do what they did, down on their luck? When you're in a deep hole won't you do whatever it takes to climb out?

He left the car in the middle of the drive and walked fast up the back steps into the kitchen. "Diana!" he called, going down the corridor to the dining room and there she was coming out of the living room with earphones on her head.

"Well hi, Love, you're home!" she reached out and hugged him.

"I called you, dammit, you didn't answer. I thought something was wrong."

"Nothing was wrong, Silly. You were supposed to fix the speakers and didn't. So I was listening to *The History Hour* on the earphones. If you'd only fix the speakers –"

"Remember that old joke, from the Marines?"

She held his cheek in her hand. "Which one, Love?"

"About when you've been deployed for months, maybe a year, and you've just arrived home, what's the second thing you do when you come in the door?"

"Oh that," she giggled. "You put down your duffel."

He took her in his arms. "So let's go do the first thing."

As he climbed the stairs beside her, palm on her slender hip, he reminded himself, *I mustn't forget to tell her about the money.*

Late that night he woke and went to the window. New snow was falling, deep already in the corral, blanketing the pastures and covering the trees. Snow. Always snow. And some day the sun will die or the earth spin from its orbit and we will become a frozen chunk of stone wandering the universe, covered in snow.

Till then we live.

Hard as we can.

THE END

CPSIA information can be obtained
at www.ICGtesting.com
Printed in the USA
LVHW02s1931090118
562394LV00013B/1162/P